13

TALLENT & LOWERY: BOOK ONE

CHAPTER ONE

Patience and Fortitude. If there was one thing Leah Tallent knew, it was that those two virtues didn't exist.

The chilly autumn wind circled the frustrated librarian but it was no use. There was nothing that could cool her anger. Leah sighed. Located somewhere deep inside her brain she could feel the heavy-metal rock band gearing up for the concert of their life. That, mixed with the incessant babbling of the horde of teenagers surrounding her, made her migraine swell to mammoth proportions.

Leah raised her gaze to the mighty lion relaxing on his pedestal. Sunlight glinted off the pink Tennessee marble eyes of Patience—one of the glorious guards of the New York Public Library.

"I wish you were real," she muttered. "You and your partner could pick them off one by one…just for me." She smiled at the quiet figure and closed her eyes, imagining what it would be like to live in that perfect, peaceful world.

"Yo! Lady! You got a bathroom in this joint?"

And just like that, the fantasy was broken. Leah's eyes snapped open. She glared at the girl with the spiked-pink hair who was rolling her eyes;

a snide smile was plastered on her face.

Throwing her arm over the regal lion's back, the teenager wiped her grubby hand on the pristine marble statue. "You're a real drag, lady."

Leah's shoulders slumped in defeat. "Life sucks," she groaned.

In response to her heartsick declaration, the teenager pulled a large, spit-soaked wad of chewing gum from her mouth and moved her hand toward the lion's mane.

Leah moved faster. "You'd be safer sticking that up your-."

"Ah-hem."

The hair on the back of her neck bristled. Turning slightly, Leah glared at the tall man walking up the steps toward her. Leaning in, he whispered strongly in his student's ear. And when he was finished, the girl crammed the gum back into her mouth and threw Leah a disgusted look.

The dirty-blond hair of the muscular teacher blew across his forehead, and the corners of his mouth twitched into a teasing grin. He gave a slight bow of apology to Leah, and cleared his throat. "You were saying… Madame Librarian?"

Leah focused on his sparkling emerald eyes and soothing voice. He was the complete opposite of every professor-type she'd ever met—far more *Indiana Jones* than the Science Guy. In fact, a fedora would've been an excellent accessory for his brown leather jacket and well-tanned skin.

"Hello?"

Leah shook the strangely disturbing thoughts from her brain. "What?"

"You were saying?" His smile reminded her of a hunter who'd spotted his prey. "About the lions?"

The heat burned her cheeks, and she forced herself to look away from the man who seemed to know exactly the effect he had on the female population. Closing her eyes, Leah went to the one place she knew was safe, and began her well-rehearsed lecture. "Our lions are two of the most recognized figures in the world. They were originally named Leo Astor and Leo Lennox, in honor of the two men whose collections formed this library. In the 1930's, during the Great Depression—." Leah stopped and stared at the teenagers; her voice dripped with sarcasm. "I assume at least *some* of you have passed history."

The teacher snickered.

Tossing him a frown, Leah continued, "During the Great Depression, our President voiced his opinion that New Yorkers would have to acquire patience and fortitude to get through the tough times that lay ahead. Thus, the lions were bestowed with these profound names. They are works of art that *should* be revered." She aimed her gaze at the girl who was now locking lips with another leather-clad deviant. Her stomach lurched.

Turning away, she noticed that the teacher was still wearing his wide grin. Apparently he found her revulsion amusing. Straightening her spine, she stared into his brilliant green eyes. "If we're really lucky their pierced tongues will get stuck together and they'll suffocate."

A chorus of giggles rose up around her; the demonic choir made her skin crawl. Leah shut out their voices, and pushed her way past the laughing man. "Follow me," she grunted.

"Nothing I'd like better…Ma'am."

His voice was like a sexy rumble of thunder in Leah's ears—deep and dangerous.

"Is there anything else I can do for you?" he asked.

As Leah headed into the warm interior of the New York Public Library, she clenched her fists at her sides and shouted back over her shoulder, "As a matter of fact, there is. Don't let these little…*people*…touch anything!"

CHAPTER TWO

Marching away from the group, Leah crossed the highly-polished floor of Astor Hall. The security team took over and began their intense search of the teenagers' belongings. Like everywhere else in the City, the safety of America's landmarks was a top priority.

Leah's high heels clicked across the red tile keeping perfect rhythm with her rapid, angry heartbeat. She walked under the soft, almost angelic light that beamed down from the original brass fixtures, and came to a stop at the hand-carved desk located in the front hall.

Skylar, a young librarian who'd been a recent acquisition of the Humanities and Social Sciences Library, looked up from her papers and offered Leah a smile. "How's it going?"

"I'd rather be practicing my knife-throwing skills with the Manson family."

"Come *on*!" She laughed. "They can't be that bad. They're only kids."

"*Only*?" Leah rolled her eyes. "Inmates on death row are more polite."

Skylar shook her head; her dark brown curls fluttered around her fresh, young face. "How can you be a librarian and hate kids?"

"I'm a research librarian not a babysitter. Even the Board was bright enough to realize that the two aren't interchangeable. They moved the children's section down to the Donnell Center years ago. Why do they keep coming *here*?" Leah's migraine intensified. She remembered how happy she'd been on that glorious day when they wheeled *Winnie the Pooh* and his pals out the front door.

Skylar reached out to pat her hand. "The Donnell Center is for *children*, Leah. Those," she continued, pointing at the motley group, "are teenagers—young *adults*. And they do research, too."

"Oh, please." Leah snorted. "Using our computers to instant message their creepy little friends does not fall under the category of research. They wouldn't know what a book was if it fell from the balcony and smacked them on their empty heads."

"You know…." Skylar smiled. "I heard the 'powers that be' are going to put a Children's Center back in here."

"Just a rumor." Leah shuddered. "It has to be a rumor."

"You're terrible. I swear. The way you talk makes me think that you're the Devil, himself. Look…just go back over there and—" The words stopped in her throat. Her eyes grew wide, as if an extraterrestrial of the worst kind had landed smack dab in the middle of the polished marble floor. Her voice suddenly turned soft and sultry, as her hand fluttered to her chest. "My God. That's two in one day."

Leah stared into her psychotic looking eyes. Panic filled her body and she whipped around, ready to confront the demon that'd caused Skylar to become speechless. After surveying the safe distance still remaining between her and the horde of teenage beasts, Leah turned back around. "What?"

Skylar's cheeks turned bright red, like a fire had erupted deep inside her belly. "Why don't you let me take this group?"

"Yeah, right. You've never been helpful in your life." Leah stared back and forth between the huddled group and her co-worker, who now seemed to be immersed in some sort of trance. "What's *wrong* with you?"

Skylar licked her lips, like a hungry tiger that'd just spotted its Thanksgiving Day dinner. "I want to help, is all."

Leah remained silent, as Skylar straightened her skirt and buttoned the tight red jacket around her slim waist. Like a magician whose hand was quicker than the eye, Skylar unsnapped the top two buttons of her thin, white shirt.

Turning away from the strange scene, Leah studied the faces that were supposedly America's hope for the future. Her pulse began to gallop as they made their way over to where she stood. They moved as one gigantic shadow across the tile, like a mass of deadly spiders journeying across the desert in search of fresh meat.

The blond-haired teacher suddenly stopped their trek, huddled the class together, and spoke in a reverent whisper befitting the room.

Leah clenched her teeth. "He better be telling them to behave like civilized people in here."

"Don't worry." Skylar tossed her heavily-perfumed curls over her shoulder. "I'll take care of him…them…for you."

"That's it!" Leah frowned. "Tell me what's going on."

"Oh, come *off* it, Leah." Skylar winked. "Don't you think he's gorgeous?"

"Who?"

The younger librarian issued an exaggerated sigh. "Him, you twit. Even the frosty, Miss Leah Tallent, must recognize the genuine goods when she sees it."

Leah looked up at the teacher's deep green eyes staring back at her from the center of the room. "You've got to be kidding."

Skylar ignored her completely. "He's even better than the first one."

"What first one?"

"A man…no, scratch that…a bronze god came in here about an hour ago looking for the private files and…" Skylar changed her course. "Doesn't matter. Anyway, he had black eyes…dark and dangerous…a deep tan, bronze hair…oh, Leah! He's the one I've been searching for my whole life."

"You haven't been alive all that long," Leah sneered. "You should have more hang time."

Skylar ignored the sarcasm. "And now a younger, *more* gorgeous, blond, green-eyed morsel walks in! I'm telling you, the Lord is being very good to me today."

Leah turned back to the teacher and his creepy little pets. "This Lord of yours certainly has a sense of humor, if you ask me."

"Please." Skylar clasped her hands in prayer. "*Please* let me take this group. You don't want to. You know it and I know it. Besides, with the gala tonight, you should be upstairs supervising. *God forbid*, Leah. Think about it! Someone could be scratching the tables as we speak!"

Leah tried to keep from laughing as she stared into the desperate gaze. "I *should* be upstairs. But I *did* promise the Director that I would be a good little employee, take my turn, and show this group around. I wouldn't want him to get mad or, *God forbid*, fire me."

"Anything you want." Skylar grabbed her arm. "It's yours."

"This could prove interesting."

"Come on!"

"Okay." Leah smirked. "You have to do all my assigned tours for the rest of the year."

"The whole year?" Skylar's voice turned into a whine of mammoth proportions. "That's a little much, don't you think?"

"Hey, now. Think about it. You're the one who wants to get closer to, Mr. Green-Eyes-Hey-Look-How-Hot-I-Am, teacher. Question is…how badly do you want him?"

"That's not it at all." Skylar aimed her chin in the air. "I love children. I think young minds should be nurtured and molded."

"Bullshit."

"Leah!"

"Make the deal, Skylar." Leah stuck out her hand. "He's coming closer. Could be the love of your life. Tick-tock."

Skylar shook Leah's hand so hard that she practically dislocated her shoulder. "You really are a stone cold—"

"Is everything okay over here, ladies?"

Leah turned and offered her best fake smile to the supposedly handsome teacher. "As a matter of fact, this is your lucky day, Professor. May I introduce Ms. Skylar Trewitt, the newest and finest addition to our library. She'll be continuing your tour."

"But—"

"I assure you. She's much more capable than I."

The professor's eyes turned to jade, and his voice took on a slightly threatening tone. "But I came here for you."

The warning bells suddenly rang out inside Leah's head as she stared into his angry face. Leah knew if there was one thing she could always count on it was her sixth sense—her ability to know that her safe world was somehow being compromised. Grabbing Skylar's arm, she practically threw her co-worker into his arms. "It was a real pleasure meeting you and your…students." Racing up the marble steps toward the Rose Main Reading Room, Leah yelled out over her shoulder, "Remember, now. Don't touch *anything*!"

*

Walking past the glass exhibit cases, Leah tried to shake the strange feeling of being stalked inside the only home she'd ever known. Her heart was

St. Jude Children's Research Hospital
ALSAC • Danny Thomas, Founder
Finding cures. Saving children.

stjude.org

Tallent & Lowery

13

Book Markers

Page 15
8 May 2014
11:22 pm

beating rapidly and she found herself briefly wondering if the green-eyed professor was a wolf in sheep's clothing.

Throwing the ridiculous thoughts from her overactive brain, Leah stared up at the large banner hanging from the ceiling. She called out to the workers, trying to stop her voice from trembling. "It's crooked, guys. Needs to be a little higher on the left."

Muddled curses rained down from above. She smiled, wondering if they would have the nerve to spit on her head and tell her it was raining. The banner was huge; the symbol of Yin and Yang completely blocked the restored ceiling and made the room feel like a cold, lifeless museum. Printed on the white side of the sign was the word Heaven; while the black half proclaimed the existence of Hell.

On top of one of the marble tables that littered the room was an invitation written in an elegant script:

The New York Public Library Presents...

Heaven & Hell: A Literary Celebration of Both Sides of Humanity.

Leah sighed. This ridiculous event that promoted the strange and eerie parts of humanity was what, she knew, was causing her real paranoia not some silly, semi-handsome teacher. In a few short hours her favorite place would be crammed wall to wall with tuxedo-clad benefactors hoping to get their pictures in the society columns. And most, if not all, would be people who'd never cracked the spine of a book in their entire lives. Leah took a deep breath and closed her eyes, trying to escape the chatter.

The deep voice of the Library Director shouting out orders ended her moment of peace. Wanting to avoid him at all costs, Leah turned to flee. The last thing she needed was to get caught up in an hour-long discussion about tonight's event. Her high heels clicked across the tile, making it sound as if an expert typist was pounding away on a keyboard. Catching her thigh on one of the six hundred pound tables, Leah swallowed her scream. She limped downstairs and made her way as quickly as possible to the old door in the darkened corner marked, *Private*.

Skylar's annoyingly-perky voice echoed behind her, joining with the frustrated teacher who was barraging her with questions about the areas of the library that were off-limits to visitors.

Taking the key from the long chain around her neck, Leah quickly unlocked the door and wrenched it open. As she limped down the staircase, she found herself wondering why the teacher was so adamantly interested in the contents of the library's basement.

CHAPTER THREE

"Talk about patience and fortitude," he muttered.

A picture of the determined librarian danced in Gareth Lowery's mind. The gorgeous hallucination appeared in the cloud of musk-scented steam that invaded every corner of the elegant bathroom. Gareth pushed open the crystal shower door and stepped out onto the thick, red bathmat. He stared at the large mirror covered in a thin layer of mist, and felt his brain switch gears. Losing the image of the stunning librarian, Gareth suddenly pictured himself in a horror movie. It felt as if he would raise his hand, clear the warm droplets from the mirror, and catch his first glimpse of the masked killer standing behind him, waiting to strike.

"You all right in there, son?"

The familiar voice broke through Gareth's strange thoughts. He shrugged the ridiculous feeling from his broad shoulders and reached out for one of the thick towels hanging from the brass rack. "Yeah. I'll be right out," he shouted back through the door.

Letting go of his childish fears, Gareth swept a large hand over the mirror and stared at his reflection. What an afternoon, he thought. It'd taken forever to free himself from Skylar, whose endless giggles had made his head ache for the past two hours. If he'd known that locating the book and stealing it from the library was going to be such a chore, he would've worked harder on devising a better plan.

Gareth sighed. So far his journey had been filled with wonder and amazement—even fear, at times—but nothing had prepared him for the mind-numbingly boring teenagers and the flirty librarian who'd been forced upon him. She'd had no answers to the questions he'd asked and he needed those answers. In order to achieve the missing piece, those answers were more important than oxygen.

It'd been such a perfect plan. With his partner's help, he'd entered Gareth Lowe's biography and resume into the school's computer system. He'd even taken careful steps to make sure that he would be picked as the substitute teacher for this one day—to scout the location that he knew was the next step toward his goal. But even a loyal member of the Department of Education hadn't been allowed to investigate the private, unlit corners of the immense library.

On another website—far from the salt-of-the-earth professor—Gareth had planted his second personality: Gareth Lowery, rich benefactor. Using that "face," Gareth had been able to forge a relationship with the Library Director through his checkbook; his large and frequent donations had bought him a place on the coveted Board. After countless meetings, Gareth had finally heard the information he'd been searching for. There was one; only one who knew every cob-webbed corner of the historic building. One who could offer him the information he needed in order to solve the greatest mystery that the world hadn't even thought of yet.

Leah Tallent was her name; and today, after all the hard work and countless hours of blood, sweat, and tears, he'd come face to face with the woman who could change his world. He closed his eyes and once again summoned the image…

The beautiful auburn hair that she'd tried to hide in a severe bun at the nape of her long, graceful neck. The sapphire eyes filled with wisdom, and her prickly sarcastic demeanor, combined to create a package that was a turn-on of monumental proportions. In fact, in their short time together, Leah Tallent had become the most interesting woman Gareth had ever met. He'd been so ready to uncover the clues from this woman who supposedly knew it all. But she'd pawned him off in seconds. It was almost as if Leah Tallent had known what he was after.

The telephone in the outer room rang so loud that the mirror trembled in front of him. Gareth heard his friend pick up the line, and he raced from the bathroom.

"Yeah?"

Donovan Barker's voice was slow…almost groggy. He always sounded to Gareth like a man who drank heavily and was in a constant state of hangover, even though Gareth knew that a drop of alcohol had never touched Donovan's lips. His appearance, too, was that of a drunken bum. His bronze-tipped mass of hair looked like he'd been stuck in gale force winds all his life. And his clothes were constantly disheveled, like he'd just woken up to a new day from his place in the alley where he'd passed out the night before.

But his eyes, thought Gareth, were what set him apart from the rest. Like a shark's, they were black in color. However, unlike the deadly predator, Donovan's were always alive and alert, as if nothing in the world could get past them. There was a bluish light that seemed to constantly shine in his pupils no matter what hour of day or night. And that otherworldly glimmer made him appear as if he was always watching, studying, and remembering everything and everyone he observed.

As the thoughts raced through Gareth's mind, Donovan turned to stare at him. The black eyes were once again alive with excitement as he thrust the phone between them. "It's Kathryn."

Gareth's heart leapt inside his chest. Grabbing the phone, he felt almost giddy when Kathryn's familiar voice flowed into his ear.

"Are you okay?"

Even thousands of miles away Kathryn was still the only person in the world able to understand every thought and hone in on every feeling Gareth ever had. He smiled at the receiver. "I'll be okay. More importantly, how are you?"

"Glastonbury."

The strange word hung between them. Gareth's pulse began to race. He stared over at Donovan who was now sitting on the bed with a smile plastered on his face.

Gareth swallowed "And?"

"True…here…mom…right."

Gareth let out a frustrated sigh and banged the receiver on the table. With the wealth of technology at his fingertips, he was always amazed that he couldn't get a clear connection when he needed it the most. "Kathryn, you're fading out. Start again."

He heard the excited intake of breath across the globe. "It's HERE! You and Donovan have to finish."

Gareth stared at the small safe sitting in the corner. He knew if he opened that door the lights would once again mesmerize him and take his focus away from the task he had to complete.

"Are you still there?"

Gareth turned away from the treasure that would change the world. "Yeah."

"Have you found it?"

He stared down at the elegant invitation sitting beside the phone. "Heaven and Hell," he whispered.

"Say again?"

"We're going tonight…into Hell."

The voice trembled. "Gareth…"

"It's going to be okay, Kathryn. You've got the fun part, remember? You just stay in Heaven."

"And you just make sure you get out of Hell," Kathryn replied. "Call me tomorrow. Let me know the minute you guys have the book in your hands."

Gareth laughed. "The second *I* know, *you'll* know, my little dictator."

"Gareth?"

"Yeah?"

"What if…even *with* the book…you still can't find them?"

"Then we'll find someone who can," Gareth replied, as the librarian's deep blue eyes flashed in his mind.

"Be careful, Gareth. Your stars don't look good tonight."

Sliding the invitation aside, Gareth stared down at *The New York Times*. Reading his horoscope, he snickered. "Come on, Kathryn. You don't actually *believe* in that nonsense, do you?"

"Very funny."

"I'll talk to you tomorrow, kiddo. I promise."

"I love you."

The words warmed his heart, as the line disconnected. He placed the phone back on its cradle and stared at Donovan.

His well-tanned friend stood up and pointed at the tuxedos wrapped in plastic, hanging on the back of the door. "To get to Heaven, you have to go through Hell." Donovan smiled.

"And what happens if we can't make it through Hell?"

Donovan reached into his jeans pocket and extracted the well-used Blackberry.

Gareth snorted. "Checking with the Google gods to see how all this is gonna' end up?"

"Oh," laughed Donovan. "You know me. Just keeping my little diary of all the things we've done so far. Don't want to lose a single second of this. We'll need all this information to write our bestseller once we discover the prize."

Gareth's voice came out sharp and cold, like the edge of an axe. "That's not what this is about."

Donovan lowered his Blackberry. "I know what this about." Reaching out, he placed a hand on Gareth's shoulder. "I loved your parents, too. Remember that. We're doing this for them. All of this is for them…to finish the work they started."

"What if we're wrong?" Gareth wondered out loud. "What if my parents were wrong? Maybe it's not our place to do this."

Donovan squeezed his bicep with all the strength he possessed. "Don't ever second guess this, Gareth. You need to honor their memory. Even Kathryn knows that. You're both doing the right thing. We can't stop now." A menacing tone entered his voice. "Your parents would never forgive you."

Gareth hung his head.

"Besides…just think." Donovan relaxed his grip. "If this works out like it should, you'll be able to see them again, son."

Gareth sighed. "How many times do I have to tell you not to call me son? You're only three years older than me, for crissake."

Donovan ran a hand through his already tousled hair and began punching more buttons on his electronic appendage. "True. But I have far more wisdom than you, Gareth Lowery. Besides, with your incredibly over-sized ego you need to be put in your place once in a while. That's why I'm here." He looked up and winked. "Of course, after what you told me about Madame Librarian, your ego may have just met its match." He grinned. "She's even more beautiful than you, I hear. Must've hurt when she tossed you aside."

Gareth rolled his eyes.

"Maybe if you can't woo her with your slow-witted brain, those movie star good looks of yours might finally come in handy."

"Comb your hair," Gareth shot back. "You always look like an out-of-work bum." He grabbed the tuxedo off the back of the door. "It's embarrassing to be seen with you."

Closing the bathroom door behind him, Gareth added, "Oh, yeah… and go to hell!"

*

"That's exactly where I'm trying to go," Donovan whispered back, as he stared at the safe in the corner. He could feel the treasure pulsing inside like small, angry heartbeats. They were yelling at him to find the other half of the power that would make them useful again. He punched in a message on the Blackberry.

> Lowery found the One. A woman who can solve it all. And his annoying sister found the location. Glastonbury. We're more than halfway there.

The return message appeared on the screen like magic.

> *Don't get ahead of yourself. And don't get cocky.*
> *The Lowery clan are a lot of things, but dumb isn't one*
> *of them. I've already begun Plan B in case you fail.*

Donovan felt the anger swell inside his chest. Hatred burned in this soul as he stared at the elegant writing. The ego of his replier was far greater than Gareth Lowery's would ever be.

> I won't fail. I'll see you in Hell.

The Blackberry screen filled with a bright yellow smiley face. The words underneath the familiar picture were big, black, and bold; a dare, if ever Donovan read one.

Race ya'.

Donovan erased the offensive message and cursed his father for saddling him with such a vile, pompous brother. "I'll win," he whispered. "I'll beat you…and I'll be in charge of the whole damn thing."

He could feel the flame burning in his soul as he stepped to the door and grabbed the other elegant outfit. Staring at the bookshelves surrounding him, he took in the horrific scenes of gleaming weapons protruding from screaming, bloodied victims on the covers of the bestselling thrillers, and felt a wave of happiness. The eerie décor of the *Mystery Room* located in The Library Hotel was beyond appropriate, Donovan thought, seeing as he was about to begin his own dark, exciting journey into Hell, following in the footsteps of the other chosen ones.

Listening to Gareth humming behind the bathroom door, Donovan felt as happy as a schoolboy with his first crush. He couldn't wait for the day when Lowery was a pile of broken bones and rotted flesh under his feet.

"Enjoy your last adventure, Gareth," Donovan chuckled. "I'll make sure you and Kathryn see your beloved parents again…sooner than you think."

CHAPTER FOUR

Leah pulled up to the valet parking area roped off between Patience and Fortitude. A young college student opened the door of her compact, reliable, gas-friendly vehicle, and offered her his hand.

Adjusting her glasses on the bridge of her nose, she stepped out and stared at the boy whose eyes suddenly filled with sadness. Following his woeful gaze, Leah saw another valet give his friend a thumbs-up as he raced away to park the gleaming silver Porsche that idled beside Leah's boring vehicle.

She reached into her tiny handbag and placed a twenty-dollar bill into her valet's hand.

The young man looked startled. "Thank you, Ma'am."

"I want *my* Porsche to be taken care of just as well as that other one. Better, in fact, because I actually *need* my car."

"Yes, Ma'am." He grinned.

Leah nodded and made her way up the steps. Her breath caught in her throat as she stood in front of the majesty that was her place of business. The dazzling lights beamed out onto Fifth Avenue. The beaux-arts building seemed to be alive; the words of the geniuses housed inside the mammoth structure felt like they were radiating from the stones.

She stopped to straighten the black bowtie that hugged the neck of Patience. She wondered who had first come up with the bright idea to decorate the statues. At Christmas, holly wreaths were placed around their manes. When announcing springtime to the City, they wore wreaths of colorful flowers; and, for graduation day, they donned square caps with golden tassels that hung precariously over their sharp teeth. Tonight, it was bowties—one black, the other white—representing the theme of Heaven and Hell in literature.

Leah sighed and continued her trek up the steps and into the building. "I could be home reading a good book right now," she muttered.

As she stepped inside the only real home she'd ever known, another young urchin appeared out of nowhere. Racing forward, he practically tore her leather coat off her shoulders. He looked bored beyond belief. Leah knew he was probably wondering why he was stuck in a room full of rich old coots who tipped like it was still 1920, instead of sitting at home and mastering the latest game on his new Playstation 46—or whatever model they were up to by now.

Leah had a strange moment of sympathy for the boy. She was sure he was confused. He was probably wondering why people would bother to pick up a book, when they could simply type in a keyword and learn all they needed to know about any subject imaginable in just seconds. This new generation, she knew, was built on simple and time-saving techniques. No one had the hours or the inclination to actually read anymore; just point and click and the world was at their fingertips.

She passed a ten-spot to the young man, and nodded at the genuine smile he offered her in return. After all, she may dislike teenagers, but at least they were working. Considering she was about to enter a room full of adults who had no idea what hard work really was, she found the boy slightly refreshing, and added another five to his sweaty palm.

"Wow! Thanks lady."

"Do me a favor?" she whispered.

"Ma'am?"

"Try not to let any of these drunks touch anything."

The boy offered a nervous laugh as another tall, gangly youth in an ill-fitting tuxedo marched up to them. A heavily-laden tray tilted in his hands. "Would you like anything?"

Leah sighed. "What idiot would serve finger food in a library? After a few glasses of champagne these apes will destroy everything in their path."

His face turned beet red.

"It's not your fault." Leah placed a hand on his shoulder. "Just steer clear of the real morons, okay? The last thing we need is a clump of caviar stuck to the pages of the Gutenberg Bible."

Both boys nodded obediently and moved away.

Leah watched in agony as the heavy silver tray wavered in the young man's hands. "This is going to be a mess," she whispered, staring up at the black and white sign that still hung crookedly above her head. At the top of the elegant staircase there were two doors. Over the first was the Yin symbol promoting Heaven. Above the other was the Yang, heralding the entrance into Hell.

"Well, I'm already in Hell," Leah snorted. "Might as well start with Heaven."

Not two seconds after her black stiletto heels clicked over the threshold, did the loud voice of Director Shaw echo in her ears.

"Miss Tallent! There you are. Thank goodness you've *finally* arrived."

Plastering a fake smile on her face, Leah turned around to meet her boss. "Director Shaw, what a lovely evening." She shook his hand, ignoring the elegant men standing on either side of him. "It seems to have gone off without a hitch. You should be proud."

He gave a slightly tipsy bow; the champagne in his full glass spilled over the crystal rim and hit the floor. Leah cringed at the sticky mess, but the Director ignored her glare. "All due to your hard work, my dear. I merely take the credit for being intelligent enough to hire the best."

Leah ripped her hand from the short man's sweaty grip when she noticed his flirtatious wink. "Yes, well…thank you, Director."

Out of the corner of her eye, Leah watched the guests set their flutes of champagne down on the white oak tabletops, and tried her best not to scream.

The Director's voice droned on at her side. Suddenly, Leah realized that her name had, yet again, been called.

She turned back to her boss. "Sorry?"

Shaw attempted to mask his frustration. "This is Mr. Gareth Lowery and his business partner, Mr. Donovan Barker. They are *very* generous patrons."

Leah reached out and shook the shorter man's hand. "Pleasure to meet you Mr.….Barker, was it?"

"It was and is, Ms. Tallent." He smiled. "My friend told me you were stunning, but he's usually a liar. I can't tell you how pleased I am that this is one occasion where he was completely honest."

Leah tried to hide the sudden shudder that raced through her body when the man squeezed her hand tightly in his freezing cold grip. She could feel her sixth sense click on like a protective light bulb inside her brain. Offering her best attempt at a smile, Leah quickly turned away from his eerie black gaze and focused on the other man waiting quietly by his side. Her eyes moved up the well-built body. A gasp of surprise escaped her lips when she recognized the familiar emerald eyes.

"We've already met." A deep growl resonated from the teacher's throat.

"Gareth Lowery."

Tearing herself away from his mesmerizing gaze, Leah quickly recovered. "I was under the impression that you were a schoolteacher." She heard the accusatory tone flowing through her words.

"Filling in, actually." The man turned to the bewildered Director and shrugged his tuxedo-clad shoulders. "I was here earlier today for the tour. Brought some students along. Doing a favor for a friend. You know how it is."

"Ah." Mr. Shaw offered a lop-sided grin. "So you *did* get the tour from Miss Tallent, after all. Good, good. She's the best."

"Actually—" Leah began.

"Unfortunately Ms. Tallent was called away before our tour could really begin." Gareth finished.

"That *is* unfortunate." The Director shot her an angry look.

Leah stiffened.

"It wasn't her fault," Gareth continued. "She was doing her job—making sure that this remarkable exhibition was ready for tonight. I completely understood. After all, she certainly didn't have time to play babysitter when the final touches had to be applied to this most elegant evening." With a perfect smile, he added, "From the basement on up, this woman seems to know your library like the back of her beautiful hand."

The scowl disappeared from the Director's face, and he beamed at Leah. "Yes, yes. She's wonderful. And her hand is definitely not the only beautiful part of our dear Leah. Don't go trying to woo her away from us now. I simply won't stand for it." Shaw offered an unmanly punch to the muscular benefactor's bicep.

Gareth's smile wavered, and he turned back to Leah. "Maybe now is a better time?"

"For what?" she asked.

"To finish the tour."

"Well...I should really see to—"

"She'd love to!" Shaw bellowed.

"I think that's a great idea," Donovan Barker added.

Everyone in the small circle jumped when his quiet voice entered the conversation. Leah had forgotten that the man with the strange black and blue eyes was still a member of their group.

Donovan aimed a smile at Gareth. "You two kids go on and I'll stay with the Director, son. I want you to learn all you can about this fantastic building."

"You two kids?" Gareth rolled his eyes. "Seriously?"

Leah moved her gaze back and forth between the two men who couldn't possibly be father and son. When her eyes came to rest on the Director's frustrated gaze, Leah jumped into action. She suddenly wanted nothing more than to escape the eerie Mr. Barker and her visibly angry boss.

She focused on the green eyes of the man who seemed much less threatening than the other two. "I'd be delighted to finish our tour, Mr. Lowery."

Hesitating for a split second, a smile finally appeared on his face. "Call me Gareth," he said, offering his arm to escort her away from the group.

Leah ignored his gentlemanly gesture, turned on her heel, and walked quickly toward the heavenly side of the exhibition. Feeling like the Devil, himself, was at her heels Leah once again immersed herself in the one subject that made her feel completely safe. "The New York Public Library is the largest free library in the world. Its size is second only to—"

*

Gareth raced after her as she marched quickly by the exhibition tables. "I must say, you're about the fastest woman in high heels I've ever met. You must have very good balance to stay up on those things."

Leah took a deep breath. "My mother's a fashion queen, which is where I got the love of beautiful shoes. My sisters, thank goodness, got the rest of Mom's female weirdness."

Gareth studied her from top to bottom. The soft auburn curls that—try as she might with the spinster—like bun to hide—still framed her face like an autumn crown, and her enchanting eyes that seemed to hold a world of knowledge in their blue depths, caused a flame of passion to ignite in his soul.

She placed her fists on her hips. "What…exactly…are you looking at?"

"This get-up doesn't work for you, Leah." Gareth pointed at her long black dress.

"I just told you that female ridiculousness is not my forte, Mr. Lowery. And you *will* call me Ms. Tallent."

He laughed. "What I meant to say, *Ms.* Tallent, is that your choice of demure dress doesn't even begin to hide your long legs. If you're trying, which I believe you are, to keep the men away, then I should tell you that clothing yourself in mystery is not the way to do it. Like any gift, Leah… the wrapping doesn't matter." He leaned toward her and dropped his voice to a whisper, "Tearing it off and getting to play with what's underneath is basically all us boys want to do."

"Who do you think you are?" Leah demanded. "Look, I don't care how much money you and your friend give to our institution, I won't be spoken to like this."

Gareth's spine straightened immediately. Panic flowed through his veins when he realized that his normal 'playboy' routine wasn't going to fly with the furious lady standing before him. "I'm sorry."

"What do you want, Mr. Lowery?" She spoke through clenched teeth. "I suggest you think before you answer. Your whole shtick," she continued, "doesn't work with me."

Gareth took a deep breath and answered honestly. "I really am sorry. I'm used to women…"

"Falling at your feet?"

He shrugged. "Makes things easier."

"Stretch yourself. Try something new."

"Look, all I want from you is-" Gareth stared into the angry sapphire eyes. "Information about your library."

"That's it?" Her voice came out like a dare.

"Yes," he replied, crossing his fingers behind his back. "That's it."

Leah turned on her heel and walked back to the double doors of the Main Reading Room. "Well, Mr. Lowery…if that's the truth—." Her eyes bore into his soul. "Then we should get this over with." She pointed to the door. "Shall we?"

Swallowing hard, Gareth glanced back over his shoulder. Donovan's black eyes were stuck like glue to the librarian's angry face. Noticing Gareth for the first time, Donovan raised his glass and saluted his friend.

Gareth read his lips.

Go get her.

CHAPTER FIVE

Keeping his mouth shut, Gareth listened to the stream of intelligent words that flowed effortlessly from her lips. He wanted to force her to speed up, to ask questions, to get the answers he needed. But, as the knowledgeable woman continued to speak, he felt himself pulled into her words like a lost soul into a beam of heavenly light.

Her eyes gleamed like the summer sun glaring off a rich blue sea, as she regaled him with the marvelous works of art that were part of the library's huge collection. Her voice took on an air of reverence as she pointed up at the restored ceilings; the recessed sky murals offered a picture of brilliant sunlight all day long—no matter what the forecast was outside. The puffy, white clouds floated above their heads as she pointed out the gold and copper leaf that'd been meticulously restored to its former brilliance.

Gareth found himself mesmerized, listening intently to the sultry voice as she told him of the seven levels that made up the library; stacks upon stacks of books that surrounded them; the words of genius flowing down from the balconies above. She pointed out the pneumatic tubes that ran from the Main Reading Room to the other floors. In minutes, someone could get any book they wanted from any level, as they listened to the "whoosh" of the canisters carrying their request to a helpful librarian.

Her voice was like a hallucinatory tonic flowing through his veins. "Director Shaw was right." He smiled. "You certainly know everything there is to know about this place."

Her cheeks flushed with color. "I work here."

"No," said Gareth. "It's more than that. You make it sound like this is your place of worship…not your job."

He followed her loving gaze to the frescoes decorating the Caen stone walls.

She cleared her throat. "I admire the workmanship."

Gareth looked down at the glass cases on the tables draped in stark white fabric. "And was it you who chose the books on display here tonight?"

Leah stared at the chalice pictured on one of the bestsellers and rolled her eyes. "Yeah, right. Like I would pick *this* to represent Heaven? I don't think so."

Gareth pushed a stray blond curl off his forehead, and smiled. "You don't believe?"

"History is much more interesting than fiction," said Leah. "Besides, if religion's what you're after our library has the actual Gutenberg Bible."

"Fiction and nonfiction living side by side. Seems balanced to me."

Leah raised an eyebrow. "Which one is nonfiction?"

Gareth smirked. "Isn't the Bible generally regarded as a nonfiction work?"

"I'm an atheist."

"No you're not."

"Excuse me?"

Gareth stepped closer. He leaned in, his mouth inches from hers, and whispered, "There's no such thing as an atheist, Leah. At some point everyone looks up."

She took a quick step back.

Catching the sudden look of fear in her eyes, Gareth altered his voice back to the charming professor. "Besides, I have irrefutable proof that there is some type of god," he stated. "Only a higher power could make anything a beautiful as you."

Leah rolled her eyes. "This is really getting old."

Gareth raised his hands in mock surrender. "There's also a devil. Do you want to know how I know that one?"

Leah waited.

"Anyone who looks like you and chose to become a librarian is like Miss America becoming a nun. It isn't fair for you to hide out here and not be seen by the world." His voice grew soft. "If I hadn't come here I would've missed you completely. And *that* would've been a tragedy of epic proportions."

Leah's glare turned angry. He knew that he was treading on thin ice. Clearing his throat, Gareth offered her what he hoped was a more intelligent avenue. "As your exhibition clearly states, you can't have one without the other." He pointed up at the crooked sign. "Yin and Yang, remember? Without Heaven there would be no such thing as Hell—and vice versa. Humanity needs both sides of the coin to survive."

Leah shrugged. "Then perhaps you should go to Hell." She pointed into the room with glittering black tablecloths. "After all, as a mere mortal you should pay homage to both."

Gareth nodded and shook the icy feeling from his spine. "You have to go through hell to get to Heaven," he mumbled.

"Then it seems we've made this trip backwards." She stared at him strangely. "We should've started in Hell."

"For me to move forward I have to go back."

Leah's gaze burned through his skin. "Do you write fortune cookies in your spare time, Mr. Lowery?"

He grinned. "Horoscopes, actually."

"Worse than I thought."

"You don't believe in the existence of God. You don't believe in horoscopes. What *do* you believe in, exactly?"

Without a moment's hesitation, Leah answered, "Books."

"Books are truth?"

"Books are real." She smiled. "Books are tangible. Most were written by people smarter than me, so they're easier to believe."

Gareth shook his head, trying to figure out how to get through the tough, unbreakable skin of the woman standing before him. "Forgive me…but isn't the Bible a book?"

"I've been told it's a Good one." She laughed.

Gareth felt his hands begin to tremble and his smile waver, as the librarian's grin disappeared and she once again stared into him instead of at him. He wondered how she did that. It was as if the strong, clear, honest eyes were like lasers radiating through his skin, uncovering the reason he was really here. Maybe she was a human lie detector, searching for any variation in his pulse or heartbeat to proclaim him a liar and cast him out of her precious building.

Her voice was quiet when she finally spoke. "What's with your friend? Barker?"

"What about him?" asked Gareth.

"He's not like you." She shrugged. "He doesn't exactly seem like the 'full of faith' type."

"You only met him for two seconds." He tried to keep his voice steady.

"Can you read people that quickly?" He watched her eyes fill with anxiety as she bit down on her full, red lip. He took a step closer. "What?"

She shook her head. "There's something not right about him."

"Donovan?" Gareth's stomach quivered as he stared across the room at a man he'd known for quite a few years. A smile was stuck to his friend's face as he stood and listened to the Director drone on, but his gaze was still locked on Leah like a starving hawk on a tantalizing rabbit. Gareth had no idea why the strange feelings exploded inside of him. He suddenly wanted nothing more than to stand in front of Leah and protect her from…what? Gareth shook the thoughts from his mind. Donovan had helped him through the hardest moment of his life, and his friend deserved nothing less than his total allegiance—no matter what the fascinating librarian said. "He's okay. I trust him."

"Forget it." Leah shook her head with disgust. "Let's get this over with so I can go home and forget about the both of you."

Gareth stepped back from her suddenly angry tone.

"Let's go play in the flames of pure evil, shall we?" she said, pointing at the other open door.

Gareth's throat went bone dry at her words. Saying a silent prayer, he took a deep breath and stepped over the threshold into Hell.

CHAPTER SIX

"Over here, we have Aleister Crowley."

A shudder of fear raced through Gareth's soul when Leah said the name he wanted to hear. He took a deep breath and tried to steady his voice, feeling the stacks of books closing in around him. He had to play this just right. "What would a lovely lady like you know about such a hideous man?"

He was awestruck as he watched her gaze darken. It was as if she were a card catalogue of knowledge. All he had to do was ask a question and her brain was off, sifting through facts filed inside her mind. The strange overprotective feeling came over him once again, and he found himself hoping that her knowledge would only contain surface facts—the type of information offered in reference books. Gareth knew if Leah held the in-depth data that he and Donovan were searching for, he would have no choice but to drag her into their dangerous world.

She turned to face him. "Our Director has seen fit tonight to promote Heaven with the Bible, religious doctrine, and other…more questionable texts. He also decided that Hell should focus on books that use the terms magick, occult, and astrology to represent the dark side of human nature."

Gareth smirked. "I've always found it amazing that the ancient religions of the world are now categorized as occult."

"Hypocrisy at its finest," she agreed.

The fire in Gareth's soul erupted into an inferno when he stared into her understanding eyes.

Clearing her throat, Leah turned away. "In Mr. Crowley's case, however, our Director was probably correct in his assumption that he would be a perfect representation of the evil side of religion. In fact, Crowley was once known as Satan by his followers."

"Okay." Gareth leaned against the wall; a feeling of dread washed over him. "Tell me what you know."

Leah stuttered at the part-command, part-dare, but her brain called up the information and sent it through her lips. "He was born Edward Alexander Crowley in 1875. He was a writer, mystic, astrologer, and even dabbled in the occult."

"Doesn't sound like Satan. Sounds like a well-rounded individual to me."

Leah grinned. "The Satan reference was started by his mother. Crowley's parents were devout in their chosen religion, but little Edward had no desire to sit around all day quoting scripture. His mother began to call him the name of the Beast, and it stuck. He loved being referred to as the Devil. He thought it was the perfect title, considering he believed that the laws of God were hypocritical."

"Still sounds human. Bit of a zealot—probably fun at parties—but not exactly a supernatural being." Gareth attempted a smile.

Leah raised an eyebrow. "Crowley used to tell people that he'd sat with The Council of Masters."

Gareth forced himself to breathe slowly when the librarian hit the bull's-eye.

"He believed that this powerful group of men lived in every time period. Crowley claimed that this Council asked him to join them in order to bring their scripture to the huddled masses." Her voice held a note of sarcasm. "Sound familiar?"

He nodded. "Almost biblical."

"Precisely." Leah continued, "Crowley always did like messing with the old school. He was the Yang, so to speak, of Heaven. Al even put pen to paper after his life-changing experience with this so-called Council and wrote, *The Book of Law*, which you see in the display case. His followers used this as their very own bible. It contains everything from normal prayers and phrases, to sexual magick practices and numerical ciphers that, according to Al, *he* couldn't even decode. Crowley believed in free will. He also believed that the only law that should be practiced was the law of pleasure."

"Still doesn't sound so bad to me." Gareth offered his best attempt at a sexy grin.

Leah rolled her eyes. "In that respect, he was just another deviant who was a proponent of sin. Not exactly a cutting edge idea."

"So his ideas weren't *all* out in left field?"

Leah seemed to stop in the middle of the open card catalogue inside her brain to select the more disturbing facts. Her voice grew serious. "He once wrote in a book of his own confessions that he didn't wish to serve or even believe in a devil—he just wanted to get in touch with the real one and become his chief of staff. He wanted to find a way to harness Satan's evil."

He shuddered at the familiar words that Donovan always spoke.

Leah took a deep breath. "Other things…darker things…began to come out."

Gareth held his breath. It was as if puzzle pieces were falling from her lips, forming the explanation he'd been searching for.

Leah stood stock still. Like a political candidate running for office, her voice was a monotone. "Stories began to circulate about practices and rituals that were being used to summon demons to do Crowley's bidding. The strangest moment came in 1902. That's when Crowley began announcing that he'd made contact with Heaven, and knew beyond a shadow of a doubt how and where to find the Pearly Gates."

Gareth's mouth went dry.

"He said that monsters had shown him the way." Leah smirked. "Crowley started talking about a Union of Opposites—a lot like our Yin/Yang symbolism here tonight. He said that if the Devil was real—which to Crowley was a fact—then the other side had to exist, too. He was the first to say that to get to Heaven a person had to experience Hell first. These 'chosen' people would have to don the armor of knights and prove themselves worthy enough to find utopia, by actually fighting their way through a dark and savage world.

"Aleister claimed that he was told all this by the Holy Guardian Angel. He also said he'd been hand-picked to hide this angel's path from the world."

Gareth shuddered. "Did he?"

"Did he what?"

"Find the gates of Heaven?"

"I doubt it." She laughed. "Theologians have decided that Al was more of a heretic than anything else. Even the house he'd lived in eventually became nothing more than a tourist trap."

Gareth took a steadying breath. "Anything else?"

"Al was a great speaker. He quieted down in his later years, though." She shrugged. "As he got older, he stopped talking about Heaven and Hell and began an obsession with the Ouija board."

Gareth raised his eyebrows. "Is that why that toy is in the display case?"

Leah looked into the glass box where *The Book of Law* was leaning against the ridiculous game board. She nodded. "There's not much published about Crowley's work with the Ouija board, but one of his followers said that Crowley would use it to try and summon the angel to help him keep the keys to Heaven's door hidden."

"Why would an angel ask a devil like Crowley to hide Heaven?"

Leah tilted her head to the side, staring up at him as if he were a complete and total loon. "That was Crowley's Union of Opposites theory. In other words, male needs female, black needs white, and Heaven needs Hell to survive. He said that the angel gave him part of the secret because a truly faithful person would never go to someone like Crowley for answers. A person of true and devout faith would never follow someone like him into the darkness, even if it meant finding the answers to life after death. Because of that, the secret would remain safe."

"What would stop Crowley from exposing the secret? Or simply walking through the gates of Heaven himself?" asked Gareth.

"I told you. Crowley was only given *part* of the secret. Just like the Yin and Yang—the balance of all things. In this instance, a devil—Crowley—held half of the answer and, I suppose, a saint held the other." She shrugged. "Only together could they reveal the truth to humanity… the locations of Heaven and Hell."

Never breaking their gaze, she continued, "If someone knew the *whole* secret, the gates of both would open. Different religions refer to this, but the most common that you might be familiar with is the Second Coming. You know? The big knock-down, drag-out fight to save the world?"

"Do you believe all this?"

"I'm an atheist, remember?" Leah grinned.

A deep voice came from behind them. "Atheists, my dear, are simply the Devil's joke."

Leah practically jumped out of her skin when Donovan Barker materialized beside her. Turning on her heel, she fell against Gareth's side.

Gareth's arm came out immediately and wrapped around Leah's waist to steady her. He glared at his friend. "Must you always pop out of the middle of nowhere? You're gonna' give someone a heart attack someday. It's creepy."

Donovan smiled. "Sorry about that."

Leah nodded, noticing that the apologetic smile never quite reached Barker's penetrating eyes.

"I couldn't help my rudeness." He continued, "I've been lingering behind you two for a while now and I must say, Ms. Tallent, you do know your subject."

"Are you a Crowley fan?" She tried to keep her voice steady as a chill crawled up her spine. Her sixth sense screamed at her to be careful.

Donovan laughed. "I've studied him…as well as others. You and I actually have something in common. I, too, believe that Crowley was trying everything he could to find a way to harness the Devil's power. He was one of those remarkable people you hear about who wanted to be the Devil's chosen one."

"You call him remarkable." Leah glared at him. "I call him a nutbag."

"Really?" Donovan leaned back on his heels; the strange blue light bounced in his eyes, making him look like an insane child laughing with joy. "It's well documented that Crowley was exceptionally smart. He had *some* kind of power in him. Some…knowledge, shall we say, that others didn't have." He grinned. "As a research librarian I would think you'd have to keep an open mind on all issues, so as not to color peoples' opinions."

"Mr. Barker," Leah began. "If you believe that Crowley had a way to bring the actual Devil inside him, than you'd have to believe that there *is* an actual Devil." Her voice dripped with sarcasm. "And if you believe that, then you'd have to believe in the other side, too."

"You really don't believe in God?" His lips twitched into a daring little smirk.

Leah took a step back from the hypnotizing beam that seemed to radiate from his eyes. "If there were one," she replied. "There wouldn't be all this ridiculousness in the world. Blaming all the horrible things that plain old morons do in the name of war, peace, etcetera, on some phantom being called Satan, is just a way to ease everyone's conscious. *Human* slime balls make the world evil, Mr. Barker. Men like Crowley."

Donovan took a long sip of champagne and stared at Gareth. "A fine upstanding Christian boy like you is going to have a hard time romancing this lovely non-believer."

"I'm not romancing her," Gareth said through clenched teeth. "I'm interested in what she has to say."

Donovan reached out to pat Leah's hand. "I'll pray for your soul, my dear."

His touch felt like that of a corpse; Leah pulled away from his freezing cold skin. "Don't bother. My soul is well protected…by me. I can see a serpent in *my* garden from a mile away."

He smiled.

"You know?" Leah tilted her head to the side. "You remind me of Crowley."

"Really?" His face brightened, as if she'd paid him the highest compliment a person could bestow. "In what way?"

"Al liked listening to the sound of his own voice, too," she stated firmly. "He also loved fame. He wanted way more than fifteen minutes of it."

Barker's black eyes flared.

"How many minutes are you looking for, I wonder?" She grinned.

Gareth cut in, "Okay. That's enough." He nodded at Donovan. "I don't think you and Ms. Tallent are on the same page. Why don't you go back to the Director and have a chat about good and evil, and leave me in the company of this fantastic lady?"

Barker raised his glass in mock salute. "As you wish, Lowery. You're in charge, after all."

Leah glared at the retreating tuxedo, as Barker sauntered away from them. "What's he mean by that? In charge of what?"

Gareth sighed. "I don't know."

"You don't seem like you'd be friends," Leah remarked. "Of course, as you pointed out, I just met you both. Maybe you're just better at hiding the fact that you're an asshole."

"Are you ever wrong?" Gareth leaned against the wall.

"My mother says I am."

He hung his head and stared at the floor.

"Look," she sighed; a touch of sympathy laced her suddenly delicate voice. "Forget your friend. It's none of my business, anyway. And, as far as Crowley is concerned, he wasn't much of a bad guy either." She grinned. "Throughout history, Gareth, the world needed people like Crowley. We've had one or more of him in every era where atrocities have taken place. Salem, Massachusetts had their witches to burn. England had its traitors who committed treasonous acts against the crown and lost their heads on the steps of the Bloody Tower. All decades had evil, and they all had their knights in shining armor who spilled blood for their land—or, their God—depending on the day."

Gareth rested his chin on his fingertips, and committed to memory the monumental knowledge of the beautiful woman. There was a part of him that wanted her to keep talking. The other part wanted to turn and run away from the woman who seemed to be the only person alive who could help him solve the mystery his parents left behind.

CHAPTER SEVEN

Leah reached out and took his hand; she looked genuinely worried. "Enough of this. You want Hell? Watch the evening news. You wanted to hear about the New York Public Library and here I am going on and on about some dead fanatic. I'm sorry."

Gareth clasped her hand in his and they marched out of the room. As they walked by the display cases and out into the hall, Gareth barely glanced at Dante dancing in the flames of his Inferno, or the eerie shadow cast by the Overlook Hotel that played home to the demons of Mr. King's imagination.

Leah, perhaps sensing his tension, went back to the words she could recite like clockwork. "Like you, Andrew Carnegie was the huge benefactor who built this place. He was the one who wanted a free library where the public—no matter how poor—would be able to come, sit, and read the words of the finest minds imaginable. We're actually the second largest library after the Library of Congress, you know."

Gareth found his voice again. He glanced at the small door in the corner marked, *Private*. "Carnegie laid the cornerstone for this library in 1902?"

"That's right."

"Carrère & Hastings were the architects?"

She smiled. "You've studied."

Gareth shook his head. "No. I've heard of Hastings before…and Carrère. He died, didn't he?"

"Yes." Leah nodded. "They were both good friends of Carnegie. Unfortunately, John Carrère was in a taxi that collided with a streetcar."

Gareth felt more puzzle pieces settle into place.

"You're standing over what was once the Croton Reservoir. There are subways, passages, and climate-controlled rooms below us." She grinned. "We keep all the things we don't want your demonic students to ruin locked away down there like our own little vault."

Gareth continued to stare at the door and pasted his charming smile back on his face. "May I see the basement?"

"Sorry. Patrons aren't allowed. Not even the ones who put a lot of zeroes on their checks can go through that door."

"Aw, come on." He took a step closer. "I just want to see what's there. I saw you go down earlier today."

Leah stepped back. "It's just old books, card catalogues that were replaced with computers, a couple of chairs, and an old coffee machine."

"Sounds…cozy."

She cleared her throat. "Rules are rules."

Snaking his arm around Leah's waist, Gareth pulled her against him. "I like Crowley's idea of free will better than rules right now. Maybe tonight our dark sides should be given a chance to play. What do you say?"

Leah's words came out loud and sharp, like a general's command to the troops. "I don't have a dark side, Mr. Lowery. And even if I did, I wouldn't explore it with you."

Gareth stepped back as if she'd smacked him across the face. He shook the lustful thoughts from his brain and buried the heat that threatened to consume his body. He tried to regroup. No matter what, he had to find a way to get through the locked door. "Leah, I'm sorry. That was stupid. You don't understand. I have to see the basement because—"

"Well, look who we have here."

Leah and Gareth whipped their heads around. Skylar, barely covered in a tight, red dress, sauntered toward them. Her face was a mask of sheer determination.

Gareth watched the wave of relief flood Leah's eyes. "You made it!"

"Of course I made it." Skylar flicked her eyes to the muscular man. "Why, Mr. Lowery. I barely knew it was you—so handsome and elegant. Let me guess, professor by day, secret agent by night?"

"Good to see you again, Ms. Trewitt." Gareth bowed, trying with all his might not to scream his head off at her rude interruption.

Skylar reached out and seized his arm. "What *are* the two of you doing standing all alone in the corner?" She batted her eyelashes at Gareth.

"Miss Tallent was giving me the extended library tour. I just can't seem to get enough of her vast knowledge of this place."

Leah spoke up, "Our tour is over, Mr. Lowery. I'll stop prattling on now. Besides, I'm quite sure that our Skylar would like nothing more than to share some champagne with you."

Skylar took her opening and pulled Gareth toward the festivities. "Leah's absolutely right. I would like nothing more than to get to know you better. Why, I've been thinking about you ever since this afternoon. And, my…the thoughts I've had."

Gareth tried not to cringe at her annoying giggle, as Plan B began to form in his mind. He squeezed the eager woman's side, and dropped his voice to a low, throaty growl. "Maybe we should shy away from the party. Now that Ms. Tallent is quite obviously through with me," he continued, looking back at Leah's flushed face. "We could grab our champagne, go through that private door, and explore more deeply some of those thoughts you've been having."

Skylar squinched up her nose. "That old place? Forget it. The last thing I want to do is ruin my beautiful dress with cobwebs and dust. Even the Director wouldn't be caught dead in that dirty, smelly old basement. That's why our Leah has the only key—the key to her kingdom." Skylar turned to her. "Why *do* you sit down there? Do you have a secret yen for dungeons or something?"

Gareth saw the spark of anger in Leah's eyes. "I'm the head of research, Skylar. There are manuscripts and resources held in that dirty, smelly old basement that directly affect the work I do here." She aimed her gaze at Gareth. "And the reason I have the only key is to keep people away from things that shouldn't be touched."

"Pssh!" Skylar returned her focus to Gareth. "Believe me, Mr. Lowery, there are a ton of secluded, *clean* corners in this old building where we can sit and examine my thoughts."

Grabbing two flutes of champagne off the silver tray of a passing waiter, Skylar walked up the staircase attached to Gareth's side. "I saw you upstairs earlier standing with our other handsome visitor from today. Are the two of you related?"

"No. His name is Donovan Barker." Hope filled Gareth's soul. "In fact…let me go get him! I'm sure he'd *love* to have more time in your gorgeous company."

"No need." Skylar held tight to her prize. "I definitely have my hands on the *right* one."

Gareth sighed. "So did I."

*

Leah's stomach churned as she heard his whispered reply. She watched

Skylar's hips move from side to side up the stairs, looking like a voluptuous pendulum wrapped in a tight red spandex shell.

Her horrible giggle sliced through Leah's brain, as Gareth Lowery suddenly turned back and flashed his emerald eyes at her. Leah's breath caught in her throat. He looked at her as if she were a beacon of hope against all the evils of the world.

When the couple disappeared to the second floor, Leah reached behind her and checked the knob, making sure that the door to her private world was indeed locked. Her brain was confused; warning bells rang out inside her skull. She couldn't help but wonder why their meeting seemed like a life or death event to Gareth Lowery. And no matter how hard she tried, she couldn't let go of the creepy feeling that his friend had spawned in her with his eerie blue-black gaze.

Grabbing her coat from the bored teenager at the door, Leah raced away from the mystery men who were now hidden on the second floor. Gareth's worried green eyes continued to dance in her head; eyes that seemed to believe that the answers to life's biggest mysteries were hidden deep inside the bowels of her library.

*

Donovan stood on the balcony and watched the tall, auburn-haired librarian rush from her beloved home. He could hear Gareth's voice in the darkness; he sounded like he was pleading with the wanton woman named Skylar to grant him his freedom.

Donovan laughed to himself as the Blackberry suddenly came to life inside the pocket of his tuxedo jacket. He looked down at the annoying smiley face staring up at him.

> *What do you think of the One Lowery found? Is she all she's cracked up to be?*

Donovan punched in his reply.

She knows more about Crowley than you do.
Impossible.
Not at all. You should envy me. I'm having the most fun. Her name is Leah. And she is stunning.
Beautiful AND smart? I do envy you. That's a first. If she's that smart there's more of a chance you'll fail.
To quote you, brother...impossible.
Why's that?
She doesn't believe.
In?
Donovan laughed.
Anything. As far as she's concerned none of this exists. She did say that she was wise enough to see a serpent in her garden, though.

The flood of type on the Blackberry's screen came to a stop. It was as if the man on the other end was considering his newest challenge.

Is she...wise enough?

Donovan mimicked his brother and waited a bit, carefully considering his response.

Maybe. But Lowery's not. And she doesn't like him enough to care what I do to him. No one as smart as she is would risk anything for the likes of Gareth Lowery.
Be careful. The genes in her family are strong.

Donovan laughed out loud. The nerve of his brother never ceased to amaze him.

What could you possibly know about this woman's family?

See that? I'm once again far ahead of you. Ciao.

Donovan slammed the device back into his coat pocket and marched down the staircase, damning his brother with each step. He knew all he needed to know about Leah Tallent and she was certainly no match for him. Gareth would find the book and follow the path his parents had left behind. That's the type of man he was—loyal, compassionate, honest—a real life hero.

Because of these ridiculous traits, Donovan knew that Gareth would put the lovely librarian to good use. She was the perfect asset he needed to find the answers, and to keep Gareth in line at the same time. After all, the woman was strikingly beautiful, and there was nothing more important to a hero than saving a damsel in distress.

CHAPTER EIGHT

If she ever saw the son of a bitch again she'd kill him, Leah swore to herself. Here it was, a beautiful fall day in New York City. Probably one of the last remaining days where a person could enjoy the crisp, fresh air and vibrantly colored leaves before the white blankets of snow rolled in, and the wind chill made you feel like a sunbather trying to get a tan on the polar ice caps.

But could she enjoy it? Could she immerse herself in the fragrance and feel of Bryant Park in the fall? Could she revel in the fact that it was a beautiful Sunday morning and she was on her way to worship at the only cathedral she'd ever known where she would enjoy a cup of slow roasted coffee and read the newspaper? No! She couldn't. Because her brain was too busy replaying the unexplainable images from her troubled sleep.

All night she'd tossed and turned as pictures of long-dead fanatics came alive inside her mind; each monster had possessed flashing green eyes that spoke to her of Hell, yet sent her to a place that could only be described as heavenly. The throbbing pulse deep inside her body had begun overnight when she'd stared into those brilliant green eyes filled with need…with passion…

"Enough!" Leah shouted, frightening the jogger coming up beside her.

"Sorry," she mumbled, as the woman glared at her and sped up—clearly wanting nothing more than to get as far away from the crazy woman as she could.

Taking a deep, calming breath Leah stared up at the only home she'd ever really known. Patting the lions on the head she wrenched the ridiculous bowties from their regal necks. Feeling better, Leah took out the ornate key and opened the door. She stepped into the confines of the massive building and closed her eyes, reveling in the silence.

Happily, she noticed that the crooked sign had been folded up and carted away. The caterers, too, had done an admirable job; not one napkin or lipstick-covered flute marred the white oak tables. All remnants of the drunken soiree had been wiped away and the surfaces polished back to their original brilliance.

Leah let her gaze wander up the large staircase to the second floor where the green-eyed man had disappeared just a few short hours ago. She willed her legs not to climb; she had no desire to see any creases on the overstuffed couches, or leftover articles of clothing scattered on the floor where Skylar had undoubtedly conquered the strange man.

Prying her gaze away from the shadows, Leah marched to her private door. Today she planned to sit with the master, Poe, and listen to the dark side of a romantic's thoughts. She opened the door and flicked on the dim light. Closing and locking it behind her, Leah descended into the basement.

As she reveled in the scent of old parchment, she walked over to the small machine and loaded it up with her favorite coffee beans. The pipes began to rattle inside the walls when she turned up the heat. They seemed to be screaming in protest at having to work on this, their one day of rest.

Leah took off her leather coat and hung it on the old rusted hook in the corner; the wonderful scent of coffee brewing filled the air. Walking down the hall of bookcases, Leah ran her fingers over the well-known titles. Spotting Poe, she reached up to grab his large book of stories when a loud crash suddenly shook the room, sending the huge tome smashing down on top of her skull. The sudden explosion rattled her teeth, and her head throbbed with pain, but she tried her best to recover. A shot of adrenalin sent her running down the narrow hall; she prayed that an animal—or, worse—hadn't broken a window.

Racing around the corner, Leah skidded to her knees. Small bits of rock covered the floor and acted like marbles underneath her boots, sending her crashing to the floor. Her eyes grew wide as she stared into the corner. The entire backside of Carnegie's marble cornerstone jutted out into the room. It looked like a monster wrecking ball had slammed into the block, sending sharp and heavy chunks of marble into the air.

Heaving herself off the floor, Leah backtracked toward the phone on the main level. She needed to call someone and get them down here quick.

A scream stuck in her throat when a hand reached out and pulled her arm behind her back. In seconds, her attacker had claimed her other arm, and was wrapping her wrists in what felt like metal handcuffs.

Leah closed her eyes. She didn't want to be killed—or, worse—in her favorite place. She couldn't even imagine the kind of scum who would assault someone in the basement of a library, not to mention blowing up the literal cornerstone of intellectual human civilization. Fear coursed through her body as a familiar growl broke through her terrified thoughts.

She whipped around to face her attacker and found herself staring into the familiar emerald eyes that'd haunted her dreams.

A smile twitched at the corners of Gareth's mouth. "I thought you didn't believe in God."

"What?"

"You looked like you were praying."

Leah took a deep breath and spoke the only words her brilliant brain could come up with. "Fuck you."

"Now, now, Leah. Is that any way for a demure librarian to talk?"

"Who the hell *are* you? Untie me, you creep!" She brought her knee up to strike, but Gareth moved faster.

Catching her around the waist, he threw her over his shoulder like a caveman. Walking down the hall, he dropped her on one of the overstuffed chairs; a cloud of dust rose from the threadbare cushions.

Leah struggled with the cuffs. Her whole body shook with anger. The hairpins broke free and sent her thick, auburn mane down over her face like a waterfall of lava. Quickly, she threw her neck back to move the curls from her eyes so she could gauge her attacker's intent. Her anger turned to rage as she watched him calmly pour two cups of coffee and set them down on the table in front of her.

Leah's muscles tensed when he made another quick move, and reached behind her. She heard the click of the manacle and her left hand was suddenly free. She lunged. But with the speed and stealth of a lion on the hunt, he re-shackled her wrist to the marble table.

Gareth dropped into the chair beside her. Remarkably, he sounded frustrated, like a father whose little girl had gotten into his den and messed up his important papers. "Leah, what are you *doing* here? It's Sunday! Don't you *ever* take a day off?"

"What am *I* doing here?" Rage mixed with confusion. "What the hell are *you* doing here? How did you get in? And why did you set off a bomb in my library?"

He rolled his eyes. "Leah, for God's sake."

"God doesn't have anything to do with this!"

"Actually…" He raised his hand in the air.

"Do you honestly think you can get away with this? Are you planning on killing me? You'll have to do it, pal. Because the minute I get out of this I'm going to throw your sorry ass in jail faster than it took Skylar to get in your pants!" She smashed her hand against the underside of the table; the mugs overturned and sent hot coffee down the leg and onto her flesh. "Damn it!"

"Will you calm down?" yelled Gareth.

"Calm down?" she screamed. "Are you out of your mind?"

"I'll assume that's a rhetorical question."

"Now is *not* the time to be a wiseass." She watched carefully as Gareth, still dressed in his tuxedo, stood up, poured more coffee, and once again set down the offering in front of her.

Gareth shook his head; bits of stone and plaster fell to the floor. When his hand disappeared inside his jacket, Leah's heart leapt into her throat. This was it. This was how she was going to die. But instead of the weapon she expected, a different sort of metal object appeared in his hand.

He placed the round, flat item between them on the table. Much like the banner from the night before, the flattened metal was cut down the middle by a line of solid gold. One side was copper with a large opal in the center; the other side was silver with a polished onyx stone. The black and white jewels made the object look like a medieval mask.

Leah held her breath when Gareth unclasped the lock at its center and opened the two sides. She exhaled. "It's a book." She blew air from the corner of her mouth to move the heavy curtain of curls out of her eyes.

Reacting, Gareth shifted in his seat and reached out his hand to help her.

"Don't touch me!" She glared at him.

Immediately, he threw his hands in the air. "Just trying to help."

"Then take the cuffs off."

Slowly, he shook his head. "Not. Just. Yet."

"This is ridiculous." Leah sighed. "Who *are* you?"

"I promise I'll tell you everything. But you have to calm down first."

"Stop telling me to calm down!"

Gareth brought the hot cup of coffee to his lips.

Anger burned inside her as he calmly crossed his legs and leaned back in his chair as if he were a normal man enjoying his Sunday morning. "I could kill you with my bare hands right now."

He held the mug out to her. "You can have some if you calm down. But you have to listen to me first."

"Oh, for crissake!" screamed Leah. "Fine! Tell me your damn story! It won't change anything."

"I want you to know that I'm taking a huge leap of faith here." Gareth took a deep breath. "But I truly think you're the one and only person who can help me. Believe me, what I'm about to tell you is going to sound a little…crazy."

She grunted. "You? Crazy? That'll be a first."

"Leah…please."

"Get on with it!" she snapped.

Carefully placing his mug on the table, Gareth put his elbows on his knees and leaned toward her. Flipping open the cover of the strange book, he took a deep breath. "What do you know about the Akashic Records?"

Out of sheer habit her brain came alive, and sent her the information. She gazed at the metal book lying open on the table. One side was filled with old, faded handwriting on pure white parchment. Hieroglyphics showing various images of the sun had been drawn on the ancient paper, like strange maps from an unknown world. The other side of the log was filled with chalk drawings on sheets of thick, black paper. As she looked closer, Leah's stomach lurched. The crude drawings depicted humans in various stages of torture and death.

She shifted her gaze to Gareth. "This isn't the Akashic Records."

His gaze eyes bore into her soul. "How do you know?"

"The Akashic Records aren't a tangible book."

"What are they?"

Leah rolled her eyes as if he were a student playing dumb. "The Akashic Records are a myth. They're a…library of the mind."

"Go on."

"Let me go," Leah seethed.

"Soon." He leaned in closer. "I promise this will all be over a lot quicker if you just cooperate with me."

Rage consumed her. "Then I suggest you quit playing twenty questions with me and get on with it."

Gareth nodded. Taking her advice, he spoke quickly, "There are people who believe that each soul records every minute of its time down on Earth in a sort of…cosmic book. They also believe that if they learn how to focus, they can read this book…view their past lives."

"The records you're talking about are a myth." She gritted her teeth. "They can't be proven because no one can ever find them. They only exist in someone's *mind*."

"Are you sure about that?"

"About as sure as I am that you're an asshole," Leah snapped. "So, yeah, I'd say I'm pretty sure."

Gareth tried not to grin, knowing that a smile would spark another screaming match. "The sooner you answer my questions the sooner you'll never have to see me again."

She sighed. Scanning the card catalogue in her mind she found what she was looking for. "The Akashic Records aren't scientific fact, or even religious texts. They're just an idea."

"What if they could be proven?"

"Who would care?"

"Leah!"

"I don't know," she shouted back. "I suppose...it would prove that there's not only life after death but *many* lives after death. But it's like proving beyond a shadow of a doubt that Heaven exists. You can have faith in anything you want but there isn't, and never has been, any actual *proof* that it's real."

Gareth's deep voice filled the warm basement, as the over-worked pipes clanged behind the walls like prisoners demanding their last phone call. "The Akashic Records prove that we're all Divine, Leah. They prove that there's a Creator. They prove that souls are real and they're inside each and every one of us—put there by a higher power that sends us back again and again. And if souls are real, in the end, Heaven is just as real as this basement."

"Do you smoke pot?"

Gareth rolled his eyes. "Do you want the cuffs off?"

"Okay," she snorted. "I'll play along. How, exactly, does blowing up my library help you find records of past lives that only exist in your own mind? Apparently you have a mess of personalities in there already, so maybe you've already zoned in on the fact that you've been crazy in *all* your lifetimes."

Gareth shook his head in disgust, and closed his eyes.

Her emotions went wild; a ball of confusion sat in the pit of her stomach. She literally couldn't believe it. The man had handcuffed her to a table and then had the nerve to act like *she* was annoying *him*. She was the prisoner, yet he acted disappointed that she wouldn't sit still and listen like a good little girl. "Hello!" she screamed.

Gareth's eyes popped opened. "I've spent years trying to find...

something. And, while looking for it, I came across the Akashic Records and their most avid supporter. Using him, I've been able to put together a puzzle of mammoth proportions." He pointed at the metal book. "This is a clue to finding the rest of the pieces. I've traveled all over the world, and I'm slowly finding the answer to the greatest mystery mankind has ever known."

"Okay…I see where this is going." Leah rolled her eyes. "I knew your friend from last night was creepy and weird, but I didn't realize that you were one of them, too."

"Them?"

"You know…one of those fanatics who see the Virgin Mary in a mud puddle; or the image of the Devil in their morning oatmeal?"

He dropped his head in his hands.

Leah's fists clenched, and the metal cuffs pierced her skin. "Look! Gareth, or whatever your real name is, I don't care if God wears white robes, if angels truly do sing, or if Jesus was married, had a kid, and owns a time share in Palm Springs. I honestly couldn't give a shit less."

Frustration filled his voice. "This is way bigger than all that."

"What then? Elvis? Aliens?"

"You're not funny," he snapped.

"I'm not laughing," she snarled.

He glared at her. "I'm very close to finding the actual location—the entrance into Heaven that's opened by twelve keys based on the astrological signs."

Leah's blood began to boil at his insane words. She was livid that her current pain and misery was due to some whack-job's quest. "You want to go to Heaven? Untie me and I promise I'll send you there."

His green eyes twinkled with mischief. "I'd love to let you take me to Heaven, but I'm afraid we don't have the time right now."

"You make me nauseous." Leah spat in his face. "Wasn't Skylar enough for you?" Fear and panic suddenly filled her soul. "Jesus! You and your friend didn't bury her down here?"

Gareth rolled his eyes. "We took your friend home last night, Leah. And, by the way, she was too drunk to get into anything…including my pants."

She grimaced. "I *really* don't want to know."

Gareth's gaze wandered from the book on the table, back to her angry gaze. "Give me thirty minutes. If I can't convince you that I'm not crazy in that time, then I'll take the cuffs off and you can call the cops. Deal?"

Leah stared into a face filled with hope. As soon as she got out of this predicament, she swore to herself that she'd comb the city for an excellent psychiatrist. After all, Leah knew she must need her head examined when she made the decision to listen to a person who should be scaring her to death.

CHAPTER NINE

Gareth stood up and began pacing the green, frayed carpet. He attempted to collect his thoughts before releasing another crazy diatribe at the woman he needed more than life.

"Get on with it already," said Leah. "Clock's ticking."

Taking a deep breath, Gareth stood straight and tall in front of her chair. His hands at his sides, he felt like a student readying for his first oral exam in front of a very angry teacher. "Rudolf Steiner was an Austrian philosopher. In 1902, he headed up an organization called the Theosophical Society."

"I *know* who Rudolf Steiner was," she muttered.

Gareth wiped his sweat-soaked forehead. "Of course you do."

"Is there anything else, or can I call the cops now?"

Gareth sat down on the coffee table and focused all his efforts on convincing her that he was sane. "Rudolf Steiner believed that people's spirits were suffocating under the stress of daily life."

"Ain't that the truth."

"He believed in reincarnation. In fact, it was the basis of all his lectures. He told people that they could see their past lives. If they learned how to focus, they would actually be able to *see* what they'd done before."

"The Akashic Records."

"Yes." Hope welled up inside him, as her skin began to return to its normal color. He prayed that her anger was fading with his explanation. "Steiner believed wholeheartedly that, depending on what you did in your past life, you would benefit or pay in the next."

"Karma."

"Exactly!" He slapped his knees.

"So?" She didn't blink; her eyes remained riveted to his face. "How does this explain why you tried to blow up my library to get an ugly metal book with pictures in it?"

"I did *not* try to blow up your library!" Gareth took a calming breath, and started again. "I did not try to blow up your library. Look. It wasn't so much what Steiner believed as who else agreed with him. Steiner gave a ton of lectures that focused on ancient civilizations, tracing the origin of humanity back over thousands of years—even before the birth of Christ."

"There goes your Heaven theory, aye?"

Gareth sighed. "Jesus was born way after the establishment of Heaven."

"And you know that for a fact because you were there."

Ignoring the sarcasm, he continued, "Steiner looked to astronomers, astrologers, and other scientists-"

"Science?"

He grimaced. "Once upon a time astrology and astronomy were considered exact sciences, like math. They were revered in intellectual circles. Those scholars not only believed in the immortal soul, they could and *did* prove—through the stars—that Heaven existed."

Her face remained blank. "Once upon a time is how all good fiction starts out."

Gareth quickly continued, "Steiner preached a theory of twelve world views. He believed everyone's soul was made up of six good and six bad traits—a perfect balance. That's why he was chosen."

"You lost me," Leah muttered.

"For every materialistic trait in your personality, you also have a spiritual trait to offset it. Your soul is made up of a mixture of dark and light. You're balanced."

"Yin and Yang."

"Exactly." His smile faded as she offered him a frustrated glare. "A perfect human being is one whose flaws exactly number their virtues. These souls are enlightened and can see their past lives."

"So what does astrology have to do with Steiner's world views?'

Gareth felt giddy. He could almost see the wheels turning in her overactive mind. He knew she was filtering information through her brain, looking for documents that could either support or destroy his theories. "Steiner said that the sun moving through the twelve signs of the zodiac represented our souls moving through various lives. Ancient civilizations founded their religions based on the zodiac. Steiner believed these twelve signs made up the map that pointed directly to the gates of Heaven."

"So what?" She sighed. "Through your soul you can find Heaven. It's like a fortune cookie. Have faith, believe, and you'll find God. It's still a theory—at best."

"But put it into a tangible thought, Leah." He slid closer to her. "There are books—your favorite things—and whole civilizations that firmly believe the twelve constellations of the zodiac are Heaven's hieroglyphs."

She nodded. "I understand what you're saying. But, in the end, it *isn't* tangible."

"What if Steiner was speaking literally?" Gareth's eyes grew wide. "Wouldn't that change the theory into tangible proof?"

"What do you mean?" Leah's voice came out as a whisper, drowned out by the loud clanging of the ancient heat registers.

Gareth forged ahead. "Steiner told his students that the *orbs* of the zodiac were the key to finding the gates of Heaven."

"My headache is now exploding."

He reached out and touched the side of her face, trying to keep her attention. "Leah, what if these orbs he talked about were real? What if there's truly a zodiac key to a precious lock that has been guarded for centuries? What if there were two people selected—Yin and Yang—who were each given the job of hiding half of these orbs where no one would be able to find them?"

"Reaching a bit, aren't you?"

"Leah," he sighed.

She jerked away from his hand; the warmth of his skin made her body tingle. "You're taking a huge leap of faith here. Maybe the word *orbs* was just a figure of speech, like when Steiner said anyone could find the Akashic Records if they just concentrated hard enough."

"Look." Gareth lowered his voice. "I can't explain everything in the next fifteen minutes but, believe me, my mother was an astrologer and my dad was an astronomer, so—"

"No wonder your head's in the clouds."

"*So,*" Gareth stopped her sarcasm. "I know what I'm talking about where this is concerned. You're going to have to trust me."

"*Trust* you?" Leah banged the handcuff against the table making him jump. "You're kidding, right?"

He began to pace the floor. "My family believed they could actually find the entrance to Heaven. Philosophers as far back as Plato left us clues. Heretics and Knights joined forces and hid the orbs over centuries. That way, if one side talked, the other side would keep the rest of the secret hidden. Good and bad will never fight for the same cause." His voice grew hard. "That's one thing that *has* been proven beyond a shadow of a doubt."

Leah closed her eyes and sighed. "It's a pretty theory, okay? Everyone likes to believe in the 'other side.' Even atheists like me feel a slight comfort in this."

"You mean both sides." Gareth stared down at her exhausted face. "The simplest explanation is a 'good' person hid six of the orbs in heavenly places on Earth, and a bad guy hid the other six. The secret would have iron-clad protection because believers in a god would never ask a devil for help. And believers in the dark side of humanity would certainly not turn to God's followers for anything, let alone begging for the secret location to His world. The bad guys wouldn't want people to find Heaven anyway; they want everyone to follow them."

"Stop." Leah rested her head on the arm of the chair. "Let's say, for argument's sake, that you're on to something. Let's say these zodiac orbs exist and have been hidden for thousands of years. How would you possibly find them now?"

Gareth felt the knot tighten in his chest, as he made the final decision to pull Leah head-first into his quest. "I've found half of them already."

"Sure you have," she muttered.

Gareth reached out and put his hand under her chin, lifting her face to meet his. "I'll show them to you. I'll tell you everything…how Donovan and I figured it all out. I won't hide anything from you. But I have to continue, Leah. This book has been hidden over and over again for ages, and has been sitting in your library for over a hundred years. It holds the only clues in existence that point to the hiding places of the orbs.

"The last time it was used was in the early 1900's, when the world began to split apart at the seams. Immigrants came from everywhere, and numerous religions began popping up around the globe. That's why they chose to re-hide the orbs, just in case there were people coming from distant shores who knew the secret."

"How do you *know* all this?" Leah stared at him; confusion blazed in her eyes.

"Steiner was the 'good' guy they chose to hide half of the orbs."

She shook her head. "He was a heretic. People called him an occultist."

"Not then," Gareth continued, "In 1902, he was still a beloved scientist."

A cold feeling of dread washed over Leah. She felt scared all of a sudden, like a tiny voice imbedded deep inside her brain was screaming at her to stop listening before it was too late. But she couldn't help herself; the need to know was far too great for the librarian to ignore. "Who was Steiner's alter ego…his Yang?"

Gareth remained silent, chewing on his bottom lip until he could taste blood.

Leah's steady stare filled with the gleam of challenge, and her voice came out like a dare. "Come on, Lowery. You've come this far. Who's the bad guy?"

CHAPTER TEN

The metallic taste of his own blood coated his tongue; even his body was trying to mutiny. There wasn't one single reason he could think of to put Leah in harm's way except…Kathryn. His sister's face hovered in his mind. She was already waiting there…at the end…counting on him to come through and finish what their parents began—what they'd risked their very lives to achieve.

"Well?" asked Leah.

Sending out a prayer to anyone who was listening, Gareth finally spoke, "You know that Andrew Carnegie worshipped libraries. He also worshipped other things, Leah. Like the Knights of the Round Table, Carnegie had a secret society made up of twelve men who called themselves the Council of Masters. Their only duty was to choose who would do the dirty work; who would hide the completely *tangible* artifacts known as the Keys to the Kingdom."

"The Council of Masters?" she whispered.

Gareth studied her suddenly pale face. "Remember? In the 1900's writers, artists, architects—even banking institutions—were basing their work and their very lives on Steiner's belief system."

"Banks?"

Gareth continued, pushing her brain to the limit. "People believed in reincarnation. That's why some, like Andrew Carnegie, gave back so much of their fortunes to institutions like this library. He believed that he would be safe in the next life by doing good works in this one. By knowing about the orbs, Carnegie also had tangible proof that there was a Heaven. Not faith. Fact."

Gareth could almost see her struggling to answer the questions zooming through her brain. He wondered if the puzzle pieces were beginning to take shape in her mind. Moving closer, he saw the thin line of sweat on her forehead and felt her warm uneven breath on his skin. "If Heaven is a historical fact, it goes to figure that—"

"Hell exists, too," Leah finished. Her eyes grew wide. "The Council of Masters? *Crowley*?"

He nodded. "Aleister Crowley."

"No way!" She scoffed. "The guy was a loon."

"Crowley was the same as Steiner," said Gareth quickly. "He was just the dark side of the coin. He knew—not believed—*knew* that souls were real entities that simply made a pit stop in Heaven or Hell before coming back to Earth again."

"The Council of Masters that Crowley talked about was *real*?" Leah gasped.

Gareth rubbed her arms, trying to warm her goose-pimpled flesh. "In 1902, Rudolf Steiner was giving lectures."

"1902?" she repeated.

"That same year, Crowley wrote *The Book of Law*, and went around telling people that an angel had appeared to him and told him the Truth. *You* told me all this last night. Of course, no one believed Crowley was being serious because by then he'd blatantly shown that he was crazy.

Who'd believe that the self-proclaimed prophet of the Devil would actually know the whereabouts of Heaven?"

Leah remained silent.

"Steiner and Crowley were chosen by Carnegie because of their views. They were invited to a meeting which was held in a hidden room on the fifth floor of Carnegie Hall. There, the Council decided where the Yin and Yang—Crowley and Steiner—would hide the orbs. Then they recorded those places in a book—*this* book—written by the angels and demons that'd been chosen over time to hide the priceless keys."

Leah stared at the metal log. "But where did this come from? How did it get into the hands of a bunch of men in 1900's America?"

Gareth gave a sigh of relief. He felt better now that the blood was once again flowing in her cheeks. "Andrew Carnegie's family was one of the oldest in Scotland. Generations of his relatives had been involved over time in keeping this information hidden. This knowledge was passed down to him like a torch, way before he made his emigration to America. He'd been searching for a long time for the right people to help him.

"That's when he attended a lecture that Rudolf Steiner was giving in New York and decided that he was the one to help. And picking Crowley, well…not a real stretch considering what Crowley was preaching at the time, he made the perfect devil."

"Carnegie did love libraries," Leah mumbled, as she continued to stare down at the metal book resting on the marble table. "They were his passion."

Gareth nodded. His voice grew soft. "It seems fitting that he would've buried the most important book in the world in a place known across the globe for higher learning. Like it is to you, Leah, this building was Carnegie's cathedral."

She gazed at him. "You said artists and architects were part of

Carnegie's circle of friends. Carrère and Hastings, the architects of this place, must've known about the book when they laid the cornerstone in 1902."

"I'm sure they did." He agreed. "In fact, Hastings helped me to come here. Without his clue I would've been lost."

"Huh?"

"I'll explain that part later."

"What about Carrère's accident?" she asked.

"I don't know." Gareth shrugged. "Could've been just that—an accident. Or, maybe someone thought he knew something and killed him because he wouldn't turn over the book. There are other people out there searching besides me, Leah. I can't even tell you for sure that the other half of the orbs will still be in the locations that are written in that book. Someone could've already figured this out and found them. I found six without the help of this book, remember?"

"Gareth?"

"Yes?" He placed his cool hands against her inflamed cheeks.

"What happens when you get them all together?" Her voice was filled with fear. "I mean…what if you succeed? Do you just put them side by side and Heaven falls down from the sky like a meteor?"

He took a deep breath. "We already know where the end is."

She sat back in the chair, as far back as the handcuff would allow. "You and your friend…Barker?"

He nodded slowly. Gareth decided to save Kathryn—the more personal part of his story—for a later time, knowing that there was already way too much information pressing against every corner of Leah's amazing mind. "But I need to find the six orbs that Crowley hid before I can even think about the end. I need to go through Hell to get to Heaven."

Leah shifted in her chair. "I still don't understand what it is you think

I can do about all this."

"I need your help," he whispered.

"Why me?" She slammed the cuff against the table. "I think you're crazy, remember?" Her voice turned cold. "Time's up."

Without a word, Gareth reached inside his jacket and removed a small, silver key. Unlocking her wrist, he slumped into the chair beside her. Gareth bowed his head in defeat, knowing that his incredible journey had just come to a screeching halt. He'd been so close. Now, just like that, it was all over.

*

Leah glanced at the staircase leading to the main floor of the library. She could see Gareth from the corner of her eye. His head was bowed and his eyes were shut tight, as if he was finally contemplating the jail cell that awaited him.

Talk about complete confusion. Leah should run; she knew that. But the sixth sense she'd trusted all her life was telling her to stay. Reaching across the table she picked up the heavy book. Checking to make sure her kidnapper wasn't making any new threats, Leah began thumbing through the pages; dark and light, side by side, she attempted to decipher clues from the past.

From Egyptian handwriting that reminded her of a book she'd once read about the lost Library of Alexandria, to a strange map with Latin text that looked like it came from the secret vaults of the Vatican Library, Leah found herself sucked in to every amazing page. There were unbelievable signatures at the bottom of each sheet that she couldn't wrap her mind around: Plato, Socrates and, oddly enough, one that she could've sworn read, Merlin. The librarian in her was exhilarated beyond belief.

Leah paused when the strangely familiar words met her gaze. On the 'good' side of the book, there was a hand drawing of Christ dying on the cross. Above it, instead of scripture, were the words to the song *Rock of Ages.*

"Without the book," she began. "Without the clues…how could you possibly have found the first six orbs?"

"I thought I was going to jail," came the sarcastic reply.

Leah tried not to smile at the man who now sounded like a petulant teenager. Flipping through the 'evil' side of the book, she quickly passed over the strange scenes of slithering serpents, and victims with mouths open wide in silent screams. She'd rather not dwell on those; she feared knowing too much about the worst possible side of humanity.

But when she came across the familiar slanted handwriting, she stopped dead in her tracks. On the dark page, opposite the sketch of what she'd assumed was ancient Alexandria, was a childlike drawing done in white chalk. The lines looked like rooftops; spires and steeples rose up into the blackness. Scrawled on each triangular eave was the number thirteen and, on the largest one, there was a chalk outline of a human being. A bullet-hole had been drawn dead center in the person's chest.

Leah blocked out the sirens and whistles that erupted inside her brain, and read the words at the bottom of the page:

To me, a book is a message from the gods to mankind…A. Crowley

Closing the cover of the strange book, buried for over a hundred years in the basement of her favorite place, Leah turned to the defeated man sitting quietly beside her. For the first time in her life, she had no idea what she was doing. It was as if Crowley, himself, was daring her to solve his riddle; taunting her with the fact that she just wasn't as smart as he had been.

She sighed heavily. Like her father, Leah had to go further than the rest. She had to excel. It wasn't a choice it was a necessity for her. Research, books, words…they were like a drug. She absolutely *had* to know.

If her father had been sitting beside her, Leah knew exactly what he'd say. He'd tell her that a gift had been dropped in her lap—a chance to literally step away from the books, go into the unknown, and solve a mystery that a true historical devil had left behind. Making a mental note to find that star psychiatrist as soon as possible, Leah reached over and touched Gareth's arm, causing him to practically jump out of his skin. "You own a laptop?"

He grunted. "They have some at my hotel…why?"

The computer clicked and beeped inside Leah's brain, searching her own database for the answer to the first clue that she knew was designed to take her into Hell.

Standing up, she stretched her back and grabbed her leather coat. Turning, Leah stared into the confused green eyes. "Let's go see these orbs of yours."

CHAPTER ELEVEN

Just a few short steps from the New York Public Library, down Library Way, they quickly arrived at Gareth's hotel

"How appropriate." Leah tried not to roll her eyes as she stared up at *The Library Hotel*.

Gareth grinned. "I thought it really fit in with the theme."

When they entered the luxurious lobby, the large fireplace immediately erased the chill from Leah's bones. The motif was truly relaxing. Stacks of books lined the walls and burgundy leather chairs offered a comfortable place to rest. Looking at the décor of the den made Leah think of Sherlock Holmes. She could imagine him coming through one of the ornate wooden doors dressed in his favorite smoking jacket—requisite pipe in mouth—and taking a seat.

"Good afternoon, Mr. Lowery." A sweet voice called out from behind the large mahogany counter.

Leah's stomach churned as she watched Gareth's face transform back into the rich, arrogant playboy. His mega-watt grin returned and he offered a wave to the young woman. "Good afternoon, Valerie. Are there any messages for me?"

Valerie handed him a stack of messages, and fluttered her long eyelashes like a butterfly on cocaine. "A lady named Kathryn keeps calling for you," she said, with an exaggerated pout.

Gareth placed his hand against the young woman's cheek. "Kathryn is my sister."

Beaming with relief Valerie leaned across the counter, revealing as many assets as she possibly could from beneath her modest red jacket. "That makes me feel *so* much better…knowing I'm still in the running, that is."

"Don't run too fast." Gareth winked. "Makes it harder to catch you."

"For the love of God," mumbled Leah. "Do I really need to be here for this?"

Gareth turned toward the elevator, and whispered in Leah's direction, "You look a little green, my dear librarian. Jealousy, perhaps?"

"My skin has a tendency to turn green when I'm about to puke."

Gareth pressed the elevator button. "Nice lady, that Valerie. I've never stayed here before, but I must say the staff is top notch."

"You make me physically sick."

"That's new." He cocked his head to one side. "I don't think I've ever had that reaction from a woman before."

"Then you might want to rethink my company, Mr. Lowery." Leah batted her eyelashes dramatically. "A few more hours with me and your over-inflated ego will be flat as a pancake."

The doors opened, and they stepped out on the eighth floor. Gareth pointed at the fancy sign on the wall. "This is the Literature Floor," he said. "*The Library Hotel* has ten floors that are all based on the Dewey Decimal System."

"How cute."

"Isn't it?" He laughed.

"Let me guess?" said Leah. "You're holed up in the astronomy room?"

Gareth pulled out the key card from his wallet. "Nope. I thought I should pick something I'm more comfortable with. Something, you could say, that's closer to my personal beliefs."

Leah was startled when he walked directly to the big oak doors labeled, *Erotic Room*.

He looked back over his shoulder. "What's the matter? You wanna' take a look inside, don't you?"

"Are you kidding?"

His eyebrows rose up his forehead. "Aw, c'mon. There just might be some literature in here that even the great Madame Librarian is unfamiliar with. Could be an interesting experience."

"Seriously," she stated loudly. "Gonna' puke."

Gareth walked to the next set of doors, laughing all the way. "Just messin' with you. I would never expect a lady such as you to even enter a room filled with such sinfully explicit material."

Leah offered a one finger salute as Gareth threw open the door. "I decided that the *Mystery Room* would be much more appropriate considering the journey of discovery I'm on."

Walking over the threshold, Leah looked at the stacks of books and paintings covering the walls. She read the well-known titles and stared at the chalk-covered outlines on the bloody covers. "Mysteries aren't all that interesting, Mr. Lowery. There have been so many written that there's no new way to kill anyone anymore."

"I wouldn't worry about that, Leah." He smirked. "I'm sure with a little time and effort you could find an intriguing new way to kill me."

"No doubt." Turning, she offered him a smile that she hoped projected the evil thoughts that were dancing in her mind. "As a matter of fact, I've come up with a few already. Scared?"

"More like…intrigued." He grinned.

Leah felt her heart skip a beat as the mesmerizing eyes seemed to burn directly into her soul.

Gareth's voice grew soft. "In fact, I find myself completely intrigued by you. The sultry voice—the unfathomable blue eyes that glitter behind those heavy glasses of yours—you're truly a mixture of passion and poise."

Leah held her breath as he took another step closer.

"I wonder how someone would go about breaking that prudish mask you wear to wrestle the animal inside."

Struggling to find a stinging retort to his blatantly suggestive words, Leah's usually loyal brain failed her. "You're so full of shit."

"You missed your calling." Gareth laughed. "With the wonderful handle you have on the English language you could've become a much beloved author."

"Bite me."

"I rest my case." He grinned. "I think I'll take a shower and change my clothes. I can't entertain you when I'm covered in plaster and sweat."

"I didn't come here to be entertained," she reminded him. "The cops can still be called, you know."

"And I, for one, wouldn't blame you if you called them."

Leah let out a yelp of surprise when Donovan Barker once again appeared at her side. "Jesus! Must you do that? Can't you cough or something?"

He grinned, wiping his hands on the small red towel. "Sorry about that. I was in the bathroom. Thought you heard me."

Leah took a deep breath, trying to get her heartbeat under control.

"Although it *is* nice to know that I can sneak up on you whenever I want." Donovan added, "That particular gift might come in handy someday."

Leah clenched her teeth at the arrogance flowing through his voice. "I wouldn't go that route if I were you. I have a tendency to shoot first and ask questions later."

"A woman after my own heart." He smiled. "Now, tell me, what has my friend done that would bring New York's finest to his door? Don't get me wrong. Whatever it was I'm sure he deserves a night in the slammer."

Leah raised her chin in the air. "He blew up my library, wiseass. And handcuffed me to a table."

Donovan looked her up and down as if she were a slave at auction. "Interesting."

Gareth moaned. "For the last time, I did *not* blow up your library!"

"But you did handcuff this beautiful lady to a table?" Donovan's voice was filled with sarcasm.

Gareth shrugged.

"Well. I don't blame you a bit, then." Donovan offered Leah a penetrating stare. "There's no shame in falling for a woman like you. You shouldn't be so hard on the lad."

Leah clenched her fists at her sides, but the eerie bluish light that beamed from Donovan's black pupils made her skin turn cold. Her throat went dry; her usually strong voice came out unconvincing. "You're an even bigger ass than your friend."

Swiping a hand through his bronze hair, Donovan winked. "I'm bigger in many departments, Ms. Tallent."

"Give me a break." To avoid the evil eyes, Leah stared down at his disheveled wardrobe. Donovan's t-shirt was wrinkled underneath the faded plaid shirt he wore. The buttons of the shirt were hanging on by mere threads and they were off-kilter, as if he'd been in a hurry to dress and hadn't noticed which button went with which hole. Leah didn't get it. The shabby garb, the tousled hair… none of it fit with his intelligent face and arrogant demeanor. She suddenly felt as if she was standing in the presence of a great actor; a man who wore his careless costume like a shield that hid the deviousness of his sharp mind.

Leah turned back to Gareth. "You have thirty seconds."

Nodding, Gareth walked quickly to the small safe in the corner. "They're in here."

Feeling incredibly warm, Leah threw her jacket on the bed, still avoiding the quiet man at her side. The weight of the world felt like it was sitting on her shoulders. She kept her focus on Gareth, watching him as he unlocked the safe and retrieved a green knapsack. Sitting down on the bed, he carefully opened the well-worn case.

With trembling legs, Leah walked forward. Her heart beat fast, as he unfolded the large green towel and set the odd-looking artifacts on the bedspread.

She gasped. They were small, able to fit in the palm of her hand. But they were humming—a fast beat like a tiny drum—and small lights danced inside each one. Inside the first orb was a small hologram of a ram. The light surrounding the miniature animal was bright red, like a flame was pulsing inside the glass ready to break the shell and set the small animal free. The bright red beam blinked on and off like a malfunctioning stoplight.

Holding her breath, she stared at the orb sitting beside it. This one held a bull. Its eyes were bright green, and the flame that burned around the figure looked like emerald fire. She was mesmerized by the blinking lights of the two orbs—red and green—like an evil Christmas tree. Taking a step back from the angry, proud faces of the ram and bull, she whispered, "They're terrifying."

"They are, aren't they?" Laughed Donovan. "Terrifyingly beautiful, as all truly great things are."

"*Terrifying?*" Gareth glanced at the orbs. "I think they're wonderful."

The evil red eyes of the ram made Leah's body shake with fear. Sitting down on a high-backed chair by the window, she took deep, even breaths to calm down. "Tell me about them."

Donovan leaned against the wall. Leah could see him out of the corner of her eye and felt his gaze pinned to her like a missile on its target. She continued to focus on Gareth. "Tell me."

"Yes." Donovan's voice came out like a command. "Tell her."

"These are the orbs of Aries and Taurus," said Gareth. "I found them in the catacombs under the site of the original Library of Alexandria."

"How did you find them?" She swallowed.

Gareth shook his head. "The story is so long, Leah."

"That's true," Donovan added. "And we *are* trying to conserve as much time as possible."

Leah waited. The strange humming that came from the orbs seemed to speak inside her head. She was so tense that a scream tore from her throat when the telephone on the table suddenly rang out like a siren in the room.

Gareth lunged from the bed and knelt in front of Leah's chair. "It's okay." Never taking his eyes off her, he reached up and snatched the phone from its cradle. "Yeah?"

Leah heard Donovan mutter, "Nothing to fear yet, my dear."

The sound of static filled the air around Leah, and Gareth's voice grew quiet. She took a long, deep breath and stared at him, trying to concentrate only on the soft husky tone of his voice. But the eerie humming continued to invade her brain. Her skin prickled, like a hundred tiny little fishhooks had imbedded themselves in her flesh. She could feel the skin start to pull away from her bones, as if the orbs' power was forcing her to stand up and walk to them so they could suck the life from her soul.

Gareth muttered something and hung up the phone. He caught her face in his hands. "Are you okay?"

Leah's voice came out cold and flat, like a corpse whispering its final goodbye. "Please put them away now."

With a strange laugh, Donovan moved from his corner, wrapped the orbs in the towel, and shoved them back into the knapsack. Tossing the bag back in the safe, he turned to face her. "Better?"

Leah forced the hypnotic hum from her mind. "I'm not sure what came over me."

"They're very powerful objects." Gareth nodded.

"Although," added Donovan. "The effect they seem to have on you is different from what Gareth feels."

The black eyes once again burned her skin.

He leaned toward her. "Do you see bad things?" His voice was almost…eager. "Do you see death?"

"Enough!" Gareth glared at his friend. "Leave her alone."

"Ah…the hero." Donovan smiled. "I almost forgot."

Leah's fear melted away. She felt her brain re-start, like an old, well-used generator coming back to life. She stared at Donovan. "What do you see when you look at them?"

His eyes grew into slits, and blood rose in his cheeks.

"Nothing." She laughed softly. "You don't see or feel anything."

"Does it matter?" he snarled.

"Apparently it does to you."

"Enough." Gareth pushed Donovan out of the way, sending him back to his corner and sat down on the edge of the bed. He looked at Leah. "My father worked for the National Laboratory Research Center in New Mexico with nuclear scientists on various projects—all very top-secret, high-level stuff."

"I thought he was an astronomer?" she said.

"He was. That was his field. But astronomy covers a lot of bases, Leah." He continued, "My dad was into his own thing—a life's pursuit, you could call it. He was intrigued with ancient civilizations and the belief they had in astronomy. At one time there were millions of people who believed they could see their past, present, and future by studying the constellations.

"My father liked to decode old notes—follow old legends. He thought that if the world could understand creation with an open mind then wars, death—all bad things would be erased. With understanding would come peace."

"Nice thought," Leah said.

"But impossible," added Donovan.

Gareth ignored the pessimistic remark. "Then Dad met Mom." A loving smile spread across his face. "There were no two people better suited for each other, I'll tell you. Mom was an astrologer which, of course, no one believes is an actual science anymore. The true science of the stars has become a hoax on carnival midways.

"But my mother," he continued, with a wistful sigh. "She knew what she was doing. She was the most enlightened human being I've ever met… not to mention the most beautiful soul in the world."

Leah began to feel warm again listening to the doting son's voice.

"My mother was part of a group that went on an archaeological dig to Nag Hammadi, in Egypt, to translate texts that'd been found buried in ancient jars."

"The Gnostic Gospels." Leah nodded.

"Of course *you* would know." He laughed. "I forgot for a second who I was talking to."

"The great and powerful Oz," Donovan snickered from his corner.

Leah followed Gareth's lead and ignored the smarmy little man.

Gareth continued, "Everyone's heard about the Gospel of Thomas, and certainly the Gospel of Mary Magdalene has raised debates, but there's one that's barely mentioned and that was the one that captured my mother's interest." He took a deep breath. "Have you ever heard of Zarathustra?"

Leah raced through the card catalogue in her brain, and shook her head.

"Wow! There's something you *don't* know? I should record the time and date for future archaeologists who want to label you the smartest person who ever lived."

"Funny." Leah felt the color return to her cheeks; the blood seemed to be flowing normally through her veins once again.

Gareth went on. "Our pal, Rudolf Steiner, believed that there was a god named Zarathustra who lived thousands of years before the Trojan War. He was said to have been reincarnated several times."

Leah scoffed. "And this was proven how?"

"One of the Gnostic Gospels was the Apocalypse of Adam—the one my mother was so fascinated with. This Gospel actually told of the reincarnated lives of one, Zarathustra. It actually documents his journeys through time."

"Okay," said Leah. "But what does Zarathustra have to do with astrology?"

"Zarathustra was the first to discuss the existence of twelve spiritual beings. In every lifetime, apparently, he spoke about the Great Twelve; the zodiac signs that would fall from the heavens and take physical forms on Earth. Some popular versions of this prophecy are Arthur and the Knights of the Round Table; The Archangel Michael and his twelve angel warriors; and, Jesus and his apostles.

"Uh-huh."

Donovan laughed. "I don't think she believes you."

Gareth ignored him. "Zarathustra was a real scientist; he documented each equal-sized zone in the sky, better known as the constellations. You see, each zone that the sun moves through is thirty degrees. Today we use his conclusions in almost every mathematical and scientific formula we have."

"We do?"

Donovan cleared his throat. "Twelve constellations multiplied by thirty degrees in each sign equals three hundred and sixty degrees—our circle. Clock faces have twelve divisions and every hour of our lives is thirty times two. Simple, but brilliant."

Leah glared at him. "Why don't you let Gareth talk?"

"I'm more learned than my colleague." He glared back.

"A," Leah began. "I highly doubt that. B," she continued, watching his black eyes fill with anger, "he has a way better voice than you do."

"Loving him already, are you?" Donovan sneered. "Good. Makes things easier on me."

"What things?"

"You're really getting annoying Donovan," said Gareth.

He snorted. "Sorry. Please…continue."

Gareth turned his attention back to Leah. "Zarathustra taught tons of people, including the prophet Daniel. He also predicted his own return, as well as twelve eternal beings in every lifetime. He was even the first person to tell the star story."

"Star story?" Leah was confused.

Donovan laughed. "My, but you *are* a non-believer, aren't you?"

Gareth spoke quickly, trying to stop the fight that was about to begin. "Based on Zarathustra's research, three star-gazing magi would journey across the desert to meet the Son of God."

"Zarathustra was Jesus?" she asked.

"No." Gareth tilted his head. "Jesus was Jesus. But the Apocalypse of Adam shows that in each time period there was a king—a savior—born on Earth who had twelve followers; twelve beings to protect and help him. Every religion preaches the One and Twelve theory—they just use different names. That's why my parents were so interested in finding the truth.

"Think about it." Gareth's eyes lit from within. "Proving Heaven exists would change the world. Wars would stop happening because everyone would finally have to admit and accept that there's one place that admits *all* souls. There'd be no more racial or religious bias because there would be proof of where we *all* came from. Everyone would be the same. Whether you believe in Egyptian gods and goddesses, Chinese animal signs, zodiacal constellations, or even King Arthur—it wouldn't matter anymore."

Leah stared into the hopeful gaze. "Why aren't your parents here? Considering all that you've done to further their quest I would think they'd want to be in on this."

Guilt erupted inside her when tears sprang into Gareth's eyes. "I'm sorry," she said, quickly. "I didn't mean anything."

He shook his head.

Donovan walked to Gareth's side and placed a hand on his shoulder. "Gareth's parents died in a car accident when he was fifteen."

She could've kicked herself for having such a loud mouth. "I'm so sorry, Gareth."

He stared out the window. "Mom knew they were going to die young. She said she could see their future written in the stars."

"My mother always said that I couldn't even read the writing on the wall," she said.

Gareth pointed up at Donovan. "He helped me through it."

"You were friends with his family?" Leah tried hard, and with little success, to keep the accusatory tone from her voice.

Donovan smiled. "I worked for Gareth's father in his lab. I learned a great deal from him. Loved him as if he were my own father."

Trying to ignore the warning bells in her brain as she listened to his cold, dead voice, Leah looked at Gareth. "So that's why you trust him?"

Gareth hesitated. "Donovan helped me a great deal. I could've just folded, you know? But Donovan told me about their stories…their quest. He wouldn't let me give up."

"What's in it for you?" Leah stared at Donovan Barker, trying to find some sort of emotion hidden in the blue-black gaze. But the feeling he gave her was still the same; a shield. A shield of protection seemed to radiate from the man. And his smile, she thought, was not that of a friend. It was closer to that of a predator, lulling his prey into a false sense of security. But Gareth Lowery wasn't simple-minded. Leah knew that in her heart. Except for blowing up her library he seemed like a man who knew the right way to do things, and the right people to do them with.

She'd no idea how long she'd been sitting there silent when Donovan finally spoke. "She still has doubts about me." He smiled down at Gareth. "What is it, do you think, that makes her question my loyalty so?"

Leah felt her own shield snap into place around her, as she came to her final decision. Donovan Barker was definitely not a friend. He was her enemy. And she hated him even more for making her feel protective toward Gareth Lowery—a virtual stranger. "Let's just say the jury's still out, Mr. Barker." Leah offered him the friendliest smile she could muster. "But you certainly don't need my approval. Gareth trusts you. That should be enough."

His face hardened for a split second before his grin reappeared.

"Actually, it's more than enough."

Leah turned back to Gareth's completely confused face. "Go on with your story."

He hesitated, but slowly his voice returned. "The night before my parents died there was a speaker at the Research Center in New Mexico. His name was Jiddu Krishnamurti. Ever heard of him?"

She laughed. "What is this, *Jeopardy*?"

"Good. Strike two," he said, with a wink. "Makes me feel better that you don't know everything."

"Let us hope there's not a strike three coming in my future." Leah threw a glance at Donovan. "It'll ruin my reputation."

He grinned.

Leah could feel her peaceful world begin to crumble. She trembled slightly, as she began to wonder exactly what she was getting herself into… and, more importantly, why?

"Jiddu was part of the Theosophical Society." Gareth tried to get her focus back on him.

"The one Steiner was in charge of?"

He nodded. "Steiner actually left the Order when the other leader, Annie Besant, announced that Jiddu was the Second Coming of Christ."

"Was he?" She laughed.

"No." Gareth smiled. "Jiddu was quite a man, though. He disbanded the Order because he felt like they were trying to coerce people down a particular path and he wouldn't stand for that. He thought people should be free to choose religion for themselves."

"Free will."

Gareth gave a nod. "When he came to New Mexico to give his speech, my mother and father went to talk to him. They wanted to tell him about the astrological secret they'd uncovered. They thought he could help them.

After all, people listened to Jiddu. No one was ever going to listen to my mother—a carnival queen astrologer; or, even my father, the astronomer with his head in the clouds."

She turned to Donovan. "What about you? You were their research assistant."

"I was just a kid," he replied. "Eighteen. I had no power."

Leah had trouble believing that. She turned back to Gareth. "Did your parents get to tell him?"

Gareth stared at the carpet. "No. Jiddu was taken out the back. They did meet with one of his staff during the event and made an appointment to see him the next day."

"And…that was the night it happened?" Leah hesitated, not wanting to hurt him anymore.

He answered in a monotone. "Our car was hit by a drunk driver. I was thrown out the back window. They were trapped inside when it exploded."

"I can't imagine something so horrible," she whispered.

Gareth nodded. "It was the only time I've ever really experienced hell."

Leah struggled to get the conversation back on track. "Maybe you can go to this, Jiddu, now?"

Donovan interrupted. "He's dead."

Leah could've sworn she heard a note of happiness in his voice, as he continued, "The speech in New Mexico was his last. Do you know what he said that night? I'll never forget it."

She waited.

"He said that it was not a 'measure of good health to be well-adjusted to a profoundly sick society.'" The catlike grin reappeared on Donovan's face.

"Ain't that the truth," replied Leah, feeling as if she was staring dead-on at one of the profoundly sick. "He certainly knew what he was talking about."

"People listened to him."

"Not well enough, apparently. Considering where the world is at now." She turned back to Gareth. "Do you believe that Jiddu was a prophet?"

"Yes."

"Did he have a group of twelve?" Leah smiled.

Gareth nodded. "In fact, he had an intimate circle of twelve who stood by him and counseled him along the way."

"Coincidence." Leah decided.

"Maybe. But that's a whole lot of coincidences: Twelve zodiac signs, twelve followers, prophets, apostles, and twelve world views based on Steiner's research." Gareth reminded her.

"Not to mention twelve orbs that supposedly unlock the gates of Heaven." Leah cringed at the cynicism in her voice.

"You've only seen two of them," said Gareth. "They're all *very* real, and I have six in that safe. All I need is the other half."

"And the clues are in this." Leah reached into her jacket pocket and pulled out the metal book. "How did you know where to start looking without the book?"

"My God! You found it!" A whisper of excitement whistled through Donovan's lips.

Leah stared at his eager face. "Did Gareth's dad tell his *research assistant* where to begin the biggest quest in history?"

"I can't take credit for any of this." He smiled. "Gareth's family are the brilliant ones."

"So you're fairly useless," Leah stated. "I figured."

Donovan laughed, but his facial muscles once again hardened underneath his skin. "I'm here to help; to keep his parents' dream alive. They would've wanted their son to continue their journey."

"Would they?" asked Leah. "They would've wanted their only son to risk dying?"

Gareth cleared his throat. "Apparently, the two of you aren't going to get along."

"Apparently not!"

"Leah...please-"

She raised her hand. "It doesn't matter. Go on. How did you find the first six without the book?"

"My sister figured it out," Gareth replied. "She'd studied the papers, manuscripts, documents—everything that my parents had accumulated over their lifetimes. She poured over the research and came to the conclusion that the old Library of Alexandria held the first piece of the puzzle."

"She was the woman on the phone?"

"Kathryn." He nodded. "She was only seven when our parents died. She'd stayed home with our grandmother that night because she had a cold and Mom didn't want her to go out." A loving smile reappeared on his face. "Man, she was mad. Kathryn hates—I mean, *hates*—to be left behind." Gareth studied her. "She's a lot like you, in fact. She's doing this mostly for answers. Kathryn doesn't hold much stock in astrological mysticism or legends. She wants the cold, hard facts."

"Sounds like a realistic girl." Leah smiled. "Smart, solid—I like her already."

"She doesn't stand for frilly, wispy, imaginative things." His eyes grew sad. "She's so unlike our mother, but she was always so mad when people mocked our parents. Kathryn didn't want our mother to have to practice her chosen occupation in silence."

"Was your mother a psychic?"

"I prefer to say that she was open-minded." Gareth offered a timid grin. "She could see things in the stars—in the constellations. She could read the signs of the zodiac and understand…things. Kathryn loved Mom, but she's always been grounded in reality. There was a part of her that wanted our mother to be normal."

"Yet Kathryn is somewhere far away continuing to search for something that's a bigger myth than Big Foot."

Gareth hung his head, and sighed. "You really disbelieve *that* much? You really think that ninety-nine percent of the world's population is having a coincidental dream?"

Leah took a deep, steadying breath. "Gareth, I believe that you believe in what you're doing. Those horrible orbs are real, I see that. And this book," she continued, "is certainly a tangible object. But I'm not sold on the fact that humming glass and ancient theories will unlock the gates of Heaven." She glanced at Donovan. "There have been some real sickos in this world. This could be some complex joke that'll lead you straight to Hell."

Donovan smiled. "Union of Opposites, Leah. If Gareth sees Hell, it'll still prove that there's a Heaven."

Gareth stood up and walked into the bathroom. "I'm gonna' shower before you blow even more holes through my theory." He slammed the door behind him.

"Don't let me disturb you." Donovan laughed. "You have a lot of thinking to do…decisions to make."

Leah remained silent, listening to the blast of water coming from the bathroom.

"I'll just head down to the lobby. Grab a newspaper," he said. "Can I get you anything?"

"No."

Halfway to the door, Donovan turned back around and stared at her.

It was as if a vacuum had suddenly sucked the fresh air out of the room leaving a stale taste in Leah's mouth.

"I can see that you like him," said Donovan.

"I don't know him."

"You're awfully protective for someone who doesn't know him."

"He doesn't need my protection," Leah replied. "He has you for that."

"True." Donovan's face grew serious. "You might not like me, Ms. Tallent, but I'm not a bad guy. Gareth believes in this. He has faith. The only hell he's ever known is the death of his parents. The rest of his life has been extremely…blessed."

Leah caught the slightly jealous thread imbedded in his voice. "Why are you telling me all this?"

He seemed to slither forward, like a snake fluctuating across the carpet. "Because there's a difference between faith and truth. He believes… but you *know*."

"I know what?" she asked.

"You know since the book and the orbs are real they must lead to something. And you're eager to find out what that something is."

Leah snorted. "I don't need Heaven; I don't need to be saved."

"Not yet." His voice turned cold as ice. "But you can help Gareth. His faith will only take him so far. I think he's grown tired of me."

"Now, *that*, I believe."

He took a step closer. "Be careful, Leah. I may not be a bad guy, but I won't be pushed."

"Uh-huh." She did her best to hide the trembling of her hands, as she stared into the evil black eyes.

He grinned. "You should be careful of other things, too."

"And those are?"

"The Devil preys on empty souls, Leah. He's always on the lookout for someone who's completely alone; someone who has shut themselves off from the world. He enters them and takes over their soul…makes them do his bidding." The blue flames pulsed in his eyes. "You seem like a prime candidate."

"I'll watch my back," she said, in the most sarcastic tone she could manage.

"You won't be the only one watching it." Laughing heartily, Donovan walked out the door.

Leah let out a deep sigh and fell into the chair. She had no idea why the words of a complete stranger would bother her so much. Moving her gaze back to the book, she stared at the white page that certainly referred to the ancient library that was destroyed so many years ago. The signatures of Plato and Socrates still blew her away. She couldn't believe that the great men had once written in the ancient artifact and held the treasure in their hands that Gareth now had tucked away in his safe.

She flipped through the pages, staring at the black side of the book. Stopping at Crowley's first entry, she gazed at the crude drawing that looked like a child's attempt at his first art project. The chalk outline of a human being, and the rooftops adorned with little number thirteen's, made her brain come to life, searching for the answers that she could feel in the far-distant caverns of her mind. God, she needed coffee.

The bathroom door swung open and a cloud of steam filled the room. Leah tried to keep her focus, but it was impossible. Gareth walked out of the mist like some Arthurian legend, sending Aleister Crowley's drawing right out of her head. Free from the elegant tuxedo, Gareth looked far more comfortable—not to mention sexy—in his weathered jeans and brown suede shirt. Flecks of gold swam in his green eyes, and Leah's pulse began to race.

Gareth stared down at himself, checking to make sure that everything was both zipped and/or tucked. "What?"

Leah shook the disturbing thoughts from her brain. "You know what I really hate about the concept of Heaven?"

A small smile curved his lips. "What's that?"

"You have to be dead to get in."

She saw her statement hit home when Gareth's legs trembled beneath him. Pulling himself together, he shrugged. "We all have to go sooner or later."

"I prefer later."

His voice grew soft. "You still think I'm crazy, don't you?"

"Crazy is in the eye of the beholder, Mr. Lowery," she replied. "I think crazy people probably have it better than the rest of us. Like your friend Barker. Loons don't have to deal with the real world; their demons are on the inside of their minds like a house full of-."

"Of...?"

Like the blinking orbs buried in the safe, a flame in Leah's brain came to life. "Wait a minute." She stared down at the strange drawings. "You said you had a laptop."

He nodded. "They're up on the second floor."

Leah threw on her jacket, and dropped the metal book into her pocket. "Let's go."

"Where's Donovan?"

"Who cares?"

Throwing open the door, Leah practically ran down the hall; the picture was burning inside her head.

Gareth flew out the door behind her. "Wait for me!"

Stepping into the elevator, Leah punched the button.

Sprinting down the hall, Gareth pole-vaulted through the almost closed doors. "What's the hurry?"

"I think I know where Crowley hid his first two." Her voice grew serious. "I have to ask. How ready *are* you to go to Hell?"

*

Donovan watched Gareth jump into the elevator from his place at the end of the hall. His excitement mixed with aggravation when the familiar beep came from his pocket. Removing the Blackberry, Donovan stared down at the new message.

Do you have the book?

Yes.

And?

And...Leah Tallent seems to have deciphered the first clue.

And??!!

Donovan smiled. He loved having power over his self-important sibling.

And what? She's telling Gareth.

Why isn't she telling you?

Relax. He'll tell me. I think it would be good for them to have some alone time. She's the catalyst we need to make Gareth Lowery go faster.

Risky. She could change his mind.

Not a chance.

Why?

She's curious. And she's looking to blow his theory out of the water.

Skeptics become the strongest believers.

Not her.

Fine. If you're going to do nothing there, then I need you here. I have a job for you.

Donovan felt the familiar rage spring to life inside him.

You're not the boss.

If the orbs don't pan out, there's another object that can help us.

What object?

A necklace that

Donovan sighed heavily when the battery went dead.

CHAPTER TWELVE

"How? When? *What!?*" A steady stream of questions poured from Gareth's lips.

"Just get me to a computer," demanded Leah.

The bell dinged and the door opened to the second floor. Gareth grabbed her hand. "This way."

They tried their best to act normal as they passed by the other tourists relaxing in the big leather chairs. When they hurried past an open door marked, *Reading Room*, Leah glanced in at the people feeding on trays of fruit and biscuits. She took a deep breath and let the heavenly scent of fresh-roasted coffee fill her nostrils. Her stomach growled when they sped by another set of French doors that opened into the *Poetry Garden*. Leah caught a glimpse of the sparkling greenhouse that offered a quiet place to sit and pass the time with Yeats and Chaucer.

Open terraces lined the hallway where, to Leah's dismay, even more people were enjoying their cups of coffee as they sat and stared at the loveliest skyline in the whole world.

Trying to shake the thoughts of caffeine from her parched brain, Leah followed Gareth into the *Business Center*. This area had been paneled with rich, dark wood; a cozy fireplace sat in the corner. Long mahogany desks and leather chairs were offered, so that businessmen could feel right at home while using one of the laptops provided for their convenience. Leah could smell the lingering scent of cigars, whiskey, and, yes, that marvelous coffee. She wondered if Andrew Carnegie had once owned a room like this in his mansion. Minus the modern-day electronic inventions, it was easy to imagine the well-known businessman sitting in a big leather chair, smoking a cigar, and devising his next master plan.

The sound of a computer coming to life buzzed through Leah's thoughts.

She sighed. Leah loathed the fact that it took no intelligence whatsoever to point and click, and get the answers she needed in seconds. To her, it was against nature to not crack open a book for research. "I hate these things."

Gareth smirked. "A librarian's worst enemy, aye?"

"The world was a much better place when people read and didn't waste their time on these horrible, mind-sucking devices. And don't even get me started on email! Penmanship is truly a lost art form."

Gareth laughed so loud that the glass rattled in the ornate French doors.

Leah ignored him. Her head was spinning, as she plugged in her keywords and called the picture up on the screen. She sank back into the soft leather chair that held her body like a glove. "I don't believe it," she whispered, handing the metal book to Gareth. "There it is."

Gareth studied the childlike drawing created by Aleister Crowley. He gasped when he saw a mirror image staring back at him from the computer monitor. On the screen was a four-color picture of a large, meandering house; numerous rooftops and steeples rose in the air like swords and spears, piercing the white, puffy clouds. Each eave was painted a different color; the bright pink, baby blue, and rich purple made his eyes ache. The house looked like it belonged on the *Candyland* game board. The only thing missing was the colorful peppermint sticks growing in the front yard. "What *is* that?"

"That," replied Leah, "is the Winchester House."

"Winchester House?" Gareth sat down beside her and stared at the screen. "Why does that sound familiar?"

"It's a tourist trap in California," Leah answered. "A haunted house if ever there was one. I read a book about it a long time ago. I was going through my 'America's Most Haunted Places' phase."

Gareth raised an eyebrow.

"Don't ask," she mumbled.

"But what does this house have to do with Aleister Crowley?"

"Nothing," she answered, throwing her hands in the air. "Not a damn thing. But it would fit. He would've buried the orbs in the worst places imaginable, right?"

Gareth nodded; his face was still set in a mask of confusion. "But this is just a house. It doesn't exactly remind me of the gas chambers at Auschwitz."

Leah grabbed the metal book and pointed to the word that Rudolf Steiner had scribbled on the opposing white page. "See the title?"

Gareth squinted at the elegant script. "*Mind?*"

"Yup." Leah flipped the next two white pieces of paper. "The one behind it reads, *Body and Blood*, and Steiner's last page reads, *Soul*."

"So?" Gareth blinked.

"So." She sighed. "I think each title corresponds to the hiding places of the orbs."

"You lost me." He stared blankly at her.

Leah tossed her heavy glasses across the polished wood table, still searching for a way that this could be some kind of galactic hoax. "*Mind*, is the title on the first page. You found that set of orbs in the Library of Alexandria—a highly revered institution that was known to house the greatest *minds* of all time."

"So…on the dark side—"

Leah glanced at the black pages. "On the dark side, I think Crowley wanted to do the same thing. Except instead of the greatest minds of all time, he chose a location that was based on the *losing* of a person's mind."

"Okay." Gareth nodded. "I'll buy that. So the owner or a resident of the Winchester House went loopy?"

Leah let out an exasperated sigh, pointed at the screen, and sat back in her chair. "Read it. I'm sure America's superhighway has it all there."

"Like you, I never trust computers." He smiled. "I don't care about the tourist trap or the convoluted ghost story. I'm looking for the facts."

Leah was amused by his serious gaze. She rubbed her tired eyes and looked away from the computer monitor—the intense glare was too much in the barely-lit room. She closed her eyelids, and thought back to the thick book that'd told the real stories of America's most haunted places.

The room was silent. Even the noisy City seemed to be holding its breath so that it, too, could hear her voice drift from the second floor window and tell the strange tale.

"Don't you wanna' find your friend first?" Leah tried to curb her sarcasm.

Gareth shook his head. "No need. I'll catch him up later."

Leah wondered if full disclosure was the right thing for her to give. She didn't really know Gareth Lowery. He could be exactly like his friend, just better at masking his feelings.

He waited patiently. "What's wrong?"

Leah never threw caution to the wind. She didn't believe in making moronic choices just for the fun of it. But as she looked into his green eyes begging for her help, another emotion hit her square in the chest. She wanted with all her heart to wipe the innocent look from his face. Maybe by proving to him that his ridiculous theory about Heaven was just that, a farce, she could take the stars out of his eyes—for his quest and his friend. Deep down, Leah knew that Donovan Barker was out to hurt the man in front of her and, for some reason, she just couldn't let him succeed.

"The house was built by Sarah Winchester," she began. "She was the wife of William Winchester."

"The gun guy?"

She nodded. "Winchester guns and rifles. They were rich beyond belief, of course. They met, got married, and had a daughter. Unfortunately, their child—Annie, I think her name was—developed a very rare illness that actually made her body waste away. So the child died and Sarah began to lose it. She struggled on the brink of madness for a long time after the death of her baby."

"God." Gareth winced. "How awful."

"That was only the first slap in the head for this woman. Her husband got tuberculosis and he died. Sarah inherited over twenty million bucks in the 1880's, which translates to about five hundred million now."

"A nice cushion."

Leah sighed. "Money, even back then, wasn't enough to save Sarah. She lost her child and husband back to back and her mind pretty much went with them. She was so confused that she consulted a medium who—no offense to your mother—was a fraud of the very worst kind. She only wanted to be on Sarah's payroll."

"No offense taken," said Gareth; a slight sadness echoed in his deep voice. "There are a lot of fakes in this world."

Without thinking, Leah reached out and took his hand. Her heartbeat began to race as she watched him stare down at their clasped hands. He stroked her knuckles with his thumb, massaging the soft skin like he was polishing a fine diamond.

Clearing her throat, Leah focused on the harsh light of the monitor, trying her best to ignore the velvet touch. "Anyway…this medium told Sarah that there was a curse on her family because of all the souls who'd been violently killed by the guns that William had made. This psychic extraordinaire told Sarah that the soldiers and victims were going to seek their vengeance on every member of her family."

Leah's breath caught in her lungs; her brain was useless under his intimate touch. Tearing her hand from his, she stood up. "Where was I?" She began to pace. "I think a lot better when I move."

"You think too much," he purred.

"And you don't think enough," she shot back. Walking to the corner of the room, Leah stared into the fireplace, trying to banish the feelings that were rapidly taking over her body. Her words came out in a rush. "The medium told Sarah that she had to build a haven for all the spirits who were taken out by Winchester guns. Unfortunately, the sicko medium went too far and told Sarah that she could never stop building."

"Why?" Gareth's voice remained low; an intoxicating sound that made Leah's mutinous body beg her brain for a reprieve from loneliness.

She focused on the intricate mantelpiece. "The medium told her that the minute the construction stopped, Sarah would die. The spirits would be mad and take her life for payment of her husband's sins."

"Thus…Winchester House was built," said Gareth.

"Sarah went mad inside its walls. If she wasn't mad to begin with—which is more likely than not. The house itself became a maze. She added rooms on top of rooms, windows that looked into other rooms, doors that opened up into walls, and staircases that went nowhere. The workers were there every day and night, in shifts, following blueprints that Sarah drew on napkins. She spent millions on building supplies until there were over seven stories on the house. Sarah even had three elevators installed so that the spirits—not her—could move around easier. Sarah barely left her room."

Leah didn't wait for a response because she knew that another shot of his sultry voice would send her to her knees. She stuttered. "Sarah communed with the spirits every night. Sometimes she even played her piano to try and calm the restless spirits."

Gareth stared at the picture of the eerie mansion. "She lived in this thing all alone?"

"She had servants; the construction workers day and night; and, of course, the ghosts who'd driven her mad."

"That poor woman." Gareth whispered a prayer for the tortured soul.

"Makes you think about who you should have faith in."

"What?" Gareth stared at her.

Leah turned around. "Sarah supposedly prayed a great deal, too. Look where it got her."

"Maybe it helped her." He sat back in his chair. "Maybe faith made it easier."

She rolled her eyes. "Right…easier." Clearing her throat, she continued, "In 1906, the San Francisco earthquake took out the top three floors of the house. It's been said that when it collapsed, Sarah was trapped for days in her bedroom. She swore that it was payback from the spirits because the construction had slowed down. So she got all the workmen back and had them build more rooms, more stairs, and more rooftops. Prayers didn't help. She lived by what she thought the spirits wanted. She even installed chimney after chimney so they could go in and out of the house if they wanted fresh air."

"Did the construction ever end?" asked Gareth.

"Not during her lifetime." Leah's voice turned hard. "Sarah supposedly held a final conference in her séance room one night, begged for forgiveness, and then went to bed. She died in her sleep at eighty-three."

Gareth focused on the metal book, and took a deep breath. "So what happened in 1913?"

"What do you mean?"

"Well...," he began. "I understand the chalk outline on Crowley's picture. I'm sure it's a reference to the Winchester legacy of building weapons to blow holes through people. But the tiny numbers drawn on all the rooftops...what are they? Something must have happened in 1913?"

Leah took a deep breath and walked back to the table. She sat down across from him, using the sturdy wood as a safe divider between her and his beguiling touch. "I think the number thirteen represents Sarah's obsession."

"She was obsessed with the number thirteen?"

Leah nodded. "There are thirteen drain holes in her kitchen sink, and nearly all the windows in the house contain thirteen panes of glass. Walls had thirteen panels, floors had thirteen boards, and the greenhouse was decorated with thirteen cupolas."

She leaned forward. "Gareth, almost every staircase in that house has thirteen steps, and the closets each have thirteen hooks to hang up the coats of visitors she never had. Sarah was obsessed."

"Or, possessed."

Leah shrugged. "Whichever...she lost her mind. It was taken from her along with her family. Sarah was a goner from the moment she began to build Winchester House."

"How would Crowley have known about all this?"

"Well." Leah's lips tightened into a thin line. "In the book I read, there were interviews and write-ups in national newspapers of the strange goings-on inside Sarah's world. The workmen at the site said they'd never heard or seen any ghosts or goblins at all. Some, however, did tell reporters that when work was completed on an area, they sometimes saw…"

"What?"

She swallowed her fear. "Orbs…floating orbs that showed up in the air."

His eyes flashed with fire. "Probably just a reflection off the glass."

"Probably. But we're talking about Crowley."

"*Not* a reflection off the glass?"

She sighed. "I'm sure Crowley didn't think so. He probably saw it as a sign. If your theory is to be believed, the suggestion of orbs would be too much of a coincidence. Of course, Crowley was crazy, too. He could've thought the stories were just funny, and fit in with the whole theme of what he was trying to accomplish."

"You don't believe that," said Gareth softly.

"No," she replied. "I think Crowley saw the orbs first hand. If, according to your research, Crowley was actually in New York in 1902 meeting with Carnegie, Steiner, and the Council of Masters, than it would've been a short trip to bury the first two orbs in a house that was known far and wide for the destruction of a woman's mind."

Leah sat back in the comfortable chair and stared at him over the computer monitor. "You really have to think this through. If we continue on this journey, you're going to be walking in the footsteps of a truly twisted man. You'll be following the ideas of a deranged individual who actually may have thought that he was Satan, or the closest thing to him on the planet."

Her voice grew louder. "You have to *really* understand this guy,

Gareth. Crowley hated women. He couldn't stand them, with the possible exception being Rose, his wife. But he said many times that the fairer sex was useless. He was also a cynical son of a bitch. You can bet that most of the locations he chose were maybe not the evilest places on Earth in terms of blood and guts, but they would definitely have been amusing to him."

Leah shuddered. "Sarah would still have been alive when Crowley went there and planted the orbs. He probably came in the dead of night and made sure to provide extra terror to the poor woman…one last nail in her coffin."

Gareth clasped his hands under his chin.

Leah watched him carefully. He looked like a man who was about to make a truly horrible announcement. "What?"

Gareth locked eyes with her over the monitor. "You said *we*."

"Excuse me?"

He took a deep breath. "You said, if *we* continue on this journey."

She swallowed. "You don't need me. You have your friend."

"Leah…Donovan is—"

"Late, as always."

The door to the *Business Center* was ajar. Leah stared through the dim light of the room to see the disheveled figure sitting in a chair behind Gareth.

Donovan smiled at her. "You didn't even jump this time."

Leah made a point to keep her gaze focused on his black eyes. "Maybe your power over me is gone."

He clicked his tongue inside his cheek. "Pity."

Gareth glanced over his shoulder. "Well? You're always eavesdropping, so I assume you heard."

"Most of it." Donovan nodded. "I agree with you, Gareth. You need Ms. Tallent's help far more than you need mine. She's certainly a lot smarter than I am."

"Not a big surprise there."

Donovan laughed at his friend's remark.

Leah could see Donovan's smile, but she also saw his clenched fists resting on his legs. The protective feeling for Gareth settled over her once again. "And what will you be doing while we're off finding your ridiculous little trinkets?"

His fists immediately unclenched when he noticed that her focus was directly on him. "I'll be in England."

Gareth turned quickly in his chair. "Did Kathryn call? Is she okay?"

Donovan held up his hand. "Kathryn is absolutely fine. But I think she's a bit tired. And her partner seems to be…questioning things." His cold voice made Leah shiver.

"Aren't we all," muttered Gareth.

"Mmm." Donovan kept his smile. "I want to see what she's found. I think Kathryn would be excited to share it with someone who believes as much as she does. You don't need my support anymore." He winked. "Seems this lovely librarian is already on the right track."

Leah leaned back in her chair. "What makes you think a non-believer like me even wants to help?"

"Because you're the devil's advocate, my dear. You want to prove that Gareth and I are wrong or, perhaps, crazy."

"I already know you're crazy." She dismissed him and returned her attention to Gareth. "Your friend wants fame. He wants his name to appear in the history books as the man who proved it all. That's normal. But you I don't get. Tell me why *you're* doing this."

"Why?"

"I need to know," she said. "Is this all for vengeance? Do you want to prove to the people that bad-mouthed your parents and made your sister sad, that your family was right all along? Or, is it the love of a son and a daughter who want to make sure their parents went to a better place? Maybe you want to cure the ills of humanity and bring us peace. Are you really one of the few righteous people left in the world? Really that faithful? Which is it, Gareth? Why are you really doing this?"

He sighed. "Whether you believe or not, Leah. When I hold the orbs in my hand I feel good things. *Only* good things. When Donovan's near them he feels nothing at all."

She stared at Donovan's slightly angry face.

He shrugged. "We all have our own protective devices, shall we say. Gareth's is his faith; he believes in the good side of humanity."

"And which side do you believe in?" Leah smiled.

"I'm on the fence." He laughed. "Maybe that's why I feel nothing." Sitting back in his chair, he stretched his long legs out in front of him. "Maybe you, Ms. Tallent, see the bad things because of what *you* believe in. You certainly put me on your hate list quickly enough…without even giving me a chance. Maybe you're just one of those people filled with hatred."

Leah shook her head. "I don't hate you. Gareth likes you…trusts you…so you must have some redeeming qualities."

"Jeez. Thanks for the compliment." He laughed.

Leah turned to a silent Gareth, apparently still contemplating her question. If there *was* a god, she mused, he was certainly having a huge laugh at her expense. She leaned forward and stared into Gareth's beautiful emerald eyes. "Well?"

He took a deep breath. "I'm not the one to figure out the dark side of this puzzle. Since the beginning of time there have always been two people working together—Yin and Yang. My faith knows no boundaries, that's true. But now that I've come to this point, I know I don't have the strength to go into Hell alone. I really, truly need you."

Silence descended, as Leah thought about his intoxicating, and somewhat bewildering words.

"What are you thinking?" he asked, after a time.

She stared at Gareth's hopeful face and Donovan's daring grin, and rolled her eyes. She had no choice…she was in too deep.

"I'm thinking it's gonna' be a real pain in the ass getting vacation time."

CHAPTER THIRTEEN

The plane lifted off the runway, and Leah's ears started popping. It felt like kernels of corn were being heated to their breaking point inside her brain.

Closing her eyes, she tried to ignore the man sitting beside her. She still couldn't believe it. The strange decisions she'd made over the last few hours boggled her mind. She'd woken up this morning dreaming of nothing more than enjoying a hot cup of coffee—which she still hadn't gotten. Instead, she was flying across the country with a virtual stranger—who could very well be a deranged lunatic—to see a house that could possibly hold a set of keys to a Kingdom she didn't even believe in. She wondered when the exact moment had happened, the moment when she had decided to go completely loco and journey in the footsteps of a madman.

When they'd left the *Business Center* and walked back to Gareth's room, they'd remained silent. She'd watched him pack his belongings, say goodbye to his strange friend, and grab the knapsack from the safe.

Leah'd caught the look of pain that crossed Donovan's face when he watched Gareth cart away the treasure. When his cold hand shook hers goodbye, she'd seen the warning in Donovan's eyes. It was as if he was telling her that he'd been in Gareth's life first, and would not be thrown from it no matter what she did in the next few days…or what they accomplished together inside the walls of the Winchester House.

Keeping her own protective shield firmly in place, Leah had wished him a safe flight, and felt a warm, fuzzy feeling descend on her when he'd visibly flinched at her sarcastic tone.

When Valerie, the overzealous front desk girl, had leapt over the counter to kiss Gareth goodbye, Leah'd kept quiet. They'd hailed a mud-covered taxi and driven to her small, dimly-lit apartment where she'd showered quickly, dressed in jeans and a t-shirt, and grabbed the only pair of shoes in her closet that had a heel less than three inches high.

She'd laughed when she looked in the mirror. With her hair pulled back in a long ponytail, her scuffed leather boots and matching duster made her look like a modern-day outlaw.

Thankfully, the phone call to Director Shaw had been brief. Leah told his answering machine that, after years of faithful service she'd come down with the flu, and had to finally use some of her hundreds of accrued sick days. She'd even added a few sneezes and retching coughs into the receiver for dramatic effect.

While she was doing all this, Gareth had stood in the center of her living room, silently observing her walls, cubbyholes, and countertops filled with books. He'd laughed.

"What?" Leah'd asked.

"Usually when there's this many, they're in some fancy rich man's library."

She'd smiled. "Books are made to be read, not used as an accessory. My father taught me that." She'd briefly thought of her favorite man, sitting in his rich man's library, pouring over huge tomes of ancient history trying to decipher clues from the past.

A lot like Gareth Lowery, in fact, thought Leah. Maybe it was just that easy. In addition to the strange, protective feelings she had for Gareth, she also saw in him the wonderful attributes that her father owned in spades. It did her good to know that there was more than one gentleman walking the earth.

The green knapsack hummed quietly over his shoulder, and her peaceful thoughts had disappeared. She'd tried to ignore it…and him, as much as possible. Yet even with all the warning bells and whistles going off inside her head, she'd still done the unthinkable and followed a total stranger on a crazy path.

Leah gave a grateful sigh as the plane finally leveled out. Her eyes shot open when she heard the familiar squeaky wheels of the aluminum cart coming down the aisle. After all, bad coffee was better than no coffee.

The flight attendant pulled up beside her. The corner of the cart smashed into Leah's elbow when the woman caught sight of Gareth. Leah rolled her eyes. The man was definitely a magnet for morons. She watched the woman straighten her skirt and take a quick glance at her chest, as if she were making sure that the perfect globes of flesh were well-positioned before nabbing Gareth's attention.

"Sir?"

Gareth jumped in his seat. "Yes?"

The woman leaned over, practically suffocating Leah with her considerable attributes. "Can I get you anything?"

"No, thank you. I'm fine." He looked at Leah. "But my lady would love a cup of coffee."

Like a terrorist had suddenly burst into the cabin and pressed a gun into the small of her back, the stewardess stood up straight. "Of course." She glared at Leah. "Decaf or regular?"

Her once helpful voice turned into that of a cross military commander downgrading a lowly corporal. Leah could almost hear the woman's thoughts: If Leah didn't exist, she would be chatting up a storm with the gorgeous man and making a date for the LAX hotel where they would make beautiful music together.

"Regular, please." Leah offered her a big smile.

The woman rattled the aluminum drawers of the cart dramatically, and shoved a small Styrofoam cup into Leah's hand. The force of the exchange caused the coffee to overflow into Leah's lap.

She winced at the sudden searing heat. "Boy, you sure are a poster child for the friendly skies, aren't ya'?"

The stewardess turned away and took off down the aisle, rattling all the way.

Leah yelled over her shoulder, "I don't suppose you have any cream or sugar in there?"

"No. I don't suppose I do."

"I hate people who can't do their jobs," Leah grumbled. Taking a sip of the thick, black coffee, her stomach revolted. She turned on Gareth. "What is it with you? Do *all* women act like complete idiots when you're around?"

He offered her the innocent look of a young schoolboy. "I'm sure I don't know what you're talking about."

"Females turn into piranhas around you. Maybe—although I find it extremely distasteful—you could flirt with her a little so I could get a decent cup of damn coffee." Leah's voice echoed in the small compartment, and a few hushed giggles filled the cabin.

"Sorry about that." Gareth produced his trademark smile. "I didn't notice."

"Yeah, right."

"Really. I thought all women acted like that."

Leah stared into his teasing face. "Oh, please. Really. Be serious. Doesn't that kind of blatant aggressive behavior get old?"

"Women just like talking to me, is all. I must have one of those faces." His eyebrows shot up and down on his forehead. "Don't I have the same effect on you?"

Leah tried to ignore the parts of her body that were screaming yes—like the Whos in Whoville singing around their community Christmas tree. "Thankfully, I'm immune."

"Well, there's one in every crowd, I suppose," laughed Gareth.

Leah threw the cup of wretched coffee on the floor, and curled her arms around her chest.

The rest of the flight was quiet. Gareth, lost in his own world, continued to stare out the window. Maybe, Leah thought, he was taking a good look at the puffy, white clouds drifting by and wondering if this might be the closest he ever got to Heaven.

Through the slightly parted curtain, Leah could see the stewardess and her friends clustered together like a pack of angry dogs, whispering and glaring in her direction. Leah wondered if they were planning her demise, in order to get closer to the Adonis sitting beside her.

Once, the attendant stepped from behind the curtain with a big smile plastered to her face, and asked Leah if she could get her more coffee—freshly brewed this time—*and* with cream and sugar that she'd magically discovered in the plane's kitchenette. Fearing arsenic poisoning, Leah declined.

After that, she'd decided to keep her eyes wide open, just in case they formed a gang and killed her in her sleep. By the time the plane hit the tarmac, Leah's eyes were watering.

Gareth reached up and retrieved their bags from the overhead compartment. As they made their way to the door, the stewardess directed her glowing smile at the handsome man. "I have a layover in town. Give me a call if you need a tour guide."

Shoving the folded sheet of paper with the private cell number into his pocket, Gareth didn't even acknowledge the blatant invitation.

Leah burst into laughter. "You have lipstick on your teeth. Did you know?"

The stewardess muttered a final goodbye, "Bitch."

"Bite me."

Gareth roared with laughter as he finally seemed to hear the conversation going on around him. "You know, until I met you, I never realized women could talk like drunken sailors on shore leave."

"I guess that's just the effect *I* have on them."

"So I see."

*

The enthusiastic driver/wannabe superstar drove them to the Winchester House, where they would try to solve a mystery that not even a Hollywood scriptwriter could imagine.

Soon they were standing before the strange-looking mansion. The eerie peaks, cupolas, and weathervanes rose into the sky; the medieval architecture, combined with the overly bright paint, created a perfect home for a modern-day Cinderella. *Well*, thought Leah. *If Cinderella were on crack.*

Leah took a deep breath and forced herself to walk across the well-manicured lawn. "Here we go."

Gareth remained silent as they made their way to the grand house, whose mammoth shadow towered over the herd of tourists. They walked slowly past the fountains decorated with statues of cupid, and angry looking cherubs tiptoeing over greenish water.

Leah glanced at a rather ominous looking statue of a hunter carrying a bow and arrow over his muscular shoulder. He seemed ready to spring from his base with a cry of war and thrust one of the sharp spears into her heart.

The flesh seemed to shake on her bones; the warm Santa Ana winds turned cold. They walked between the two tall palm trees and past the hedges, stepping onto the meandering front porch that was the length of five football fields laid end to end.

Leah craned her neck to stare at the top balcony attached to the front of the house. There, stood a lone door looking out onto the property. She found herself wondering if there were invisible spirits perched up there taking aim at the unknowing visitors.

Her imagination kicked into overdrive. A deathly chill washed over her and made her skin prickle, until the large, warm hand reached out to take her own.

Gareth spoke softly in her ear. "Leah, there's something I need to tell you before we go in there."

She looked into his worried gaze. "God, what now? Something horrible you conveniently forgot to tell me?"

"No. But…" Gareth stuttered, looking around at the people crowding the front porch. He pulled Leah into the shadows. "When I was in the maze under the Library of Alexandria something…funny happened."

"Blood and death funny, or Jon Stewart funny?"

Gareth's jaw clenched. "I saw things, Leah. Strange things…from the past. It was like I could see people studying in the ancient world, writing words from thousands of years ago. I could even swear that I saw—"

"Whoa." Leah put her hands in the air. "Are you talking about ghosts and goblins?" She tried her best to sound like her normal, sarcastic self. "Don't worry, crazy man. I don't believe in ghosts. I have my feet set firmly on the ground, thank you very much. You're the one who's nuts, remember?"

Gareth took a deep breath and tried to continue, but Leah pulled away and walked to the front door. A chatty older woman stood before the large front entrance, talking about the wonderful mysteries of the tour they were about to embark on. Leah barely listened, as the woman went over facts that were already deeply imbedded in her well-read mind.

Gareth began to whisper in Leah's ear when suddenly, out of nowhere, a word that meant everything flew from the gray-haired lady's lips.

Leah immediately interrupted her memorized speech. "I'm sorry. Did you say there's coffee?"

The guide threw her an indulgent smile. "Yes, my dear. On the grounds we offer a very fine café with a variety of coffees, teas, and baked goods, as well as a lovely gift shop where you can pick out some—"

"Where's the café?" Leah cut her off again.

The gentile manner of the lady evaporated. She now glared at Leah as if she were nothing more than an insolent tourist. "The café is only open until five. Seeing as that it's already six o'clock, and this is the last tour of the day, I'm afraid you'll have to come back and visit us tomorrow."

Leah's heart wept.

"We open at nine. You'll find that there's so much to see here at the Winchester House, that you'll actually need at least two visits to take it all in." The woman gave Leah a strict, school teacher's glare and then reaffixed the smile to her face. "Now, if the rude interruptions are over, we'll get on with the tour."

As the woman turned away, Leah stuck out her tongue, and followed along behind.

Gareth's laughter dissipated when they entered the dimly-lit foyer. They stood in silence, staring at the maze laid out before them. It was unbelievably sad to know that the haphazard mess had been created by a troubled mind who'd lived day-in and day-out in the depths of her very own hell.

CHAPTER FOURTEEN

Leah and Gareth could hear the well-versed voice of the tour guide coming from somewhere near the outer edges of the large house. It certainly hadn't been difficult to break away from the rest of the group, step through another door, and trek deeper into Sarah Winchester's world.

Leah's mouth fell open as she stared up at the immense skylights. Instead of letting in the lovely sunlight, the glass panes had been placed under the brown wooden ceilings; strange barriers that kept the outside world far away. She opened doors that led to boarded up panels, and followed water pipes that fell from the ceilings—connected to nothing. She peered into the empty chimneys; some opened into the sky while others led to nowhere. Following hallways that ended abruptly at a closet door with no knob, or a broken window that'd most likely been demolished when the earthquake hit, Leah followed Gareth's lead and kept silent. Whether to not disturb the ghosts of the past, or simply because she was straining to hear the slight humming of two orbs buried somewhere inside, she didn't quite know.

As she and Gareth moved further toward the center of the house, stepping over numerous thresholds and walking up staircases that had thirteen steps leading into the next slanted room, a light seemed to grow brighter. Leah followed the small beacon into a beautiful ballroom. Against one wall stood a huge, ornate pipe organ that seemed to be waiting for its master to blow the dust off and get back to work. On the opposing wall was a large fireplace. Unlike others scattered inside the mansion, this one was made of red brick; the white mortar was scuffed and chipped from a lifetime of use. However, the intricately carved mantelpiece seemed like it'd been polished to within an inch of its life only yesterday. And, above it, a huge mirror gleamed.

Leah stopped suddenly, and grabbed Gareth's arm. The glass seemed to be moving; their reflection wavered in front of her eyes. In the mirror, orbs of every shape and size soared around their heads like a swarm of translucent fireflies.

Leah turned and studied the rest of the room. She looked behind her, searching for the flying objects that appeared in the mirror. But there were none.

Gareth looked at her, and shrugged. Taking one last glance at the flying globes in the mirror, he walked quickly to the open door in the corner of the room.

"Where are we going?" Leah ran to catch up.

Gareth remained silent, as she followed him into another room. Unlike the brilliance of the ballroom, this area was sparse and…frightening. The walls had been painted a brilliant white with bluish-gray trim. Leah suddenly felt like she was locked in a cell of an institution, waiting to lose her mind with the rest of the inmates. There was a rickety round table in the center of the floor with one lone chair that'd seen better days. The walls were bare of pictures and mementos. Only hooks, an array of strangely shaped coat hangers, decorated one wall.

Leah focused on the brass hooks. There were two in the center, spaced apart like eyes, while another set ran vertically between them, forming a nose and an evil mouth that seemed to be stuck in the middle of a scream. She tried to turn away, but the horrid face of hooks was mesmerizing. It felt like it was ordering her to sit down in the broken chair and stay forever.

"According to our lovely four-color guidebook," Gareth whispered. "We're now standing in Sarah Winchester's séance room."

"Uh-huh," she replied, still staring at the wicked brass face.

"This is where she sat, night after night, communing with the dead."

Not noticing her trancelike state, Gareth took Leah's hand and led her through another small door. As they walked along the narrow hallway, Leah felt her flesh begin to peel away from her bones. It was like some malevolent spirit was pulling her in the direction it wanted her to go.

Her eyes noted the crooked closets as they passed by. Each held nothing more than a single row of thirteen brass hooks. They looked like a line of servants waiting for guests who would never arrive to hang up their soaked overcoats.

Around the corner they entered Sarah's private bedroom. A tray with an old cracked teapot sat on a thick comforter that covered the hand-carved four-poster bed. The clean white sheets had been folded down, as if the maid had just left after preparing the room for her employer's nightmarish sleep.

Leah heard Gareth's distant gasp and she came back to herself with a start. Turning on her heel, she stumbled over an old rocking chair sitting in the corner. The chair began to creak back and forth, awakened from its long slumber by the human contact. Practically racing through the small door, Leah followed the sound of Gareth's heavy breaths into yet another hallway filled with a brilliant yellow light.

Coming up behind him, Leah stood on her toes and stared over his shoulder at a huge Tiffany glass window that illuminated the small space.

It was the most beautiful thing she'd ever seen. The top of the glass was a dark shade of purple which slowly faded into the soft blue hue of a summer sky, before ending in a bright yellow sun.

Leah's mouth went dry. Inside the metal framework that held the pieces of fragile glass were orbs of every shape and color. They were blue, yellow, green—twelve in all—floating around the bright yellow sun.

A far-off drumbeat began inside her head. Leah felt the invisible force press against her body like a well-educated lover. She turned around and faced the odd-looking staircase behind her. "Gareth." Her voice came out like a ghostly whisper in the small hallway.

Gareth turned and looked at the tiny stairwell. The thirteen steps stopped at a low, narrow ceiling. They led…nowhere.

"Don't tell me. Let me guess." Leah let out a nervous giggle. "The stairway to Heaven?"

Gareth's lips twitched as he pushed past Leah and walked up the stairs. Sitting on the center step, he reached up and tapped on the ceiling. The flat, dull sound of a solid object was the only thing they heard as he moved his knuckles across the panel.

Leah's heart leapt into her throat when the next knock produced a hollow echo in her ears.

Gareth removed a pocketknife from his jeans and raised it toward the ceiling, ready to thrust the blade into the wood and tear it apart.

"Wait," whispered Leah. The caress of an invisible hand pushed her slowly up the staircase to sit beside him. Slowly, she reached up to the thirteenth step and lifted the wood. The top of the step gave way, opening like a pirate's treasure chest.

Leah's breath caught in her lungs when she heard the familiar humming begin. She carefully reached her hand into the empty void of the thirteenth step and searched for the orbs that she knew were inside. Her fingertips touched the soft, suede fabric. The heat of the colorful flames inside the orbs made her hand feel like it was caught in the middle of a raging fire. She panicked. Tearing the package from the step, she threw it at Gareth, and raced back down the hall.

Leah fled into the bedroom of Sarah Winchester; her brain felt like it was on fire. Closing her eyes, she tried everything she could think of to calm her breathing and banish the powerful hum from her mind.

Blink. The rocking chair in the corner creaked. Leah's eyes snapped open. She couldn't believe that the rickety piece of furniture was still moving. The scream stuck in her throat when she gazed at the little old lady rocking nervously. She was there—Sarah Winchester—wringing her hands and moving her lips, muttering words that Leah couldn't understand. In fact, all Leah could hear were the busy workmen hammering floorboards and ceiling panels, building yet another useless level on to the house. They laughed as they worked; laughed at the old woman who was buried somewhere inside their work. They called her crazy, deranged—a ridiculous millionaire who'd lost her mind. But they were happy to have a full-time paycheck, whether or not it was at the expense of a madwoman. They loved the fact that the "crazy old bird" kept making sketches of new rooms—up and up, out and out, wall after wall—giving them job security.

Leah gazed at the terrified woman. Worry lines were carved deeply into her gray, pasty flesh. Her small round cheeks were like little scoops of ice cream, making it seem as if she'd been born to smile. But, for Sarah, there wasn't anything to smile about.

The defeated woman stood up, walked down the hall to her séance room, and sat down on the rickety chair. Leah followed, keeping her gaze turned away from the eerie mask of hooks. The dead woman's hands trembled as she lit the candle in the center of the table, and began to speak. A steady stream of words came from her cracked lips; Sarah apologized over and over to the empty room. She pleaded to be taken, begging the invisible entity to let her have peace. She'd had enough, and wanted the curse to end.

Suddenly…there were screams. Turning quickly, Leah stared into the large ballroom where hundreds of people were now crammed between the dark paneled walls. Some were holding flutes of champagne, while others sat at the huge pipe organ and pounded away on the keys. There were men dressed in uniforms of blue and gray, crawling across the polished floor because their legs had been literally shot out from under them. Others sported bullet holes in their heads and chests. These were the corpses, Leah thought. These were the consequences of weapons that'd been created to take human life.

The orbs floating in the mirror suddenly burst from the glass and turned into physical beings right before Leah's eyes. Their faces were masks of blatant hatred, and their evil voices grew louder when they walked by the open door and screamed at the frightened widow.

Leah turned back to Sarah. The old woman's eyes were closed, but her lips kept moving—praying, apologizing, begging to be freed from the wrath of the Devil. Her marriage vow had killed her. To these angry souls who haunted her every waking hour, Sarah's husband had been their murderer—even though he'd never fired a single shot.

Leah followed Sarah as she stood from her chair, walked back down the hall, and crawled into her bed. The scene wavered slightly in front of Leah's eyes when a tall shadow marched into the dimly lit room. Leah released the scream that'd been sitting in her throat, when the shadowy figure reached out and grabbed her by the shoulders, shaking her body and yelling her name.

Blink. One by one the images disappeared. Feeling like an addict who was slowly awakening from the worst hallucination of her life, Leah's eyes popped open and she recognized the familiar face. She threw herself against Gareth's broad chest, and gasped for air.

"Shh, breathe." His voice was deep and soothing. "Breathe slowly."

To Leah, he was like a beacon of hope in a howling windstorm, calling her back from the dark and evil past. The rocking chair stopped creaking, and the invisible workmen hammered their last nail. Leah breathed in Gareth's musky scent and slowly began to calm down. She stepped back and stared into his worried face. "That was *not* cool."

His green eyes remained wide and alert. His spine was ramrod straight, and his fists were clenched, as if he was preparing to fight for Leah's life.

Her body was cold as ice, but her hair was pasted to her forehead by the sweat pouring off her.

Gareth led her to the rickety chair. "You should sit down."

"No!" She jumped back from the table. "I just want to get out of here. *Please* just get me out of here."

Blink. Like the flames inside the orbs, the pictures of the past reappeared. Leah clung to Gareth for support, as he pushed her through the ballroom in search of an exit.

A young soldier sat at the grand pipe organ pounding on its keys. He offered Leah a horrific glare as she raced by. His mouth opened wide, and he released a sound that reminded her of a dog howling in pain. She leaned against Gareth, as he continued to pull her across the floor.

The translucent orbs floated in the air and then fell to the floor, forming humans who'd been massacred by the Winchester invention. The broken souls reached out their hands, trying to pull Leah into their world, so she could dwell inside their nightmare forever.

Leah wrestled against their invisible grip, as Gareth practically threw her out the front door.

"There you are!" The angry voice of the gray-haired tour guide shook the thirteen panes of glass in the small window. "I *told* you to stay with the rest of the group! Don't you realize that you could've been lost in there forever?"

Leah struggled to breathe. "You have no idea."

Offering an apologetic smile, Gareth tightened his grip around her waist and led Leah off the porch, into the gardens below.

He sat her gently on a green park bench under the twilight sky. The guide marched to her car and slammed the door, racing down the driveway. She was probably thankful that her horrendous day filled with tourists of the worst possible kind had finally come to an end.

A chill overtook Leah as she stared up at the house. One by one the lights were extinguished, and the mansion fell into blackness. The numerous dark windows made the house look like the macabre mask of a hideous monster. Leah shook her head, banishing the frightening thoughts from her brain.

Gareth rubbed her shoulders. "Are you okay?"

She took a deep breath, trying to settle her raging stomach before she threw up on the well-manicured lawn. She put her head between her knees. "I *really* need a cup of coffee."

Gareth laughed softly. "We'll go to the hotel after you get your bearings, I promise. And if we pass a coffee shop along the way I'll buy it for you. Really—the whole shop'll be yours."

A trembling giggle escaped her lips, and Leah felt the blood slowly return to her limbs. She leaned back against the bench. "Did you see?"

He shook his head. "All I saw was you—white as a sheet. You looked like someone was coming at you with a machete. Your eyes were all glazed over…you scared me to death."

"I saw…things. I saw…Sarah."

"I tried to warn you." Guilt swam in his eyes. "It seems that the finder of these…relics…gets a firsthand look at the things that happened in their burial places. Past lives still exist, Leah. They're like a videotape that keeps rewinding and playing over and over again until fate gets it right. We just can't see it from where we're standing."

"What did you see in Alexandria?"

"You won't believe me." He grinned.

"After today's experience, I'll believe anything you say."

"I saw Cleopatra."

A guttural laugh came from deep inside her body at the mention of the most beautiful woman in the world during her era. "Figures. Get a date, did ya'? Does your charm work in all time periods?"

"See? I said you wouldn't believe me." Gareth continued to grip her hand like a vise. "Do you want to see them?"

"No!" The sharp command left Leah's lips like a shot from a Winchester rifle.

"Why not?"

Resting her head on the back of the bench, Leah stared up at the clear sky stippled with stars. "They make me feel awful…horrible things. When you showed me the first two back in New York I felt…impatient. When I looked at the ram I wanted to grab a gun and start shooting because I felt…invincible. And when I stared at the bull, I felt power. I felt like I could literally pick you and Donovan up and throw you through the wall just because I wanted to. The feelings were…violent."

Gareth's eyes grew wide. "You've just described the negative traits of the people born under those signs, Leah. An Aries is quick to arms; they raise their rifles first and think later. Taurus treats the people they care about like possessions. They can be quite powerful individuals."

Leah waved her hand in the air. "I don't believe in any of that horoscope crap, Gareth. People are what they are—good or bad—because of how they *choose* to be. Besides, my horoscope's always wrong. I used to read it religiously, and it would always say that I was going to get a promotion or meet the love of my life. Newsflash! Neither one ever happened."

"I'm not talking about daily horoscopes." He smiled. "I'm talking about scientific, astronomical, and astrological theories that've been debated for centuries. Very bright philosophers could actually tell a person's character—good and bad—based on where the sun was in a particular constellation at the time of the person's birth. But I can't say I'm altogether sure why you're only feeling the bad things."

Gareth stared up at the stars, as if looking for answers from the source. "When I hold the Aries orb in my hand, I feel ambitious and courageous, like I could go out and save anyone from anything. With Taurus, I feel reserved and methodical, like I could solve the hardest puzzle in the world. I feel like I have the patience to decode and decipher any clue that's thrown in my path. These traits are overwhelmingly good, and I can feel them. It's like they run through my veins."

Leah tried to keep the sarcasm from her voice. "You're just lucky, I guess."

Gareth reached into the knapsack and unwrapped the suede pouch; the two new orbs beamed their lights into the night sky.

Leah tried to move away, but Gareth caught her wrist. "Please try for me. There's so much good for you to feel."

Gareth placed the pink flashing orb into Leah's palm. "Ancient worlds are speaking to us through these. The feeling is truly magical, Leah. I promise."

She stared into the glass, as he continued, "Besides, it was probably just Donovan being there that made you angry. He apparently has that effect on you."

Leah could barely make out the miniature figure inside the glass holding the scales of justice in her hand. As the pink flame warmed Leah's skin, Gareth whispered in her ear, "This is Libra. It should make you feel full of idealistic dreams, charm, and elegance. Tell me, what do you feel when you hold the power of justice in the palm of your hand?"

Leah's voice came out strained; the angry emotions overtook her. "I feel like lying, Gareth. I feel deceitful and *un*just, and I really, *really* want you to get it away from me."

He sighed. "One more."

"I don't want to see the stupid things!" Leah smashed her hand down on the bench. "I've already gotten way more than I bargained for out of this."

She glanced at the yellowish-orange orb now resting in his hand. "Maybe non-believers like me can only see the bad stuff," she whispered. Leah could feel the intense power coming from the topaz flame, as the scorpion's tail swept back and forth inside the glass. Her body suddenly felt like it was on fire. Unbridled passion seeped into her bones. The emotion was electrifying, and her body tingled as the fantasies raced into her mind.

*

Gareth stared at her amazing face, and tried with all his might to not react to the woman who'd transformed into a seductive temptress before his eyes. If Leah was experiencing the bad traits of the Scorpius constellation, he was sure that her overwhelming passion could eat him alive. Sinful thoughts raced through his brain. He debated whether or not he'd be okay with meeting his maker early, if he could immerse himself just once in the passion that burned in her sapphire eyes.

With a heavy heart, Gareth put the orb back into the bag. The humming increased as the signs came together.

Standing up from the bench, he stared down at her beautiful face. He forced himself not to take advantage of the situation by crushing her soft lips under his own. "Leah." He shook her shoulder.

Leah's eyes cleared; the hungry flames of lust and desire disappeared, and a bright red blush flooded her cheeks.

Gareth offered a teasing smile. "What'd ya' get from that one?"

Much to his dismay, Leah kept her mouth shut. She was not going to share her innermost thoughts. "I had the urge to kill you again," she snapped. "But I probably can't blame that on the orb."

"Scorpio has always been my favorite sign." Gareth grinned. "Life would be very dull without their…desires."

"Whatever." Leah cleared her throat. "I told you I don't believe in all that crap."

Gareth put his cell phone back in his pocket, as the taxi he'd summoned magically appeared in the driveway. "Time for that cup of coffee, lady."

Getting into the cab, Leah stared back at the eerie mansion.

"There's nothing you can do about the past." His voice was filled with understanding.

Leah nodded. "Maybe Sarah was reincarnated and had a good life the second time around."

"If you believe in those crazy things."

"Shut up."

Gareth gave his instructions to the cab driver and sat back in the seat. "So you believe in reincarnation now?"

Leah stared straight ahead. "I had a friend named Brian in high school. He was somewhat of a…well…I guess you could say class clown, but I prefer idiot. He said that the next time he came back he'd be the President of the United States."

"Why was that?"

"Because he believed that his mission in every life was to be a huge waste of space."

Gareth let out a roar of laughter inside the vehicle, and threw an arm over her shoulder. "When were you born, by the way? I should at least know the character—good and bad—of the person who's going to lead me to Heaven's door."

Leah looked back at the vacant eyes of the Winchester House. "Never mind."

"You're a Scorpio."

She blushed. "I said, never mind."

"Don't you wanna' know what my sign is?" He teased.

"I didn't know there was a sign for pain in the ass."

Gareth laughed out loud as they sped away from Leah's first horrible nightmare.

CHAPTER FIFTEEN

The hot water finally erased the chills from her body. Leah emptied the last few troubling hours from her mind, leaned back in the claw-footed tub, and reveled in the fact that she was very much alive.

Gareth padded softly across the plush carpeting in the next room. Leah heard his muffled laugh and the lethal charm drip from his lips. A giggle floated under the bathroom door. From the sounds of the exchange, he'd quite obviously met up with yet another female fan who'd been sent to deliver their dinner.

The muffled laughter ceased, and the door closed. Leah waited to hear the announcement that what she desperately craved had finally arrived.

His knuckles brushed softly against the door. "Can I tempt you?"

Her body trembled at the intriguing invitation. "Excuse me?"

"I have a beautiful silver carafe out here and, from the smell of it, I'd say there may be a magical liquid inside that's calling your name."

Leah's heart jumped for joy. She practically pole-vaulted from the tub, wrapped her long hair up in a fluffy towel, and threw the luxurious complimentary bathrobe around her warm shoulders. Wrapping the tie around her waist, she raced from the room. Gareth was right. She could feel the coffee calling out to her, pulling her in with its promise of fresh roasted taste—the true nectar of the gods.

Stray droplets and fragrant suds flew from her figure as she ran from the bathroom. Leah stole the steaming mug from the smiling man and brought it to her nose, drawing a deep breath of life. "Now, *that's* Heaven."

Gareth laughed. He picked up his ice cold bottle and sat down in the overstuffed chair. Taking a swig, his gaze never wandered from her face. "You've shown more courage in the two short days that I've known you than most people have shown to me in my entire life."

"Barker's not courageous, is he?" Leah snorted. "What a surprise."

Gareth grimaced at her tone. "He took me on as a brother. He helped me with my sister when he didn't have to. I'd say that was courageous for a man of eighteen."

"I'm sorry," said Leah quickly. "It's not my place."

Gareth waved his hand in the air, dismissing her apology. "You just don't know him."

She looked at the pain that was evident in every line of his handsome face, and chastised her unforgiving nature. "Okay…enlighten me."

"Donovan has a brother he's only met once or twice in his life. His father disappeared with his brother when he was very young, leaving Donovan to fend for himself. That's probably why he got so…hard."

"What about his mother?"

"Died," Gareth replied. "At least, I think she's dead. He never talks about her."

Leah nodded, although her mind still couldn't see Barker as a poor lost orphan, or the honorable man who helped Gareth through his pain.

"Without him looking out for us, and pushing me, my parents' dream would've been lost. He kept me going in the right direction."

"And the payment?" asked Leah, before she could stop herself.

"What?"

"What does your noble friend get in return for all his kindness?"

Gareth shook his head. "Boy, you don't trust anyone, do you?"

Leah searched for an appropriate response that wouldn't make her look like a textbook case of the spinster librarian.

"I'm sure Donovan wants a bit of fame, Leah." Gareth smiled. "He wants to write a bestseller. I certainly don't think he's a saint."

"No." She leaned back in her chair. "That's your job."

"Far from it," he said, with a laugh. "You wouldn't say that if you knew what I was thinking about half the time."

Leah ignored the flirtatious green eyes, and stretched out against the velvet seat. Blowing on the hot coffee, she carefully enjoyed sip after blissful sip.

"What are you thinking about?" he asked.

"You go first."

"I was thinking about how beautiful you are," he whispered.

Leah looked away from him, trying to hide from the piercing gaze. "Oh." She began to dry her heavy, wet mane.

"See? Sainthood is probably not in my future." He laughed. "Now you."

Leah answered quickly, struggling to change the subject, "I was thinking about the coffee, to tell you the truth. Although," she continued, draping the towel across the back of her chair and throwing her long legs over the arm. "I have to say you look good this way—more comfortable. The tuxedo-clad, mega-watt grin guy is annoying. You're more in your element in blue-jean casual."

"This is true." Gareth laughed. "I am much more comfortable. Although, I *do* like my creature comforts."

"Such as?"

He looked around the ornate room. "This hotel, for instance. I love overstuffed cushions and silver platters brought to my door. I've worked my butt off for years, going after treasure to sell to the highest bidder, just to keep me in the style I've become accustomed to. I enjoy being pampered."

"Sounds girlie," she teased.

Gareth stole an appetizer off her plate. "What about you?"

"Of course I love to be pampered," Leah said, as she rubbed her cheek against the incredibly soft bathrobe. "It's okay for *me* to be girlie, though. I'm a girl."

Gareth tilted his head. "I just noticed something…girl. You haven't worn your glasses since we left New York. Considering the size of those coke bottles, I'm amazed that you could see anything in the Winchester House."

Leah bit into a warm sweet roll. "I think I left them next to the computer at your hotel. I don't really need them. I picked them up at a pharmacy a few years back." She shrugged. "Just easier."

"Easier?"

"I don't like to be looked at," she replied, quietly.

"I've said it before." Gareth grinned. "You're going to need a heck of a lot more than frumpy costumes and big glasses to get men not to look at you. You're very much like Wonder Woman, sweetheart. Diana Prince was still hot—with or without the bulletproof wristbands."

"I always wanted that magic lasso of hers."

Gareth's eyes twinkled. "You seem more the whip type to me."

"Thank your lucky stars I don't have one, pal, or you would've been beaten into the ground by now."

Gareth tore into his steak like a starving animal. "Of that, I'm sure. I suppose we both use costumes to our full advantage. We're a great deal alike."

Leah choked on her coffee. "Yeah, sure. If I must remind you, Mr. Lowery, your costume is used to *get* attention—not that you need any."

"And yours is to hide from it."

She sat quietly, savoring every bite of the delicious dinner.

Gareth wiped his chin. "Why do you want to?"

"Want to what?" Leah mumbled through her over-stuffed mouth.

He threw the napkin in her face. "Why do you want to hide? There's a shortage of really amazing people in this world. It would be a shame to bury one as interesting as you."

Without thinking, Leah began to explain the trials and tribulations she'd experienced at the hands of her three supermodel sisters and her well-meaning, but annoying mother. Gareth's laughter filled the room like a refreshing breeze.

"So," Leah continued, taking another sip of coffee. "I figured it was better to be able to spell pageant than to actually win one."

They bantered back and forth, lobbing story after story at each other. As the dessert crumbs disappeared from their plates, Gareth wiped the tears from his eyes. "You should've been a comedian, not a librarian."

"When I was younger, I wanted to be a serial killer." Leah patted her well-fed stomach. "Or a cop."

Gareth's eyes grew wide. "Go back to the first one."

She grinned. "I thought I would have a knack for the profession. I was always so angry, but my mind was like a steel trap. I would've been the one to get away with it. And I wouldn't be one of those boring, 'my father beat me and I was in love with my mother,' kind of people." Her voice was very professional, as if convincing a prospective employer that she was the right woman for the job. "I'd simply do it for educational purposes. After all, everyone should learn at least one other trade. Have something to fall back on if the whole librarian gig didn't work out, you know?"

"You're seriously messed up."

Leah burst into laughter. "True, but I had you going."

Gareth rolled his eyes. "You did miss your calling. You're definitely mean enough to be a serial killer."

Leah poured the last of the coffee. Carefully tapping the sugar packets and gently adding the cream, she found herself more relaxed than she'd ever been.

Gareth put his elbows on the table. "Why are you helping me?"

"Well…" Leah reached for a punch line.

"No. Really. The truth."

Taking a long sip from her mug, Leah thought about the consequences of opening herself up even more to a virtual stranger. But when she met his gaze, her fear faded. Perhaps she was getting soft, but the more time she spent in his company the more she found herself trusting him. Choosing to keep the strong emotions she felt for him a secret, Leah decided to let him in on the other reason she had for following him into the darkness.

"When I was thirteen," she began. "My mother took me to the beauty salon. I can't tell you how much I hated that. They were forever crimping my hair so that all my curls were flattened out like damp laundry. Then they would rip my eyebrows out, plaster makeup on my face like I was some two-dollar hooker, and all the while sit and chat with my mother like she was the queen bee of some invisible hive of idiots. All they cared about was looking good."

Leah shrugged. "I would put up with this ridiculous treatment twice a year because it made my mother feel good. I mean, what the hell? It was a minor thing compared to some. One night, after one of these spa sessions, we got home and my mother announced that we were going to have a formal dinner and we all needed to dress accordingly.

"I can't tell you how upset my father was." The love for her favorite man warmed her heart. "He didn't like frivolous things. He liked to come home and, as he always said, spend quiet time with his stable full of fantastic girls."

Leah walked over to her purse and took a picture from her wallet. She handed it to Gareth.

He let out a soft whistle. "Wow! This picture should be on the cover of *Victoria's Secret*. You certainly have good genes in your family."

"We're okay, I suppose."

"Yeah, that's it." He laughed. "You're all just…okay."

"Anyway," she continued, "we got all dressed up and the doorbell rang. In walks this Ivy League punk; one of those people who don't have to actually succeed at anything because his father had already paid his way through life."

Gareth nodded. "I'm familiar with the type."

"All through this atrociously uncomfortable dinner he aims his nose up in the air, and yaps on and on about how wonderful he is, all the things he has, and all the things he'll accomplish during his lifetime. My mother kept up with his ego step for step, listing my accomplishments." Leah felt the anger swell in the pit of her stomach. "I wanted to hurl when she only listed the ridiculous ones. It seemed she was too embarrassed to mention the science awards and the Humanitarian award. Most Likely to Succeed was a title that my mother thought was secondary to when I took first place in the New York City Pre-Teen pageant." A shudder of disgust rolled over her shoulders.

She sighed. "After dinner, she practically threw me into the back seat of his fancy car because he was the 'right kind' of guy. And ten minutes later, I kicked him in the balls and got out of his fancy car because he'd mistaken me for 'that kind' of girl. Makes me sick just thinking about it."

"Where does he live?" Gareth's eyes turned to jade. "I could find him and kill him for you."

"See?" She grinned. "Hang around me long enough and I can turn anyone into a serial killer."

Anger infused Gareth's voice. "I don't particularly like people who can't take no for an answer."

Leah offered a teasing smile. "You'll never have to worry about being one of them, since no female will ever say no."

"You did."

"Oh…that's right." She laughed.

"So you're helping me because some scum tried to force himself on you when you were a teenager?" His eyebrows climbed up his forehead. "Let me guess. If you prove that Heaven exists, then you'll go find the gates of Hell and throw him through?"

"Hmmm. Nice thought. But, sadly, no." Leah's grin disappeared. "When I got home that night I told my mother exactly what I thought of her perfect male escort, and she simply shook her head. I'll remember her words for the rest of my life. She looked at me, and said, 'You have clothes, personality, the right makeup, but I just can't get you to be impressive. That's all I wanted tonight, Leah, for you to impress him.'"

Gareth shook his head.

"Can you believe that?" Her voice grew louder. "She thought it was *my* fault. I didn't cater to his whim, bat my eyelashes, or giggle enough at his stupid jokes. I was simply supposed to dress like a Barbie doll and act like a Stepford wife to impress the heck out of him. *Why*? I mean, he sure as hell didn't impress me."

Leah reached across the table and took Gareth's hand. "I've lived my whole adult life in a building that holds the words of geniuses. These writers changed lives and altered the course of humanity. I've touched no life, Gareth. I've changed nothing. I want to be impressive, but for the right reasons. And I gotta' tell you, I'd really like someone to impress me for once.

She took a deep breath, unable to stop her diatribe. "If what you say is even remotely true, and the end of the rainbow is really what you think it is, than I want to be a part of it for a whole lot of reasons. I want to stand in front of that…power and know that my little life has meaning; that I'm here for more than just the amusement of others. I need the answers that I can't find in the pages of a book, Gareth. I *need* to know that I was meant for something." She came back to herself, and snorted. "Of course, I already know you're wrong. So, I suppose I'm really here to scrape you off the pavement when you find that out."

"Lady." His voice was like velvet. "I'll make it my life's pursuit to impress you. And you should know that there's at least one life that I can state quite honestly has been completely blessed by your presence."

Leah held her breath; his intense gaze moved from her eyes to her lips.

"I've never met anyone like you," he continued. "You're the most beautiful lady I've ever seen but, and this absolutely boggles my mind, the most breathtaking parts of you are *inside* your body. If my journey ended tonight, that fact alone would prove to me beyond a shadow of a doubt that Heaven exists."

Leah gasped at his powerful statement. She wanted to respond. She wanted to rise from the chair and throw herself into the world that belonged to the green-eyed god. But the warning bells beat in time with her rapid pulse. They weren't done. There was no way for them to take that leap when they still had to focus on tomorrow.

Pulling her hand from Gareth's grip, Leah reached for the metal book. She shuffled through the pages, past the lovely picture of Cleopatra sitting inside her well-known library. Directly behind it was a drawing of what looked like a papal decree with an 'X' drawn over top of it. Sitting alongside it was a miniature map; a tiny cross had been drawn in the center. Constellations orbited the cross like planets around the sun. Leah took a long drink of ice cold water before turning back to Gareth.

"I want to be with you," he whispered.

Leah choked on the water. After suffering through the wracking coughs, she tried her best to change the subject. "Where did you go after Alexandria? Where did you find the next two orbs?"

Gareth sighed. He looked extremely uncomfortable as he rearranged his body against the soft cushions. Reaching into her glass, he stole a piece of ice; his perfect, straight teeth chomped down on the cube. "Rome."

"Huh?"

"Another library. In Vatican City, to be exact."

Leah read the small words printed by Rudolf Steiner's hand. "Body & Blood," she whispered.

"What better place to find religion?" Gareth laughed. "But I didn't go there because I was hunting for the house of God. I went there because Ptolemy sent me."

"Ptolemy?" said Leah. "He was the Director of the Library at Alexandria."

"That's him." Gareth squirmed in his chair. "When I found the first two orbs buried in Alexandria's catacombs, Cleopatra wasn't the only person I saw. Ptolemy was the beginning for all astrologers and astronomers. He was revered in his time as being the smartest person who ever lived. His research was treated like a bible that told of the secret world of the stars. These texts were translated by scholars who formed the largest Ptolemy library collection in the world."

Leah nodded. "Which is now located in Vatican City."

"The secret archives."

"If it's such a secret how did you get in?" She grinned.

"Money can buy a great deal, and I have a lot of it."

Leah was hardly surprised. Anyone could be bought…even a man of God.

Gareth continued, "Before your experience at the Winchester House, I probably couldn't have made you understand the strange journey I've been on. When I came in contact with the orbs in Alexandria, it was like the past came back to life. I watched Ptolemy's life overlap my own."

Wonder and awe filled his voice. "He was sitting at a huge desk where the Library's underground would've been located at the time; the place where scholars would go to transcribe new ideas for Egypt and Rome. I watched him title his work—*The Almagest*—which is the document that all astronomers live by. In this book, Ptolemy wrote all about his planetary theories, and mapped out new stars and constellations that he'd discovered. Even Columbus used his maps when he made his way to the West." He grinned. "Columbus was yet another, like me, who believed that something was out there, even though it took him a while to actually prove it."

Leah listened quietly. Glancing down at the opposing page, she noted the strange pictures of white chalk drawn against the black background.

"I actually sat there, Leah, and watched the greatest mind in Egypt at work." His green eyes were wide; his voice was filled with wonder. "I watched him literally create the words that would lead someone like me, eons later, to the gates of Heaven. I can't prove it to you, Leah. But I felt a caress on my cheek and a voice whispering in my ear, letting me know that the Papal Curia was the next place to go."

"So you went to Rome." Leah smiled. "You went—you saw—you conquered."

He laughed. "The next two orbs were buried in an old storeroom in a boarded up tunnel that the Vatican once used to deliver mail in and out of the city. The book they were hidden in was buried under thousands of layers of dust. It'd fallen behind an old wooden shelf, locked inside a room that no one had entered in years. I can't tell you how Rudolf Steiner got in. All I can figure is that, with Andrew Carnegie's immense wealth behind the mission, Steiner probably could've hidden the orbs inside the Pope's robes if he'd wanted to."

"What was the book?" she asked.

"It was untitled," he replied, quietly. "But the cover showed twelve orbs rotating around a golden sun."

"Sounds familiar." She shuddered, remembering the stained glass window inside the haunted house.

Gareth nodded. "There was a huge map inside all folded up. When I opened it, the orbs were sitting inside. They blinked to life when I touched them. The power—the sheer excitement of knowing that I'd done it was startling. I must've sat there and stared at that work of art for hours. It was a perfect midnight sky, with all the constellations of the zodiac pulsing with light. At one point—." His eyes were stone-cold serious as he gazed at her across the table. "And I will swear to this on my deathbed—a beam of light came out of the map. I watched this…spear of fire rise into the ceiling of that small room, and disappear."

Leah watched the dazzling green light radiate from his eyes. She turned off the switch of cynicism inside her body for a split second, and offered him a genuine smile. "Sounds extraordinary."

"You believe me?"

Leah tilted her head to the side. "Why not? After the day I've had, I'm willing to believe just about anything."

Gareth let out a small sigh.

"What did Donovan think of the spear of fire?"

"He wasn't there. Stayed in the hotel."

Leah thought out loud. "Wasn't he ever with you…when you actually found these things?"

Gareth stared off into space, as if trying to remember. "Now that I think about it…no. He was never there at the actual discovery."

"Didn't want to get his hands dirty," muttered Leah. "Unlike our friend Crowley." She returned her gaze to the dark page opposite the papal images. The title of Crowley's drawing mimicked the other side; the words *Body and Blood* were scribbled on top of the page. Leah noticed the sinister slant to the lettering, like an evil snake had etched the script on the paper with its forked tongue.

Leah read out loud the almost indecipherable handwriting, "It is wrong and weak to reject any part of one's personality." She stared at the childish drawings below the puzzling statement. The first was a church, completely colored in with white chalk. Written in the crooked steeple was the number thirteen—once again making a prominent appearance in Crowley's next twisted clue. At the bottom of the page was a picture of a top hat and gloves; the elegant clothing looked completely out of place against the sinister background. Beside the hat, was a jumble of miniature letters. Leah squinted. "I can't make this out."

"Let me try." Gareth leaned over the book. "It looks like…well…that doesn't make any sense."

"What do you think it says?"

Gareth looked at her with a deeply perplexed expression. "I think it says that the miller went to court."

"The miller went to court?"

"Told ya." Gareth shrugged. "Makes no sense."

Leah stood up and began to pace back and forth across the carpet. She crossed her arms over her chest and bit into her lower lip, as the card catalogue opened inside her head. "What are you trying to tell us, Al?"

she mumbled. "What does a top hat have to do with a miller? Court… church…a church owned by a miller? A judge who sent a miller to jail?"

She could feel Gareth's gaze burn into her back as she tried to piece the puzzle together. Shuffling through the wealth of information in her brain, Leah discarded any data that didn't fit.

"Let's take it separately," said Gareth, trying to help. "The biggest drawing is a church. Maybe, like the Winchester House, there's a chapel somewhere with thirteen steeples?"

"Chapel," Leah mumbled.

"Maybe a miller went mad and built a haven in the middle of nowhere and…what? Sacrificed bodies? That would account for the Body and Blood angle. Then he went to court for his crimes? Maybe—"

"Jesus."

Gareth stopped talking and stared up at her. "What? You think because I found the 'good' orbs in the Vatican that this has something to do with Jesus?"

Leah shook her head. "Miller's Court…thirteen…you're right, Gareth. It's not a church. It's a chapel."

Gareth glanced at the bright white building drawn on the black page. "I'm not following."

Leah knelt on the soft carpet in front of him. She took his hands and stared into the wide mesmerizing eyes. "Thirteen Miller's Court is an address, Gareth. A rather famous one."

He shook his head. "I don't know it."

"Yes. You do. Everyone does." Leah swallowed hard. "The chapel in the drawing is white. Whitechapel. The top hat and gloves were part of the costume that the worst murderer in any day and age wore—the only killer in history who got away with the whole damn thing. He could certainly stand for body and blood, considering they were his two favorite things."

Gareth's face went white.

Leah wished with all her heart that he would kiss her hard and stop her from saying the last words that either of them wanted to hear. She knew he couldn't go there and, more importantly, that he wouldn't want to risk her seeing those truly hideous pictures from the past.

She choked on her fear. "Number thirteen Miller's Court in Whitechapel is the location where he took his final body—spilling gallons of her blood in the process."

"Body and blood," whispered Gareth.

Leah nodded; her blood turned to ice in her veins. "It's the place where Mary Jane Kelly was viciously mutilated…by Jack the Ripper."

CHAPTER SIXTEEN

As the engines of the plane roared beneath him, Gareth thought back to the night before. Her eyes, usually filled with an intelligence not known to modern man, had been wide and fearful, like Leah had been named as the next victim to face the wrath of a long dead killer.

He'd held her in his arms last night, offering her the only comfort he knew how to give. When she'd finally drifted off, Gareth had remained awake, listening to the quiet hum coming from his knapsack. He cursed himself, Crowley, the heavens—everyone he could think of—for letting him pull this woman into the clutches of a devil's joke. He beat himself black and blue inside for having the nerve to thrust Leah into this horrible mess. He even thought about gathering his things in the middle of the night and making a run for it. She'd be so much safer, far away from this twisted quest, back in her precious library. Perhaps she'd been right the first time. Perhaps deep down he *was* crazy—crazy for ever beginning this journey.

His part had been so easy, following in the footsteps of a millionaire who'd enlisted a man of science to hide six orbs in places of peaceful brilliance. Gareth knew he'd been lucky. His flashbacks had included the great minds of all time, leaning over their books and creating masterpieces that the world would someday base their very existence on. Gareth's stomach lurched with the turbulent plane. The sights and sounds of 1800's Whitechapel were going to be far more difficult than a few macabre ghosts who'd been shot by a Winchester rifle.

He'd thought about this all night…how hard this would be on Leah. He'd even left the room after she'd fallen asleep to phone Donovan for his advice. But his friend had been right. There was no abandoning Leah now, not after all she'd given to a man she hardly knew. Donovan had even labeled him a low-life, if Gareth even thought to leave the damsel in distress behind.

Gareth believed him, but he so wanted to be the one to follow in the footsteps of the madman and take the brunt of the horrible visions. Although he knew it wouldn't work that way. Leah was the bearer of the darkness; the chosen one who would face the worst of humanity. Donovan had reminded him that there had always been two. One dark and one light—each with their own talents—to keep the secret that'd been hidden from mankind for centuries.

Besides that, Gareth knew from the determined look on her face that Leah would board a plane for Whitechapel alone, if she had to. He felt so useless. All he could do was pick up the pieces and hope to God that she was strong enough to survive it.

When morning came, he'd made sure to stand close, hug her, place his arm around her waist, and pull her to his side—anything to let Leah know that she wasn't alone. He wanted with all his heart to make sure that when she traveled through death she'd hold on to him. Because his heart was most definitely hers.

The bells echoed in the plane, announcing their arrival into yet another hell. Gareth stared at Leah. Her hair was no longer in a nice, neat ponytail; it flowed over her shoulders like a river of lava. Her blue eyes were lifeless as she stood from her seat.

Gareth grabbed the knapsack and took her hand. Holding on tight, they departed the claustrophobic area through the terminal, and into the waiting cab without a word.

"Where to?" The man's accent made Gareth feel like he'd already stepped back in time. He couldn't remember when a cab driver had offered such a genuine smile of welcome, while tipping his jaunty, old-style cap.

Gareth smiled back. "Whitechapel, please."

"Should've known." The man snorted. "You Americans still want to see that place. Bit o' voyeurism in ya', aye? Love all that psycho stuff, do ya'?"

Gareth nodded. "We Americans are more than a little odd."

"Jack the Ripper and Buckingham Palace seem to be the places."

"We'll visit the Queen later." Gareth laughed.

The driver offered a smile to the silent female. His brows furrowed, as he turned his worried gaze back to Gareth. "She okay?"

*

The new voice broke through Leah's troubled thoughts. She nodded at the man's kind face, and began to steel herself against the bloody juggernaut that she was sure would come. She was so mad at herself for her childish fear. Jack the Ripper was dead and buried. Even the old cabby judged him to be nothing more than a ridiculous tourist attraction.

Leah raised her chin in the air and offered him a smile. "I'm just fine, thank you. Jet lag, is all."

He tipped his cap. "I must say you Americans know how to grow em'. You, my girl, are a real beauty."

A flush rose in Leah's cheeks; it was the first warmth she'd felt since lying in Gareth's arms the night before. "Thank you. Would you mind giving us a tour while you go through the area? I've never seen any of this except in books. And your voice is extremely comforting."

"Ha!" The old man laughed. "Tell my wife that, Miss. She says she can't stand the sound of it most days. I have a hard time shuttin' up, you see."

Leah was grateful for his happy face and glittering brown eyes. "Well, I like it just fine."

"Maybe I'll toss her out and spend some time in your company, aye?" He winked.

Leah's laughter came easily, as the man drove out of the busy airport. He shook his fist at the bad drivers who were cutting in and out of traffic. "Be hard for ole' Jack nowadays. He'd never get away. He'd be caught in this god forsaken bloody traffic!" He glanced in the rearview mirror. "My apologies, Miss."

Gareth leaned over and whispered in her ear, "And you say *I* have that effect on people."

"He's a nice man."

"He's a scamp if I ever saw one." Gareth chuckled. "Believe me, all of us are nice old men. We'll be anything you want us to be to get a smile like yours aimed in our direction."

"Look out your window," ordered Leah. "You're missing all the sites."

Gareth pressed his body into the corner of the seat, and gazed at her. "Seems to me I'm already looking at the best sight London has to offer."

She rolled her eyes, trying to ignore the wanton woman in her soul who was begging Leah to enjoy the handsome man.

The jovial driver turned a corner, and spoke in his soothing tone. "You're enterin' Whitechapel, folks. The road we're travelin' is called Whitechapel Road." He grinned. "Not very creative folk this side o' town."

Leah laughed.

"Anyway," he continued, "in the old days Whitechapel was a place where bein' poor was the main job o' most folks. Odd, when you consider that fancy Buckingham Palace and Westminster Abbey are just a hop, skip, and a jump away. Down here was mostly breweries, foundries, and the like. Good things came out o' here, though. Matter o' fact, we cast your Liberty Bell right o'er there at the Whitechapel Bell Foundry."

"Really?" said Gareth.

"You bet. Made Big Ben, too. Down the way there were slaughterhouses, and then south was the Billingsgate Fish Market. They say it smelled about as bad as it looked back then. Not a place where a lovely lady such as yourself, Miss, would be found shoppin'." He smiled in the rearview mirror.

Leah stared out the window at the pristine view; easels and carts lined the busy sidewalks. "What's the main business here now?"

"Mostly you got your artists and creative types. Think they like the mystery that surrounds the place—gets those creative juices flowin'. The Ripper may have made it famous, but the likes of Jack London, George Bernard Shaw—even ole' Vladimir Lenin was here. He led rallies right down Whitechapel Road when he was kicked out o' Russia."

He pointed out the window. "The Elephant Man was in that shop o'er there before Dr. Treves took him to the Royal London Hospital. He was here when The Ripper got down to business. There's a museum to the poor man at the hospital if you want to go by and see it."

Leah shuddered. "No, thank you." She cleared her throat, trying to disguise the slight quivering of her voice. "What about Jack? I'm sure you're up on the history, considering how many crazy Americans want to see this spot."

He laughed loudly.

Leah was thankful for his large voice because it blocked out the hum coming from the knapsack between Gareth's legs. It was growing louder.

Gareth put the bag behind his back and pressed further into the leather seat.

Quickly, Leah resumed the conversation, hoping that the man wouldn't notice the strange noise. "Are we near any of his…spots right now?"

The cab slowed, and the man pointed out the window. "Matter o' fact, young lady, that corner store used to be Thirteen Miller's Court. That's where Jack's last girl was killed. Worst one they say."

"That's not the original building?"

"Nah," he replied. "Place was leveled. They destroyed almost everything on this street. It was a mess. You have to imagine it. I mean, there's poor all o'er the world, but this place was about as close to Hell as you could get. Garbage in the gutters, prostitutes and thieves prowlin' the streets—was the way o' life here. When you ended up in Whitechapel there was no gettin' out."

His voice took on an almost reverent tone when he continued, "Down that way is Mitre Square. You walk though the ole' Church Passage and you'll find the spot where a young miss named Catherine Eddowes was sliced up by The Ripper. Not much there 'cept for a park bench and some flowers. Very clean now. We tried real hard to wipe away the memory o' that awful time."

"Jack the Ripper never seems to fade," said Gareth.

"True." The driver nodded. "Ole' Jack's more of a bloody legend by now. No offense to them dead ladies, but our Ripper seems tame when you compare him to the ones strappin' bombs to their babies and takin' out whole city blocks. Those people are way worse monsters than Jack, you ask me."

Leah nodded at the kind face staring at her in the mirror. "Thank you."

"For what?"

"You just put this whole business into perspective for me." Leah felt the fear fade from her body. No matter what she would see—it was over. It would be a horror flick at best. Considering the life and death struggles that the world's men and women were going through nowadays, Jack the Ripper was more like a Hollywood movie monster. Disgusting, but completely harmless where her life was concerned.

"Want me to take you o'er to Mitre Square?"

The humming in the bag grew quiet, and Leah stared into Gareth's bewildered face. "Actually, Mr.—?"

"Sorry 'bout that. Wainwright is what I go by. But a pretty woman such as yourself can call me George. Makes me feel young."

"Okay…George it is." Leah laughed. "I'd actually like to hear more about Mary Jane Kelly, the woman who lived in that corner apartment back there."

George pulled a U-turn and parked across the road from the clean, white building that took up the bloody block from long ago.

Leah stared at the storefronts. The windows gleamed in the brilliant sunshine, and vibrant-colored awnings hung like rainbows over the doors. As tourists and shoppers went from building to building, the melodious chimes on the shop entrances tinkled merrily. It sounded as if the whole block was being serenaded by a choir of angels. Leah could see the early signs of the holiday season approaching. Christmas lights would soon be hung, calling out to wayward shoppers to spend their money.

George took off his cap, and turned to face his passengers. His face was filled with anxiety. "This is a horrible subject for such a nice lady. Wouldn't you rather see Big Ben, or Parliament? There's interesting' stuff in our city. Really…can't miss attractions."

"It's okay, George." Leah offered him a smile. "I'd really like to know, if you don't mind telling me. I actually like ghost stories."

George glared at Gareth. Leah was startled by the disappointment in the man's gaze. She watched in silence as Gareth's shoulders slumped, like a monumental weight of guilt had just fallen on them.

She spoke up. "George, this trip was all my idea. I'm a librarian back in New York and I'm setting up an exhibition on serial killers. *I* came to get this information. My friend is just a protective escort."

"Oh." George's face softened a bit. "Disgustin' choice for an exhibition, if you don't mind me sayin'. But who am I to stop a lady from doin' her job?"

"Thank you. I want everything to be as accurate as possible. You know us Americans—we tend to get things wrong."

George didn't argue. "Okay…let's see…Mary Jane Kelly. O' course, you know what The Ripper did. Came out o' nowhere in 1888, and from then til' 1891, he got many o' the poor dears. Some say he was responsible for six—some say eleven—nobody'll ever really know. All the women he preyed on practiced the oldest profession, as it were. All them gals were poor, homeless, and, in most cases, had no family or friends to speak of." George shook his head.

"Still happens," said Leah.

He sighed. "All too often. They say Mary Jane was different, though."

"She wasn't a prostitute?"

"No," George replied. "People agreed she was into that too. Had to feed herself. But there were those who thought she was killed by someone other than Jack; someone who just wanted to make it look like all the others so it'd be blamed on The Ripper."

"What made people think it was a copycat?" Gareth asked.

"Well, for one thing, Mary Jane was beautiful. Amazingly beautiful, they say. Auburn hair, blue eyes—" He glanced at Leah. "Sounds like I just described you, don't it?"

Her stomach heaved.

"Anyhoo, Mary was also smart as a whip. She came from very well-to-do folk who had thrown her out. No one knows why exactly, but there's a lot o' mystery around her. She didn't fit the mold of a poor, uneducated prostitute like the other Ripper victims had."

George continued walking them through history, "Up until Mary, Jack had always killed in back alleys at night. But this corner was quite a busy place back in the day. I've seen a picture of the small apartment house before they leveled it, and it had two pretty large windows that faced right out onto the street. The bars, the girls…street was never empty. And considering the mess he left, that girl had to have screamed up a storm. The police were amazed when no one came forward to say that they'd seen or heard anything.

"After Mary Jane, Jack just left. Just like that. No more killin's. You could say that Miss Kelly was The Ripper's swan song, and he saved the most gruesome for last."

"What do you mean?" Leah leaned forward in her seat.

He shrugged. "Jack's kills were horrible, but Ms. Kelly…well…she was a downright massacre. They said that the room looked like gallons o' blood had been used to paint the walls. He butchered her. Before her, the others had been dissected; they was clean, like a doctor had done 'em. But Mary was mutilated. It was like Jack didn't want just her body and blood—he was diggin' for her soul."

Leah's brain screamed at the familiar words.

George stared over at the small corner shop. "She loved singin' Irish songs. People said her voice was as lovely as a nightingale's."

"It seems impossible that someone didn't hear something?" Gareth remarked.

George nodded. "Man named Barnett came forward after a bit. He'd been livin' on and off with Mary at the time. Seems he'd gotten upset that she always let her friends live with 'em and not pay any rent. Barnett got mad and left. That was about a week 'fore Mary was killed. He was a suspect for a while."

"What about the roommates?"

"They were out. One girl, Mary Cox, said she'd seen Miss Kelly at her home around midnight, and that she was singin'. She could see lights in the window, even though a large sheet had been hung up for privacy."

"But," Leah began. "If they could hear the girl singing from the street, how is it that they didn't hear her scream?"

"Don't know what to tell ya'." George shrugged. "Man named Hutchinson said he saw her around two a.m.. He told the constable that she'd asked him for a loan, but he was broke. He also said that when he was leavin' a man came down the street—an elegant man dressed all in black. He had on a top hat and gloves, like he'd just come from the opera. Hutchinson gave a detailed description to the police, right down to the man's polished cane and black leather bag.

"He also told police that Mary led this man into her apartment, where they stood talkin' for a time with the door wide open. Miss Kelly was upset about losing her handkerchief, and he said that the mystery man pulled a bright red one from his pocket and gave it to her. She laughed, they went inside, and the man closed the door."

"That's it?" asked Gareth.

"That's it." He nodded. "Mary Cox said that when she packed it in for the evenin' at around three, Mary's lights were off and she'd stopped singin'. She told the police that she thought she heard a door slam around six, but she couldn't be sure."

"No noise?" Leah was confused. "How can that be? The walls sound like they were no thicker than paper?"

George looked at her curiously. "One woman came forward who lived down the street from Mary; the woman said that around four a.m. she heard someone scream, *Murder*! But no one else heard a thing…not one."

"Maybe they were too scared to talk," offered Gareth.

"Nah. I think by that time they were all so sick of bein' afraid that if they'd heard Mary's cries for help they would've gone after him. They were sick and tired o' livin' in fear." George tilted his head, as if coming to a definitive conclusion. "Nope. If there'd been any sounds that night from Mary's apartment, there would've been at least twenty bodies bangin' down the front door to rescue her."

"That poor woman," Leah whispered.

Gareth shuddered. "He just…disappeared? You'd think a man who'd gotten away with it for that long would've continued."

"Some say his master called him back to Hell," George stated. "Who knows? He's certainly gone now."

"But not forgotten."

George sighed. "Never will be, I spose'. Everyone seems to love an unsolved mystery."

Leah took a deep breath. "I think we'll get out here and enjoy the fresh air."

"You sure?" George's voice was filled with concern. "I can wait…take you to the Palace."

"We'll be fine." Leah forced a smile. "Thank you so much for your time and wisdom, George. You've helped me more than you know."

The cabbie stared into Leah's eyes, and whispered, "You're sure you'll be all right with this one?"

Leah laughed, noticing Gareth's chastised look. "I'll be fine. I can take him."

"Just like the wife." George snorted. "Good luck, Mister. I see you've got your hands full."

Gareth grunted, and paid George his fare. Adding a generous tip for his informative tour, he shook the man's hand. "Thanks."

George returned a few bills to Gareth's palm. "You go buy that lady somethin' nice."

"I'll do that." Gareth smiled.

"She's too good for you." The voice was kind, but genuine.

As the cab pulled away from the curb, Gareth laughed. "You ain't just whistlin' Dixie on that one."

Leah tried to steady her trembling hand as she reached for the brass knob. The welcoming chimes echoed out into the cold day, announcing their arrival. Flinching, Leah found herself hoping that the bell hadn't been loud enough to awaken the past, and call forth The Ripper.

*

Donovan stared at the duo from his place across the festive street. The librarian's face was completely ashen—void of all security and peace. He almost laughed out loud when he turned his attention to Gareth. The usually big strong man looked like he was about to lose his lunch on the pristine sidewalk.

The Blackberry suddenly beeped.

Are you there?

Outside.

Did you get it?

Donovan rolled his eyes. His sibling was an idiot. Why on earth he even cared about some silly piece of jewelry when victory was so close, Donovan just couldn't understand.

Did you get it?!

Donovan sighed, as he typed in his response to a person who he really truly believed couldn't possibly be related to him.

Lowery's in the store.

You were already in England! How could he have beaten you there? Are you really this useless?

Donovan wanted nothing more than to smash the electronic device on the sidewalk.

Lowery isn't here for the stupid necklace. No one cares about it except for you!

You'd better hope so.

You're story is ridiculous. All we need are the orbs. I've seen the cave and all of it is very, very real. Jewelry isn't required.

I told you. There are many ways to enter and if you don't succeed, the first thing you're going to do—

Donovan hit the power button. He was so happy when the picture of his brother in a complete and utter rage appeared inside his mind.

"The first thing I'm going to do is kill you, you moron," he said with glee.

After all, he didn't need his brother. With Lowery's faith and Tallent's brain, Donovan knew that success was only a heartbeat away.

CHAPTER SEVENTEEN

A cheerful lady with a great big smile affixed to her face waved them inside. "Come in. Come in. We are most assuredly open for business. What can I do for you today?"

Leah offered the worst of all shoppers' remarks. "We're just looking."

The woman's smile evaporated…until her eyes landed on Gareth walking in the door.

Leah tried to hide the exasperation and, oddly enough, the amusement that bubbled up inside her. The air seemed to change in the shop. Gone was the icy gaze that'd glared at Leah, replaced quickly by the heat of a lioness who'd just caught the scent of her mate.

The woman moved so quickly that she caught her thigh on the sharp corner of the counter. Wincing with pain, she recovered quickly and surged forward.

Leah couldn't believe her eyes. She felt like she was watching the National Geographic Channel, when the woman—oblivious to her newly sliced flesh—raced forward to place her claim on the rugged male in the room. Stifling a giggle, Leah wondered if the saleswoman would go so far as to lift her skirt and pee on Gareth's leg—mark her territory before any other female dared to enter the small shop.

"Well, now. Who are you?"

Blood rushed into Gareth's cheeks, and his green eyes widened with anxiety. Leah wondered if the fear she saw on his face was because of the horrors they were about to witness, or if he could sense that this female had the strength to hog-tie him to her bedpost with whatever fabric she had on hand.

Gareth cleared his throat. "Good afternoon…Mrs.?"

"Miss!" she shouted with glee. "Patricia. *You* call me Trish." She grabbed his hand and shook it up and down like she was striking the bargain of a lifetime.

Leah tried to focus on the task at hand, but she found it impossible to pull her gaze away from the visibly uncomfortable man. She chose to lean against the case filled with ribbons and jewels, and plaster a great big smile on her face.

Gareth shot an angry look at her over the shopkeeper's shoulder. His voice came out strong, like a lion's roar. "Actually, Trish." His dazzling smile appeared. "My *wife* and I are on our honeymoon. We were just passing by your lovely shop when she begged me to come inside."

Trish's face fell so far, so fast, that Leah imagined there was a cement block attached to the bottom of her chin.

The woman turned to Leah and extended her hand; her voice sounded like a prisoner walking his last mile on death row. "Newlyweds. How lucky for *you*."

"Thanks," replied Leah, with a giggle. "He's quite the man."

"I'm sure." Trish turned back to Gareth and replaced her lustful signals with those of a businesswoman, determined to make a sale. "What are you looking for today? I assume you'd like your new bride to have anything and everything her heart desires?"

Good for you, thought Leah. *If you can't get the guy, get his money.*

"Absolutely. Anything she wants."

Trish turned her attention back to Leah. "Where should we start? You heard *your* man." She failed to mask her envy.

"I like jewelry." Leah smiled wide. "And I *love* shoes."

Dollar signs appeared in the owner's eyes.

Gareth winced. "Looks like this is my part of the nightmare," he mumbled.

Trish broke her rigid stance and practically skipped behind the curtain to retrieve the latest styles.

Leah burst into a fit of giggles. "You look like you'd rather take on The Ripper live and in person than Trish, the scary shopkeeper."

Gareth groaned. "You're going to pay for this."

"Does this mean the honeymoon is over?" Leah batted her eyelashes.

"Shut up!"

"Here we are then." Trish parted the curtain with a flourish, like it was opening night on Broadway; glossy boxes were piled high in her arms. "Size seven, am I right?"

Leah pushed Gareth out of the way and sat down on the soft bench. "How did you know?"

"It's my job, dear. This shop has the best shoes in all of London. I've picked several colors and styles." She glanced at Gareth. "I'm sure you'll need *all* of them for your journey."

"You know what, Trish?" Leah stared into the woman's hopeful face. "I just bet that I will."

Gareth spoke up, "Don't you want to browse in other places before making a final decision…sweetheart?"

Trish leaned in closer to her new best friend. "We also have the loveliest lingerie available. I have tons in the back if you wish to try on a suitable ensemble with some of the more…sexy footwear?"

The veins pulsed in Gareth's neck. "You know what, hon? Go crazy. Trish seems to have all the bases covered."

Leah rolled her eyes, and the shopkeeper beamed.

"You begin with those, dear." Trish patted her knee and turned to Gareth. "Anything for you, sir? Can I get you a spot of tea? Coffee, perhaps?"

"Coffee would be great." Gareth smiled. "Thank you, Trish."

"I'll be back in a jiff."

Gareth winked at Leah. "Lingerie seems like a good idea, don't you think? You shouldn't be caught off-guard."

"You're a funny guy."

"It *is* our honeymoon."

"Pot's a brewin'." Trish reappeared like the chaperone from Hell. "How are we doing over here?"

Leah quickly dove into the boxes of shoes and began trying them on, intimidated by Trish's commanding presence. "All of them are so great. In fact, we were just saying that your whole shop is dazzling."

"Thank you." Trish sighed. "It's a bit of both blessing and curse, I'm afraid."

"Why's that?"

"Well…I rarely get just shoppers." The woman sounded melancholy. "You wouldn't believe the amount of tourists I get in here. They don't even buy anything. They just bother me with ridiculous questions."

"Questions?" said Gareth.

Trish turned in his direction. "Of course. After all, you're standing in the spot where Jack the Ripper killed his final victim."

Silence descended on the room.

Trish's eyes grew wide. "Please don't let that run you off. This isn't the same building. This is all new."

"Don't worry." Gareth smiled. "Leah and I don't believe in ghosts."

"Thank goodness." Trish let out a sigh of relief. "It's crazy, really. It happened over a hundred years ago. Who could possibly care now? But you wouldn't believe some of the awful inquiries from people—really sick stuff too. Some even wish that it was the same apartment so they could take pictures of the dried blood stains. How gross is that, I ask you?"

"Disgusting," Leah agreed.

Trish slapped her knee. "That's what I think."

"Happens everywhere," Gareth remarked. "I have a friend who lives in Roswell, New Mexico. Every July 4th—the anniversary of the so-called crash—people flock to the town and ask all kinds of ridiculous questions about alien sightings. My friend decided a while back that he'd just tell them that he didn't remember anything before 1947. He just woke up in his spaceship and, boom, he was living in Roswell."

"Don't tell me people believe that?" Trish chuckled. "That your friend is an alien?"

"Oddly enough, Trish, people will believe just about anything—especially if it's a myth or a legend," said Gareth. "Everyone loves a mystery."

She nodded. "But at least your American aliens didn't rip women apart and steal their hearts."

"Steal their hearts?" Leah's voice cracked.

"That's what they say." Trish stared at the old, rusted pipes in the corner. "I should dump this place anyway. It's starting to crumble around my ears."

Gareth stared at the corner. "Mildew?"

"The plumber says there's something wrong with the foundation. He thinks that there's some kind of hole in the cement where the water has gathered over time." She sighed. "It doesn't really surprise me. When they leveled the old building they kept the original foundation and basement."

"That's odd," Gareth muttered, staring at the square section of rotted floor.

"Not really. Cheaper, is what it was." Trish scoffed. "Oops, forgot the coffee. I'll be right back."

"Could you pick me out some lingerie to try on while you're back there?" Leah added, "I like purple."

"Purple? *Really?* With your hair?" Trish put her hands on her hips. "No, no, that won't do at all. Something green, I think."

"You're the boss." Leah shrugged.

When Trish disappeared into the back, Leah kicked off the stiletto heels, and raced to the corner.

"Lingerie?" Gareth grinned. "Good for you! Finally comin' around to my way of thinking."

Leah sighed. "I wanted to give us more time, you moron."

"Just married and she's already calling me names."

Leah tapped on the warped wooden panel. "This is hollow, Gareth."

She stole one of the thin high heels off the floor. Using it as a wedge, Leah inserted the heel into a tiny hole in the board and pulled; the rotted wood splintered.

Sitting back on the balls of her feet, Leah stared at the dark piece of burlap sitting inside the hole. She reached for it, but Gareth grabbed her wrist. He stuck his hand in and ripped the package out of the floor. He smiled. "Maybe if you don't touch them I'll get the…brunt of it."

Tears flooded her eyes at the concern filling his voice.

Gareth held the package tight, and the familiar hum filled the room. He pulled his knapsack off his shoulder and jammed the new set of 'keys' into the bag. Zipping it shut, he tried to mute the humming that was increasing with each new orb they gathered. It was as if they were excited about being reunited with their long lost friends.

"Mildew's green, Gareth." Leah's voice was dull. "The stains on that bag are red. I think it's been soaked in—"

"Forget about it." Gareth kissed her cheek. "Let's just leave."

They carefully replaced the small pieces of wood in the rotted floor.

Leah raced back to her chair just as Trish re-entered the room with a shiny silver platter. "Coffee's on!"

Gareth spoke. "On second thought, you really didn't need to go to all that trouble. We have to be moving on."

Trish's face fell. "Oh."

Gareth took the tray from her trembling hands and placed it on the table in the center of the room. Walking back to Trish, he offered her one of his most brilliant smiles. "Not to worry, though. We love everything. We'll take it all."

"Don't be silly." Trish fell to her knees before the young bride. "She hasn't even tried them all on. Now, come on, let's have a look at the rest."

Leah heard a distant rumble of thunder, and felt the walls of the tiny shop shudder.

Blink. The bed appeared out of nowhere—old and mildewed—the sheets wrinkled and tattered. The uneven floor was covered with garbage, dirt, and cigarette butts, and a horrible stench hung in the stale air. But the lilting voice of the singing girl made the room almost cheerful.

Blink. Leah turned her head and focused on Gareth. She could hear the incessant babbling of the woman beside him, but her voice was like thunder—too far away to decipher the words that were coming from her mouth.

Blink. The twinkling silver bell on the pristine white door was gone. In its place, stood an old wooden entrance. The boards were torn to shreds, and the weathered paint was chipped and broken. A man removed his tall, black hat and closed the door soundly, as the girl continued to sing her lullaby.

Leah watched him place his gloves down on a dresser with a broken leg sitting under the sheet-covered window. Leah could hear the sounds of people talking outside on the street. They sounded like they were fighting—no, bartering—trying to get the best price they could for their precious, flesh-covered wares.

Blink. The lights seemed to brighten again. Gareth was staring at her from across the room. Trish was standing beside him, pointing out various items in the glass case, and chattering away about the shiny baubles that made Leah's eyes ache.

Blink. The man slid across the dirty floor like a ballet dancer. His movements were graceful; his feet left no prints in the inch-thick dust. The broken floorboards didn't utter a squeak of protest under the pressure of his tall, willowy frame. His large, sharp nose shadowed his thin, white lips. He offered a small, almost shy smile, to the young girl who was now kneeling on the foot of her bed.

He leaned in and whispered to the lark, "Let's play a game." The voice was hollow, like a child shouting at his friend through a set of tin cans tied together with string.

The beautiful girl quieted her singing, and wrapped her arms around his neck. "What kind of game, luv?"

He pushed the long, auburn hair over her shoulder. His right hand reached around and stroked the sensitive skin on the back of her neck, as the left played with a bright red handkerchief. "Let's see if you have a heart, my dear."

Her blue eyes gleamed, and her red lips parted. "It's in there…just for you."

Blink. Leah wanted to scream at Gareth and the shopkeeper as they took a shiny gem out of the case and discussed the lovely, vibrant color. She watched Gareth sip his coffee; his green eyes stared over the lip of the cup. Leah tried to get his attention, but she could no longer feel her own body. She realized that Gareth was waiting for the pictures of the past that would surely cause her visible pain. She wanted to yell at him—to tell him that part of her was stuck in the horrifying scene—but her mouth just wouldn't open.

Blink. The red handkerchief hung from her mouth like a bloody tongue; her screams were smothered so the neighbors wouldn't hear the violence being played out inside the thin, dirty walls. The lilting Irish song had died in her sliced throat. Leah watched the gleam of the sharp instruments as they moved up and down, in and out, like the baton of a psychotic conductor as he strove for the ultimate crescendo.

Thick, red droplets rained down from the ceiling like a cloudburst of pain. Soon the figure stood, wiped the sweat from his brow, and cleaned the grotesque instruments on Mary's severed arm. He arranged the body parts like he was putting the final touches on an artistic masterpiece of flesh and bone.

Leah turned away from the mutilated face of Mary Kelly, but not before she'd seen the evil grin that'd been slashed across her once beautiful face from ear to ear. Her long hair was even more red, now that it was saturated with her blood. Leah turned her gaze to the door and waited for the monster to exit the horrific scene. The Ripper had claimed her body and her blood. Thankfully, the fatal blow had come quickly, releasing her soul to Heaven before his real work had begun.

The Ripper threw his cape over his shoulders, put his hat on his head, and replaced the gloves on the hands that'd just ripped a woman to shreds. Leah almost passed out when she saw him place Mary's lifeless heart into the folds of his overcoat. The Ripper opened the door and stared out into the night. He seemed so calm as he took a deep breath of the dank air. He blew a kiss to the hideous mass on the bed, and closed the door behind him.

Leah heard his deep voice as he disappeared like a phantom in the night. "I can get no better than this. I am done."

Blink. The picture dissolved when the bell rang out in the small shop. The door flew open and the rain came pouring inside.

Trish ran to her new customers. "My goodness. This came on quickly, didn't it?"

Gareth left the counter, and kneeled in front of Leah. Her eyes filled with tears.

"No!" He panicked. "But…you didn't make a sound! Jesus, are you all right?"

Leah reached down for her boots and pulled them on. Her body shook when she stood up and stared into his horrified eyes. "He didn't hurt *me*, Gareth. He's already dead."

"Christ, I'm such a jerk."

Trish skipped over and stared at the newlyweds. "Are you dears okay?"

Leah sighed. "I just need some air."

"*Air?* Honey, its pouring buckets out there!"

Leah patted the woman's shoulder and walked out the door. The cold droplets felt wonderful against her overheated skin. Sitting on the stoop, Leah put her head between her legs. She took deep breaths, enjoying the cleansing rain that ran down her back. She ordered herself to let it go. "He took enough victims in his time. I'm not about to become one of them."

Raising her chin, Leah opened her mouth and let the pure, clean water soothe her parched throat. She took the bloody images and placed them on cards inside her head, burying them in a locked cabinet with other memories that would never again see the light of day. The large raindrops knocked against her forehead as if they were being sent down from Heaven to erase the pictures from her mind. Leah took a deep breath and let go of the scents, sights, and sounds that belonged to a dark and rainy night in Hell.

The rain turned to sprinkles, and Leah opened her eyes. The clouds parted; a ray of sunshine broke through and warmed her face. Leah thought of Mary Jane Kelly. She hoped that the girl was now surrounded by beautiful things and wonderful people in a place that, Leah suddenly hoped, truly existed.

Pedestrians started filling the sidewalks again, and the bell rang out behind her head. Gareth sat down beside her on the curb; his arms were full of brightly-colored shopping bags. "I'm so sorry."

"Don't be."

"You looked like you were praying just now."

"Never." Leah teased. "Just letting Crowley know that he lost this round."

"Thank God."

The yellow cab pulled up in front of them. A familiar voice burst from the open window. "Hey there, pretty lady. Had enough o' London's dark side for one day?"

Leah giggled, and Gareth hauled the overstuffed bags to the trunk. "Yes, sir," she said. "It's time to see this Buckingham Palace I've heard so much about."

George smiled at Gareth. "Did a little shopping, I see."

"Yes, sir." Gareth smiled. "I bought her everything she wanted."

The old man winked, as he turned the wheel to drive them out of Whitechapel and away from the blood-soaked ghosts of the past.

*

Donovan crossed the street as the cab pulled away. His heart was pumping a mile a minute. He knew, simply from the look of pure exhaustion on the librarian's face, that she'd found what she was after. Not to mention, Gareth's emerald eyes had been filled with pain, and a look of pure guilt had hung on his face like a neon sign; he looked like a man who truly despised himself. Every single movement they'd made told Donovan that he was only two orbs away from using the Keys to the Kingdom.

He thought briefly about powering up the Blackberry and telling his moronic brother, I told you so. But that could wait. Let him stew; it was good for him. It was about time he learned that he would always be second best.

Donovan shrugged. Since he was here anyway, he might as well get the silly piece of jewelry. After all, it never hurt to have a Plan B.

Turning the handle, Donovan stepped inside the lovely little shop. He was positively tickled that he was walking in the footsteps of one of the chosen few. The Ripper was indeed one of Donovan's idols.

"Goodness! *Another* handsome customer." The shopkeeper called out. "The Lord is certainly smiling down on me today."

"And which lord would that be, exactly?" Donovan laughed as he shut the door behind him, quietly turning the lock. "For your sake, my dear, I hope it's the nice one."

CHAPTER EIGHTEEN

Burning water that scalded her skin; fragrant soap with lather so thick, that the scent of lavender took up permanent residence in every open pore; and, hurricane force winds that blew from the industrial strength hairdryer—all combined to erase the last remnants of the historical monster from Leah's mind.

At least the afternoon hadn't been a total waste. George, the taxi driver with flair, had personally escorted them through Buckingham Palace. He'd even dared Gareth to show his rude American side by goading the Royal Guard. Leah had laughed until she cried when Gareth had jumped up and down, and scratched his armpits like a chimpanzee in front of the highly serious men dressed in red coats and black fuzzy hats. True to form, they hadn't cracked a smile or wavered in the slightest from their very important duty.

When Gareth had finally given up and come to the realization that the only one looking like an idiot was him, George whisked them away to Westminster Abbey for a highly informative tour. Then, past the Tower of London they drove, where George had pointed up at the famed Bloody Tower looming in the distance. "Still into historical blood and guts?"

Leah had laughed. "I've had enough guts for one day, thank you."

"I wouldn't recommend our food then, Miss." George winked. "You never know what part o' the animal they'll be throwin' on the plate."

The nightmare had ended with a tourist's dream, as they'd born witness to the most beloved sites that London had to offer.

Leah flicked off the hairdryer and used the coarse brush to tame her wild mane. Her fear was gone. The shower had taken away the horrible pictures, and exhaustion was setting in. She felt like a kitten, wanting nothing more than to curl up in a ball and enter a dreamless sleep.

She grabbed for her robe. One good thing about these fancy hotels that Gareth loved so much—the robes were sheer heaven. But this place, the gorgeous Melia White House, was even more generous than the others. Leah sighed blissfully, as she stared down at the shiny cappuccino machine that was just about the best complimentary item she could possibly think of. Gareth might be girlie, but he had excellent taste.

She opened the door and stepped into the cool air of the adjoining bedroom. Leah glanced at the huge canopy bed that sat in the center of the room, and smiled. Spread out on the luxurious comforter was a gorgeous green dress and matching shoes. She walked over to the ensemble and rubbed the pure silk between her fingers. Sitting beside the lovely outfit was a large pink and white box with a card taped to the top.

Lifting the lid, Leah gazed at the lingerie made in the same exquisite color as the dress. She read Gareth's small note: *Some things should remain a mystery. Our new friend Trish picked these out and wrapped them for you. I really hope they are what I think they are.*

Leah ran back into the grand bathroom, clinging to the clothing like a drowning woman to a life preserver. It'd been forever since she'd seen an outfit that, from head to toe, would cover her in the finest fabric that Gareth's money could buy.

The outer door slammed, and Gareth's familiar growl entered the room. "Honey, I'm home."

"Funny," Leah shouted back.

"I got a table downstairs for dinner. God knows we deserve a little fun."

"Did you check the menu?" Leah giggled.

Gareth's laughter echoed under the bathroom door. "Yup. No animal guts were listed on the specials, so we should be okay."

She reached for the door handle. "I can't thank you enough for the beautiful clothes, Gareth."

"Don't worry about it. It was either buy them, or have Trish cut off parts of *my* body. I chose the easiest route." He snorted. "Let's just hope that her taste is better than her manners."

Leah stepped into the room. "I think her taste is pretty good."

Gareth turned around. His body shuddered. It looked like every part of him, including his brain, had been hit with an electric shock. His mouth dropped open. "Good God! I'd say her taste was spectacular."

Leah twirled around in a circle. "Like it?"

Gareth cleared his throat. "Give me a minute. I'm trying to piece together a semi-coherent statement." He stood as still as a statue; his lips were parted, and his hands were balled into fists at his side.

Leah laughed. "Aren't we going to dinner?"

Gareth nodded his head slowly. "Um—"

"Um…?"

Gareth slapped himself across the face, as if he were trying to wake up from a fantastic dream. "This must be how He felt on the seventh day."

"He, who?" She laughed. "God?"

"Yeah."

"Exhausted?" Leah grinned.

He shook his head slowly. "Complete…awe at seeing such a creation."

"I was created by a Yankee and a debutante." Leah winked. "I think that's a couple rungs lower than your Almighty."

Gareth leaned in and kissed her cheek. "Leah, if you've never believed before, I suggest you take a good long look in the mirror. After that, you'll have no doubt that miracles truly exist."

She stood speechless under the thirsty gaze.

"Let's go to dinner before I lose the gentleman that must be buried in me somewhere." Gareth muttered, "I *hate* that guy."

*

Leah was thankful that she'd taken Gareth's arm, considering he'd almost stumbled for the third time on the polished marble floor of the lobby.

When they entered the dining room, Leah couldn't help but giggle at the foolish grin that Gareth wore. "You look ridiculous," she said.

"You look stunning," he replied. "I wish I had a dollar for every man who will feel the pain of whiplash in the morning because they wrenched their necks in order to get a better look at you."

Leah laughed, as Gareth pulled out her chair. She took the menu offered by the elegant waiter, and smiled. "This is going to be a really boring dinner if you just sit there and stare at me all night."

"Lady, I couldn't take my eyes off you if the Devil, himself, was at the bar buying drinks for the house."

"Oh, please." She rolled her eyes. "How many dates have you been on? Hundreds? Thousands? Stop me when I get close."

Gareth leaned across the table. "Actually, with my…pet project…I haven't had time for dates."

"Uh, huh."

"Seriously." His green eyes filled with hunger. "But when this journey comes to an end I'll be able to explore that area of my life again."

A strange feeling of depression rose in Leah's throat when she thought of the hordes of women who would jump at the chance to volunteer for that particular journey. She picked up her glass of champagne. "Well, I suppose there'll be other adventures for you after this one. Maybe you can go find Atlantis next time?"

"I can't swim," he said, with a laugh. "Besides, I like the whole God thing better. I'm more partial to it."

"Why's that?"

He shrugged. "He's cool. After all, He's the one who said, 'be fruitful and multiply.' I'm all for that." Gareth leaned across the intimate table. "What about you? You think you'll ever multiply?"

Leah choked on the champagne. "God, no. I despise the little monsters."

"Really?" Gareth roared with laughter. "I hadn't noticed. The first day we met, you offered a look of such pure love to that precious teenager on the steps of your library."

"Again…you're funny."

"You can't be the end of the line." His voice turned serious. "You need to carry on. You owe it to God."

Leah snorted. "My own scion?"

"Exactly." Gareth winked, as he picked up his glass and proposed a toast to her future clones. "And please keep in mind that I am always at your service—*especially* in that area."

Leah picked up her menu and began to read. "What a selfless guy you are."

"Anything for the procreation of world beauty."

"You should be sainted."

"Nah," he said. "I'd have to be dead."

Leah peeked over her menu and gasped at the blatant invitation beaming from the electric eyes. He made her feel like she was the lost city of Atlantis—a treasure that he wanted to discover, unearth, and explore with his own two hands. Blocking her face with the menu, Leah tried to cool the heat that was invading every molecule of her body.

She heard his soft growl through the flimsy partition. "Trish really turned out to be good at her job."

Leah nodded.

"I assume that the things in the box were just as good? Fit, do they?"

Leah lowered the menu, and picked up her champagne. "Yes. And it was so thoughtful. After all, it *is* winter, and I *do* need a new jacket, so—"

"A *jacket*? That's what was in the pink box?" Gareth's loud voice shattered the quiet ambience.

"Yes," said Leah in an innocent voice. "What did you think was in it?"

Gareth picked up his menu and glared at the selection. "Nothing." He mumbled, "Maybe there'll be time in the morning to revisit Whitechapel and strangle Trish."

Leah wanted to laugh out loud as she stared at the man who'd suddenly transformed into a sulking schoolboy. She tapped him on the hand. "Calm down. I just wanted to see if you'd peeked."

"I would never peek." Gareth raised an eyebrow. "I'm a gentleman."

"Sure you are."

"So?" He smiled wide. "Did they match the dress?"

"I am *not* having this conversation with you!"

"Oh, come on, be nice." He whined. "Were there bows and stuff? Lace?" He grabbed his chest. "God help me—see-through? Please say it's see-through." Gareth's voice was teasing, but his eyes looked like he was fighting the urge to launch his body across the incredibly small table and find out for himself.

The waiter returned. Gareth made a hasty pick of foods he thought he recognized, and Leah followed suit.

"Hopefully, no guts." She laughed.

*

They eyed their half-eaten plates.

"Guess I really am one of those ugly Americans at heart." Leah giggled.

"Yeah," he agreed. "Where are all those fast food joints when you need 'em?"

"That's not real food either, trust me." Leah picked up the smaller menu of decadent desserts. "Let's have coffee and dessert. No one ever went wrong with that combination."

Gareth squinted at the small letters and stuck out his tongue. "What in the world is a spotted dick?"

"Okay, then," said Leah quickly. "Coffee it is."

Gareth sat back in his chair as the unappetizing food was cleared from the table. "Oddly enough, this is the best dinner I've ever had," he said. "Must be the company."

"Right back at ya.'" Leah smiled.

His eyes grew dark. "I'm sorry about today."

She shrugged her shoulders. "Why are you sorry? *You* didn't do anything."

"Exactly." He sighed. "There was a part of me that really thought if I touched the orbs first you'd be spared any...trip down memory lane."

"That's all it was, Gareth," she said softly. "I've seen horror movies before. And the Winchester House taught me a great deal. I just distanced myself from it all and let it play out like a film. Besides, George was right. Jack was a horrible, lethal, malicious killer, but he didn't take out city blocks full of women and children in the name of some god. The Ripper was a man—a psychopath, sure—but just a man, and a dead one at that."

His green eyes sparkled with guilty tears. "Even so."

Leah covered his hand with hers and offered him a genuine smile. "I don't want you to think about this anymore. *I* certainly won't. Besides, for ten pairs of the finest shoes money can buy, you could get me to watch just about anything."

Gareth laughed.

"I did come to one conclusion, though," Leah continued, "I'm going to forget about the serial killer career path. I definitely couldn't do that stuff."

"Mess up your new shoes, too."

"Exactly."

"You know." Gareth hesitated. "I hate to bring down this lovely evening with talk of more pain coming our way. But I took a look at Crowley's third page and there's not much there. It's just a simple drawing of a table with twelve chairs around it."

"I know," said Leah. "And there's a thirteenth one at the bottom of a staircase."

"Could you make out Crowley's message?" Gareth asked.

"I think it says, 'If you believe in the teacher and not me you're a hypocrite.' Something like that, anyway." She sighed. "These evil beings had horrible handwriting."

"What is it with the number thirteen and Crowley?" he asked. "In that illustrious mind of yours, is there any data on that? Like…maybe he killed thirteen people, or saw the Devil at the age of thirteen? Anything like that?"

"No." Leah shrugged. "But certainly the number thirteen has been associated with evil for years."

"I saw Friday the 13th—it sucked."

Leah grinned. "I was thinking more along the lines of religion…your favorite. If you look back at the roots of Christianity versus everyone else, you'll find quite a difference. In Muslim culture, Friday is regarded as a

Holy Day for their people. In Norse mythology, Friday was the day they celebrated their goddess. But when Christianity labeled all goddesses witches, the day was pronounced evil."

She leaned forward. "If you really read that bible of yours, you'll see that Friday is the day given for the crucifixion, Noah's great flood, the temple of Solomon coming down, Abel's death at the hands of his brother Cain—even Eve gave Adam that apple on a Friday and changed the world as we know it forever."

"Yeah, boy, that was a bad day for us." Gareth sighed. "Just think…if things had worked out differently you'd be sitting here naked instead of having to wear your emerald fig leaf."

She rolled her eyes.

"Just saying." Gareth shrugged. "Things could've turned out better."

Leah took a sip of her coffee and gave a comforted sigh. At least there were some things that never changed no matter what continent you were on—Gareth's heart-stopping smile and freshly brewed coffee were two of them.

"So how come us wretched Americans always say TGIF?" He grinned. "Doesn't that kind of throw it in the face of the Lord?"

"The Devil makes us do it." She laughed.

"Answer for everything." He raised his mug in salute. "That's why I love you."

Leah stared into her cup as silence descended over the table. The warning bells in her brain dimmed, and her raging heart took over.

She cleared her throat, and tried to return to what she knew best. "Of course, the Last Supper is also quite big in the number thirteen category. As you know, Jesus and his twelve disciples attended, and it was there that the Son said someone would betray him. Supposedly, Judas was the thirteenth attendee."

"Some believe it was Peter," added Gareth.

"As with everything in that book, it depends on what part of the country you're standing in as to what people believe."

*

With his napkin, Gareth wiped the sweat from his brow. He continued to replay his words over and over inside his head. Had he said them? Had he meant them? The answer to both seemed to be a great big resounding, Yes! But Leah showed no signs that he'd just poured his heart out on the tablecloth. His mind swirled, as he listened to her beautiful voice.

"Of course, the Judas Papers now say he was innocent," she said. "Not to mention the Magdalene Gospel absolves Peter, too. If the Church isn't careful, they're going to have to scramble for a new bad guy pretty soon." Leah took a deep breath. "In the end, there are a lot of answers to your question, Gareth. But I wasn't there, so I couldn't really tell you what went on."

He felt as if they were the only two people left on the planet. Gareth wondered if Leah knew his heart was dancing the mambo inside his chest.

"Anyway," she mumbled. "There was also Apollo 13, which was launched on the 13th of April at 13:13."

He reached out and stroked the back of her hand. "But they survived."

"Barely," she whispered.

Gareth smiled at the slight tremor in her voice.

Leah quickly continued, "Even the Knights Templar—America's best-selling superheroes—were decimated on Friday the 13th, 1307. The Romans took them out. They probably thought that the Knights had gotten too big for their chain-mail britches."

Gareth snorted.

"After what we uncovered today, the strangest coincidence to me is that most serial killers have thirteen letters in their name. Jack, of course.

The Ripper was the biggest, but you also have Charles Manson, Jeffrey Dahmer—even Ted Bundy."

Gareth counted like a child on his fingertips. "That's eight."

"His given name was Theodore," she replied.

"Well, I'll say this, there seems to be nothing you don't know."

Leah concluded her informative presentation with a bow.

"Why do you think Crowley hid his orbs in such public places? I mean, anyone could've found them by mistake."

"I think it was just fun for him." She swallowed. "He believed there was no one in the world who could actually see the truth—Divine or otherwise. Crowley thought humanity was basically a bunch of dumb robots with no imagination, and no brains to find anything…let alone the keys to a Kingdom that may not even exist."

"After all this…you *still* don't believe?"

Leah sighed. "I believe what you and the rest of your family have fought to learn. I also believe you're trying to find this place for worthy reasons. But I still can't go along with you on the whole 'Heaven's Gate' thing. It's extremely hard for me to believe that there's an Almighty who supposedly protects us all, when you look at the world. Blaming all our bad traits on the Devil is certainly a way to go, but it's entirely too easy."

She stared down at their clasped hands. "Men pick up arms. Men become serial killers. Not the Devil—men. Even Crowley, who went down in history calling himself Satan, was just a man; a man who, from the looks of the book, was possessed by self-importance—not the Devil. I think if the actual Devil had hidden these orbs—not even a man of immense faith such as yourself would ever have found them."

"But the Devil was supposed to have been the original hider of the orbs."

She looked up at him. "Where does it say that?"

Gareth stroked her soft, smooth skin. "The Devil met Jesus before the Last Supper and tried to get Jesus to help him go home. Basically, Jesus said forget it, and moved on. Then, the Father came. There they were—the original Yin and Yang. That night the fallen angel struck a deal. He was forgiven, because that's what God does, but he'd never be allowed back into the Kingdom of Heaven. That night was when they came to the decision that it would be best to hide the Keys once Jesus ascended."

Leah shook her head; her breath seemed to come fast and furious, as she struggled to speak. "If what's there is there, and the orbs do what you think they do, you're opening a door that's remained closed for a reason. If you believe the Bible, this particular gateway was created for the Second Coming. It's not for you, your sister, or anyone else to open that thing." She stared at him. "They'll open it and walk through when *They* want to."

Gareth released her hand and sat back in his chair. "I understand your view, Leah. But we haven't made a decision about anything. I'll just have to cross that bridge if and when we come to it."

"The 'if' is getting smaller with every pair of orbs we find."

"I want peace."

"For you or for the world?"

"Both." His voice grew hard.

She sighed. "Maybe it's not your job to supply it."

Gareth stared into the sapphire eyes of brilliance. "Do you want to stop?"

"I'm not pulling my support, Gareth," she said. "I'm just pointing out the downside, is all. That's what I'm good at."

"The voice of reason," he whispered.

Leah drained her coffee mug. "Why don't you tell me where you found the last two 'good' orbs? Maybe that'll lead us in the right direction to find Crowley's."

"You think they're related?"

"Seems that way." She shrugged. "The first page you followed was titled *Mind*, and you found the orbs in a place that was dedicated to people who had the greatest minds of all time. Crowley was the opposite. He put his in a place where a mind was lost. Sarah Winchester had lost everything…except her demons."

"Those spirits were real," Gareth spoke.

"Maybe," she said.

He felt the frustration build in his soul. "How can you say that?"

Leah's gaze never left his face. "Now that I'm away from it all, I wonder if it wasn't just a hallucination that my over-active brain put on for me. I knew Crowley's reasons for putting the orbs there before we went inside, and people do tend to see things they think they should and not what's really in front of them. The same could be said for The Ripper. George had filled my head full of facts. So even before I entered that shop, my imagination was already primed to see what I saw. "

"Okay, you overly-educated debater." He felt a challenge coming on. "I found the next two 'good' orbs in a mail tunnel under the Vatican City library. Where's the correlation with Whitechapel? What could The Ripper and the Pope possibly have in common with each other?"

"Legends in their own mind?" she snickered.

He rolled his eyes. "I'm serious."

"So am I." Her voice grew louder. "You're talking about Aleister Crowley; a man who thought there was nothing worse than organized religion. Even Rudolf Steiner, his Yin, believed that. They were two people who had far different ideas than the Church did. The strict rules and regulations of the Church were created during a time when people had none of the pressures they do today."

She continued quickly, "During Crowley's time, people had started to come out with ideas like reincarnation—ideas that the Church flagrantly abhorred. I'm sure if they could still get away with labeling everyone pagans, they would. But things have been found buried out in the desert." She stared at him. "You told me that. There have been huge discoveries that prove beyond a shadow of a doubt that some of the globally-accepted facts that the Church preaches, are actually built on imaginative myths. The old regime just isn't doing well anymore."

Despite his frustration, Gareth smiled at the slight sarcasm in her voice.

Leah smiled back, "Even though bestselling novels go on and on about the wretched events from history, some of these stories have actually been verified. Christianity was born from blood at the hands of the Emperor Constantine to the detriment of scholars and academics."

"Astronomers," Gareth added.

"And astronomers." Leah agreed. "The Church once held the widely accepted views of the world, simply because it said it did. And, at that time, there was nobody strong enough to go against them. I have no trouble with people believing there's something better, Gareth. I never have. But I hope, for your sake, it doesn't turn out to be all faith and no fact."

Gareth sent up a prayer.

"Look around you," Leah said. "It's very likely you're in Hell right now. You certainly don't have to go far to find it. That's one reason why I'm here with you. You've taught me that people should have faith in something, Gareth. Whether or not it'll be what you say it is, I don't know. You're basing a lot on a book written by men for the love of their new Emperor, and commissioned by their religious leader who was a *man*. Believe me, if God was running the show down here, things would be a heck of a lot different."

"Better."

"Couldn't be a whole lot worse." Leah grimaced. "To Crowley, The Ripper legend would've just been his way of saying that there are many different ways a soul can be harvested and blood can be spilled. Sometimes a serial killer is at fault."

Her eyes filled with a truth so powerful, that Gareth shuddered.

"But, more often than not, death lies in the hands of the righteous."

CHAPTER NINETEEN

Gareth leaned back in his chair. "That would make sense, considering I found the last two orbs in France."

"France?" She looked confused. "Rome's in Italy, last I heard."

Gareth took a deep breath. "When I was sitting in that room under the Vatican City library and opened that map, I swore to you that I saw a spear of fire—of light—rise from the pages and go into the ceiling."

"I remember." Leah nodded "The light came from the center of the constellations and you thought it was the sun."

"I thought about that, Leah. But the sun is an orb, not a spear. This actually looked like a weapon. Then the orbs took over and I started getting flashes of the pictures we love so much. I held them in the palm of my hand and I saw images of…blood and death. I have to say, you did much better than I did. I threw up."

"Blood and death?" said Leah. "I thought your half of the orbs represented the good side of life?"

"They do." Gareth nodded. "But like you just said, sometimes blood and death comes from the supposedly 'good' side of life."

Leah tilted her head, as if trying to understand his words. "Good blood?"

"I assume you've heard of the Spear of Destiny?"

"It was the weapon that pierced the side of Jesus." Leah's eyes grew wide. "You saw the crucifixion?"

"I'm pretty sure that's what it was."

Her stomach heaved. "I'll take The Ripper any day," she whispered.

Gareth felt his smile return as he realized that Leah was probably the only person who would ever understand the power, even though she may not believe in it. "Me, too."

"I thought the spear was in St. Peter's Cathedral?" she asked.

"For a time, it was. There are lots of theories about it. One has it coming into the hands of Hitler, then to General Patton, who brought it to the United States when old Adolf went belly-up."

He searched his mind, trying to remember all the research he'd done. "There's also a spear in the Vatican, although they lay no claim to its authenticity. There are those who say the spear is in the basilica of Mount Zion in Jerusalem beside the Crown of Thorns, while others say the spear was transferred to the church of Hagia Sophia in Constantinople. There are a number of spears nowadays. So many, in fact, that no one can actually confirm that any of them are the real thing."

"I don't understand." Leah shook her head. "How did this get you to France?"

Gareth explained. "The strangest part of the documented journey of the spear came during the French Revolution. It's written that the spear was housed in Sainte Chapelle up until the eighteenth century, when it was moved to the Bibliotheque Nationale in Paris for safe-keeping."

"The King's Library," Leah whispered.

Gareth nodded. "You'll notice the recurring theme. But the strange part about this particular stop-over for the spear was that this was when it supposedly vanished and the fakes started appearing. No one heard anything about the Spear of Destiny—the real one—after it moved into the Bibliotheque. The artifact didn't crop up again until the lower half of the weapon supposedly appeared in St. Peter's Basilica in Rome. But the whole spear never resurfaced."

"So you thought the library was the key?"

He nodded. "Seemed fitting, considering. There's a beautiful new library in Paris that was opened in 1996, but I was interested in the original—The King's Library."

Leah shrugged. "To be honest I don't know very much about that library."

"Well…New York is where your loyalty lies." He smiled. "You probably don't spend much time thinking about the competition."

"Once again my pompous American side rears its ugly head." She laughed.

Gareth laughed with her. "The National Library of France was located inside the Louvre. Over time, the collection grew a lot bigger. In 1868, the spear disappeared right before the opening of the newly constructed building on the *rue de Richelieu*. The opening was, to say the least, eerie."

"Why, eerie?"

"Under extremely tight security, with unusually dressed guards, the collections were moved into the new site," he said.

"Troops of heavily armed guards just to move books?" Leah's mind went in search of an answer. "Strange."

"The information given to the public was that the library held priceless manuscripts that had to be protected," he said.

"But you think that they were protecting the spear?"

"Never know." Gareth shrugged his shoulders. "I'm sure they felt that the Vatican had enough."

"As others do." Leah smiled.

"France's collection contained original works by Charlemagne," he added.

"The first who believed in reincarnation."

Gareth nodded. "Yet another clue that made me think I was on the right track. The old site is still there and holds many state collections—manuscripts, maps, and major historical documents."

"Let me guess?" She smiled. "There was an old room inside the building marked private that held the Spear of Destiny. And on either side of it were the orbs?"

"Too easy." He grinned. "Although, much like your own sacred library, they do have a basement beneath the old site. It was laid out like the catacombs in Alexandria; a labyrinth of old manuscript rooms and reading areas—mostly for scholars to do their work in peace."

"Any guards?"

"No. No menacing men with crosses on their tunics," Gareth said, with a laugh. "But, I must say, the library staff had some scary looking bouncers who were patrolling the secure areas."

Leah grinned.

"I went through the catacombs one Sunday afternoon."

"Breaking and entering again?" she snorted. "How is it that you've never been arrested?"

"I'm on a mission from God." He winked.

Leah rolled her eyes. "I had to ask."

"I could feel the orbs, Leah." Gareth's voice grew quiet. "I could hear them humming. When I found them they were wrapped in…for lack of a better phrase…swaddling clothes."

"Were they lying in a manger?"

"You'd think so but, no," he replied. "There was a storeroom in the basement. Inside there were old rags, broken chairs, ripped books, cleaning supplies…you know, normal things. And in the corner, covered in dust, was a small desk."

He felt the power of that day flow through his body. "I can't tell you how beautiful it was. The desk had to have been carved by masters of the art world. There was a picture of two men dressed in robes; one wore a crown and the other was holding a jar. Around them were the constellations that we've grown so fond of, carved in the beautiful rose wood."

"Who was the man with the jar?" asked Leah.

Gareth took a deep breath and readied himself to crash through her next wall of doubt. "I think it was Lucifer. I think it was the scene that I was talking to you about earlier—the night he tried to strike a bargain to gain entry into Heaven again, instead of having to walk the Earth forever."

Leah held her tongue.

"I reached under the desk and found the orbs." Taking advantage of her silence, he forged ahead. "When I touched them, I could swear I heard Lucifer begging Jesus to let him talk to the Father. He wanted to go home. Jesus declined the offer, but forgave the fallen angel, like They always do. However, his punishment stood. That was it for the Devil. As Jesus laid his hands on Lucifer's head to forgive him, Lucifer ran away…mad.

"Of course, Lucifer's soul was black. No amount of forgiveness would ever have changed that." His voice trembled. "I had to sit down then. I'd never felt pure evil in all my life. Lucifer wanted so badly to kill the Son for getting to go to a place that he'd never again be permitted to enter. The Devil is powerless before God. He'll never be able to slither through Heaven's doors again."

"Without help," she muttered. "The Bible doesn't have a scene like that." Leah bit into her lower lip, and offered a half-smile. "Does it?"

He laughed. "Like you keep telling me, not everything's in that book. But after seeing and hearing this incredible conversation, I certainly believe it happened."

Leah spoke quietly, "Your theory has more holes in it than a block of Swiss cheese."

Gareth shook his head. He could tell from her troubled look that Leah was struggling to put her finger on something she couldn't quite reach.

"The Second Coming *shows* the good guys winning again." She cleared her throat. "These theories of yours are useless, Gareth. God and His Son exist—the bad guy exists—I get that you believe. But Satan, per your Book and belief system, loses. Why bother enlisting the Devil to help hide the Keys to the Kingdom?"

"I told you." Gareth sighed. "God knew that for humanity to follow either entity it was up to humanity, itself. Free will is very big in all religions. It's the one thing that neither entity has control over. The Devil doesn't want souls to go to Heaven; he *needs* people to be evil. That's his job. So what better person was there to help make sure that the gates of Heaven remained closed?"

Leah shook her head. "I'm sure that the Devil's smart enough to realize that when the Second Coming happens, God has the power to open the gate. He can't lock Them *in*."

"Of course not. But he can continue to get as many souls as possible to fight for his side before that day happens." His voice grew sad. "More and more people have stopped believing. Now is probably the easiest time in history for the Devil to find recruits."

"You sound pretty angry at humanity." Leah dropped her head in her hands. "People *need* proof, Gareth. We need something tangible to believe in. Every second of our lives the overwhelming amount of crap that this world hands us puts a choke hold on our faith. Wouldn't God—if these gates do exist—just walk through them once in a while and pat us on the head? Wouldn't He take the time to let us know that everything's going to be all right? He could *stop* people from listening to the Devil in the first place."

"All I can tell you is that there's a time for everything," said Gareth. "Humanity let Him down."

"But He forgives us anyway." Leah snorted.

"Yes. He does," Gareth stated matter-of-factly. "He also pats you on the head, Leah. People just don't listen anymore. We're all too busy wrapped up in our own little minds, worrying about our own lives, that we simply miss Him. I believe that He sent me on this journey, and I believe that He put you in my path. We were destined to be together, Leah. I have no doubt."

Her eyes grew wide. "To be together for this journey."

"No." Gareth caught her hand before she could pull away and close herself off. He could see the sweat break out on her forehead, but he held her gaze, trying to read the raw emotions that he saw beaming in her eyes.

"I still don't understand," said Leah. "Why was the Devil carrying a jar?"

Gareth grimaced when she once again side-stepped the subject he most wanted to talk about. "Jesus told his apostles to go to the city and meet a man carrying a jar of water. This was the man who would lead them to a house where the Teacher had a guest room. This room was where they prepared the Passover; the room where Jesus would eat his last supper."

"He invited the Devil to the Last Supper?" Leah looked confused.

"Of course. The Devil had been forgiven. Yes, he was the bad guy, but he was also about to become an ally, in a way, by hiding half of the orbs," Gareth explained. "God wasn't worried, Leah. He knew that the Devil would lose the big fight if it ever happened. But, most of all, He and His

Son believed that God's creations—us—would never side with Lucifer."

"Then you're saying God was wrong?"

"No." Gareth sighed. "I'm saying that He put more faith in us than we did in Him."

"Wait a minute." Leah felt a ripple of understanding flow through her brain. "That's the connection."

Gareth studied her face. "What did I miss?"

"Crowley's clue," she whispered. "The thirteenth chair wasn't reserved for Judas or Peter. That's why it was down at the bottom of the stairs away from the other twelve. The chair was for Lucifer." She thought out loud. "He wasn't invited to the party, Gareth. He crashed it."

"But Jesus and his disciples make thirteen. Why would there only be twelve chairs around the table?"

"I don't know." Leah shrugged. "Maybe Crowley couldn't count."

"Oh, come on."

Leah sat up straight in her chair. "Gareth, Crowley was making a point that the Devil *was* there. With the chair being set away from the others, Crowley's saying that he did attend the Last Supper. But not as a guest. The man—the Son—who sat at that table was on His way to Heaven, but the Devil had to stay behind…alone. Crowley's saying that God made the wrong choice that night by not letting Lucifer back into Paradise. With Jesus off the earth, the Devil had no one left to stop him…*down here.*"

Leah continued, "Crowley's saying that the chosen people—*all* people—would eventually follow the being who did *not* sit at that famous table. The Beast believed, with time, he could tear the souls from humanity, which explains the title of *Soul* on the page."

Gareth's body was rigid in his chair. He didn't say a word.

Her eyes were on fire. "You found the last set of 'good' orbs in a place where the spear resided; the weapon that killed His only Son in order to save the souls on earth. Crowley used his page for a statement from the Beast. He thought it was a hypocrisy that Jesus, the Teacher, was giving up His life to save us. The Devil knew if he heaped on enough pain and anguish, wars and death, that we wouldn't be strong enough to stand against him. We would fold. That's what his note meant. You can not believe in the Teacher without believing in him too. If you do, you're a hypocrite."

Images sprang to life in Gareth's head as the pieces came together. "God didn't believe His people would turn away from Him because he gave them proof He existed—showing them that His only Son would give up His life for us."

Leah nodded. "But the world will believe in the bad guy faster, Gareth. Because there's no longer any proof that everything's going to be okay. Most people nowadays just feel alone."

"You're saying Crowley buried the orbs on Mount Zion?" said Gareth.

"Crowley buried the orbs in the room where the 'man with the jar' sat. I'm saying Crowley was pissed off about this one. The Winchester House and The Ripper were just funny to him—sick entertainment. But the final orbs, the last pieces of the puzzle, were put in a place where Crowley thought the *actual* ripper of souls ate His final meal. They left the Devil down here believing that Their people would overcome any challenge and stay faithful to *Them*. Crowley's saying, no. He's telling you that the Devil *has* won, and that by the time the Second Coming happens, it'll be too late."

Leah took his hand. "Crowley was filled with self-importance, Gareth. We know this. He loved putting his manic thoughts down on paper and delivering them to the masses. Andrew Carnegie played on this self-important streak by giving Crowley the job in the first place telling him that he was being given power that at one time Satan, himself, had enjoyed."

Her voice lowered. "The Devil's everywhere, Gareth. In fact, there's only one other entity who gets more publicity, and Crowley didn't like it."

Gareth attempted a smile. "Madonna?"

"Close. Very, very close."

Leah's words sent chills up his spine, as the image of the beloved Mother and Son sprang to life inside his mind. He swallowed his fear. "I have to call my sister."

CHAPTER TWENTY

Donovan remained silent until Kathryn set down the receiver. He tried not to laugh out loud at her pale white skin and frightened eyes. She reminded him so much of the happy Whitechapel shopkeeper when he'd tightened the noose around her neck.

"Well?" he said.

"They're going to Mt. Zion," the small voice replied.

Confusion raced through Donovan's mind, along with a surge of fear. Even though he'd had fun, his ultimate mission in Whitechapel had failed; the horrible woman had already sold the precious necklace that his brother had needed just in case Plan B had to be put into place."

He shook the mutinous thoughts from his brain. Plan A was still in play and, apparently, right on track. "Why would Crowley bury the orbs in a biblical place? He was the bad guy, after all. Shouldn't he have chosen another…location of pain?"

Kathryn shrugged. "Leah says Mt. Zion so they're going to Mt. Zion." She stared out the small window. "Maybe she's looking for faith. I can't wait to meet her. She must be really something for my brother—the life-long bachelor—to be mooning over her like this."

"Leah Tallent has zero faith and would certainly be the last person looking for it!" Donovan snapped without thinking.

Kathryn took a step back from the cold, harsh tone.

Checking himself quickly, Donovan rearranged his face into his ultimate role of calm, helpful friend. "Sorry. You know how angry I get at non-believers. And I certainly don't want your brother falling for one of them. She'd bring him nothing but trouble."

Kathryn stuck her chin in the air. "I think she's good for him." Her small fists clenched at her side. "And maybe she doesn't need to believe in God. Maybe she only needs to believe in my brother."

"Maybe you're right," said Donovan softly, trying to get the angry color to leave her cheeks.

Kathryn's voice transformed into that of a drill sergeant. "Gareth told me about all the things she's done. I think she sounds like a very great lady."

Donovan could almost feel the tide begin to turn. It was certainly time to change strategy. "She is a great lady." He smiled wide. "Truly. I'm just being overprotective of Gareth again."

Kathryn's glare remained on her small, round face.

"Just think." Donovan filled his voice with wonder. "Maybe the place where Jesus, himself, once stood, will push her over to our side. Maybe she'll find herself believing in the Divine."

Kathryn hesitated, staring into what, Donovan hoped, was his innocent gaze.

Quickly, he continued, "I worry about her, though. She's a loner, you see. And I think darkness…evil…attacks people like Leah Tallent. If you're alone, you're unprotected."

"She's not alone." Kathryn reminded him. "She has Gareth."

"True."

"And Jesus didn't stand at Mt. Zion. He sat," Kathryn added, flippantly.

"He wasn't the only one." Suddenly the answer was staring him directly in the face. Donovan practically had to stop himself from bouncing up and down with joy. Of *course* Crowley would've picked Mt. Zion. Crowley was just like him, Donovan thought. He, too, wanted to visit the place where his own beloved idol had once sat, unbeknownst to the rest of the world.

Kathryn squinted up at him, as if trying to understand the tone of his words, and his blatantly giddy expression. "I'm going to find Emmanuel. Tell him where they are." Throwing open the door, Kathryn quickly left the room.

When the door shut behind her, Donovan laughed so hard he cried. He could feel the change happening deep inside his soul. It wasn't the tide turning, it was the feeling of absolute power surging through him; the power of a true friend who'd chosen Donovan to be his next acolyte.

The time was nearly here; the true evil was coming home.

CHAPTER TWENTY-ONE

Explosions thundered in the distance. It was like listening to a constant stream of backfires from old rotted-out trucks. The sounds of rapid gunfire coming from the surrounding hills resembled a band of happy children shooting off fireworks to celebrate their freedom—a gift that these people would probably never have. Here she was standing at the site where a true miracle had taken place, yet people were still trying to tear it apart.

Following Gareth, her head covered, Leah tried to grasp what had happened here so long ago. But she still couldn't believe that she was actually here. Through the Old City of Jerusalem they'd traveled to the place known as the Upper Room; a place where remarkable men had gathered for a feast that would be remembered for all eternity.

Leah shuddered, wondering what she would see. Her brain still hoped that the orbs would show nothing more than an empty room. Still...Leah could feel a slight flutter in her stomach, as if something strange was inside her waiting to be set free. She'd meant what she said to Gareth. For the first time in her life, she needed faith as much as oxygen. If she didn't find it, Leah knew there'd be no hope for a future with Gareth. It wasn't 'dog people versus cat people.' His faith in the Divine, and hers in the world of skeptics, would eventually kill any feeling they had for one another.

Leah swallowed hard, staring up at the crumbling site. When they entered the room they found it bare. The only signs of life were the slight imprints on the floor. They weren't footprints, Leah knew. The rounded impressions had been left behind by the believers who fell to their knees and prayed for a savior to deliver them from pain.

Gareth bowed his head and closed his eyes. Leah tried to follow his example, but she couldn't. She wouldn't be a hypocrite.

"I still don't get the chairs, Leah." Gareth turned and stared at her. "Jesus and his apostles made thirteen."

She shrugged "It was just a theory." The humming in her brain began. It was a rhythmic beat, like a distress call being sent out to the first Good Samaritan who could hear.

Leah walked to the center of the room. Without thinking, she moved the dirt aside and stuck her hand in a narrow gap between the rocks. In seconds, she'd extracted the orbs from their hiding place beneath the ancient floor. They weren't wrapped in any type of burlap or cloth; the colorful flames blinked on and off like clockwork.

Leah handed the humming duo to Gareth. He took a quick glance, said a silent prayer, and buried them in the knapsack beside the rest of their supernatural family.

Amazing music lifted from the green bag and grew louder, overtaking the distant sounds of war. The orbs were all together again and ready to go home.

Leah walked to the open window and stared out at the eerily quiet street. There were no shopkeepers, no tourists—not one person wandered the sidewalk. All was silent.

Blink. A glass rattled. Leah turned around slowly and stared at the table. She gazed at them in wonder as they sat and talked with one another, staring up at their host. Leah suddenly understood. Crowley must've known; he must've seen the images when he placed the orbs in their hiding place for the rest of time. There were only twelve chairs in the room…Jesus wasn't seated. He walked around the huddled group placing a hand on each one's shoulder, offering the most beautiful smile of friendship Leah had ever seen.

Blink. Gareth fell to his knees; his body trembled as the beautiful music radiated from his knapsack.

Blink. Leah saw the man holding the jar; he sat in a small chair at the bottom of the staircase. Looking up at her, he smiled. Leah shuddered when she noticed that the smile was familiar, and never reached the evil one's black eyes. Pure evil radiated from his skin. This man was worse than any serial killer could possibly be, she knew, because this man wanted souls.

The voice that slithered up the stairs was cold and lifeless. The blue flame pulsed in his eyes when he hissed, "I'll be waiting for you." Standing up, he bowed at the waist and slinked away into the night

Blink. Gareth's eyes were aimed at the ceiling and his lips moved in prayer.

Blink. Leah turned away from the stairwell and came face to face with the one person who she'd always thought of as a character written by wise, overly-creative minds.

He reached out and took her hand. The other men at the famous table vanished from sight, taking with them the fear and doubt in Leah's soul. But the Teacher remained.

He glanced at Gareth. "He's a good man."

"He loves you," she stuttered.

"And I love him." He walked to the window and stared out at the smoke rising from the mountain in the distance.

"I'm sorry," Leah whispered.

"It'll be all right."

"I hope so." Leah nodded at Gareth's quiet figure. "He is a good man. But is he right about…doing this?"

His smile filled her with hope. "He's free to do what he thinks is best."

"People are rarely right," she mumbled.

"You just said that you hoped everything would be all right someday. Your hope is justified. You should know that every person, no matter who they are or what they believe, have our protection. *We* believe in *you*."

"Still?" Leah heard the gunfire in the distance.

"Always."

Blink. Leah tried to keep his hand, but the Son faded from sight. Her eyes filled with tears and she, too, fell to her knees and cried for the life that'd been lost.

Always. His promise rang in her ears, and she ended their meeting the only way she could think of, "Amen."

Gareth raced across the room and wrapped his arms around her, as Leah cried for the man who'd finally made her believe.

*

"Back to England," Gareth proclaimed, as they boarded yet another plane.

"Again?" Leah smiled.

Gareth's heart did a back flip when he saw the new light in Leah's eyes. It was as if all her worry was gone, now that the proof she'd craved was swimming in her soul.

She stared up at him. "Please don't tell me we're facing The Ripper again. I don't think I can take Trish for one more second, even if the clothes *are* nice."

"You're close." Gareth laughed. "She may not be a serial killer, or a manic shopkeeper, but I bet my sister could give old Jack a run for his money. Hell would be a picnic compared to Kathryn when she's angry—especially at me."

"Your sister's in England? Why didn't you visit her when we were there?" she asked.

Gareth smiled. "We were on our own path, Leah. But now the time has come to join together. Besides, Donovan's there. Kathryn's taking us to the end. She always did like to work backwards; she used to read the last page of a book to see if she'd like the story."

Leah squirmed in her seat. "I really hate people who do that. Ruins the whole thing if you already know how it ends."

"Precisely." Gareth squeezed her hand. "Kills it all if you know the conclusion. For me, it's the roller-coaster ride that's the fun part—makes me feel alive."

Leah's cheeks turned red. "I suppose this story is almost over."

Gareth leaned over and pressed his lips against hers. "And the beginning of another?" His heart leapt in his throat when Leah kissed him back with a passion that was overwhelming. Disregarding the flight attendants who mumbled as they walked past, Gareth kissed her harder.

Leah laughed.

"What?"

Her eyes held a mischievous twinkle. "I can almost hear the poor female hearts breaking all over the world…not to mention on this very plane."

"You're happy?" he whispered.

"Very."

"You believe?"

"I can hardly say no *now*."

Gareth rested his head against the scratchy seat. "We can stop all the crap, Leah. We hold the power to literally make war and pain disappear."

Leah's hand grew cold. "Let's not get too far ahead of ourselves, okay?"

Gareth nodded and closed his eyes, as exhaustion overtook him. His soul was jubilant. He now knew beyond a shadow of a doubt that this was the right thing to do. He could hardly wait to finish what his parents started, and reveal the truth to the world.

CHAPTER TWENTY-TWO

The taxi ride was long and lovely as they rode over the most breathtakingly beautiful countryside Leah had ever seen. With the new dusting of snow that covered the landscape, the whole place looked to be exactly what people thought it'd been for centuries…pure magic.

Finally they reached the outer edges of the mythical town, which was located one hundred miles away from the busy streets of London. Gareth pulled the handle, and grabbed the knapsack from the trunk. Hiding it under his coat, he tried to diminish the joyful hum.

Leah looked at the cozy bed and breakfast; an old iron sign swung from ancient hooks above the door. Through the inviting front window, she could see the warm glow of a friendly fireplace, and heard the happy sounds of a neighborhood gathering.

Suddenly, a shout burst from the doorway like gunfire, and a small woman ran over the threshold and jumped into Gareth's surprised arms. He caught the tiny fledgling in his grip and hugged the stuffing out of her, laughing and kissing her cheeks.

Gareth twirled her in the air and set her down on the sidewalk. "Well, I can't say you've grown, Kathryn."

"Shut up, you big tree." His sister scowled and punched him in the arm. When she turned around, Leah jumped, as a squeal tore from the young woman's throat. Kathryn quickly marched over to her and stuck out her small hand. "It's so nice to meet you, Leah. I can't tell you how much you've helped us. Without you, we would've given up."

Leah felt a pang of guilt at her words wondering, yet again, if she'd made the wrong decision. She shook the small hand. "Um…thank you."

Gareth winked. "I call her from the cell phone a lot. I'm telling you, if I didn't this girl would get extremely angry—and fast. Don't let the petite frame fool you, Leah. There's a beast inside that small package that can tear you limb from limb."

Kathryn glared up at her brother. "Don't listen to him. *I'm* the nice one in the family. I'm sure after all the time you've spent with him, you already know that he's a blow-hard. He's got his head so far up—"

"Kathryn!"

She smiled innocently. "I was going to say, in the clouds."

"Sure you were."

Leah laughed, as the unusually strong woman pulled her inside the warmth of the bar.

Kathryn pointed up at the old sign. "Welcome to the Round Table, Leah."

"Of course." Leah smiled. After all, when in Glastonbury, you must certainly be prepared to witness the Arthurian legends around every corner.

Kathryn's small, strong voice filled the air. "You're going to love this, Leah. I promise."

*

Leah couldn't remember a time when she'd laughed so hard, or been around a family who was so close that they knew each other's every secret.

She was also more than relieved when Kathryn told her that Donovan wouldn't be joining them.

"Where is he?" Gareth had asked.

A strange look had crossed over Kathryn's face. "He's in the cave. We take turns making sure that no one else finds it. But ever since he arrived, he's wanted to…protect it himself. We'll see him tomorrow."

"Can't wait," Leah had muttered.

Soon all thoughts of Donovan Barker had disappeared and Leah was pulled into the Lowery family fun, as they shared their most embarrassing moments.

"Remember when you saw that commercial on television and asked Mom what reptile dysfunction was?" Gareth smirked at his sister.

Leah laughed. "*Reptile* dysfunction?"

"Yeah, she was five years old and said it wrong." Gareth winked. "Mom told her that it was an alligator with a sore foot."

"I was only a baby!" Kathryn's face turned beet red. "Why do you always tell that story?"

"Because it's funny."

"Like *you* were perfect." Kathryn's girlish laugh was completely infectious. "He was such a geek, Leah. Romantic, of course, a Pisces to the extreme. He always thought that life was fun in the sun and love ruled the world. I always said he missed his calling. My brother would've been a shoe-in to work for Hallmark. You'd think, the way he looks now, that he would've been a real ladies' man, but the dork couldn't be graceful or cool to save his life."

"You're seriously damaging my reputation here, sis." Gareth reddened.

Kathryn let out another happy squeal. "My brother's first love was a schoolteacher's daughter. That girl was as smart as a whip—had it all over Gareth. He took every book out of the library that he could get his hands on and studied for weeks. Then, after all that cramming, he struck up a rather intelligent conversation with the girl of his dreams about… John of Arc."

Leah stared at Gareth's bright red face. "Don't you mean Joan?"

"He was so nervous that he messed it all up. At least the girl was nice to him before she walked out of his life forever; she probably thought he'd been dropped on his head a lot as a child. My poor brother couldn't sleep for weeks." Kathryn burst into a fit of giggles and pounded her fists on the table. "He spent all his time writing sonnets for his lost love who now thought he was the biggest moron in the world."

Gareth offered a hang-dog expression. "I can't believe you…laughing at my pain. That moment redefined my life, you know."

Leah laughed until tears ran down her cheeks, as she imagined the tall, gawky boy who had not yet grown into the stunning man that now sat across from her. "Well, I guess he's studied a lot more since then."

"Yet I *still* find myself picking women who outdo me in every facet of research. After all these years of studying, I'm still the dumb one." Gareth winked at her.

Kathryn stared at Leah. "Not only that, bro. You wanna' hear something even worse? If this is the one you've picked for life, not only will you be the dumb one, but you'll no longer be the pretty one either."

Gareth agreed. "Yup, I'm screwed."

The young man sitting beside Leah burst into laughter. His name was Emmanuel, and was the other half of Kathryn's own magical partnership. Leah had learned throughout the jovial evening that he, too, had a head filled with amazingly innocuous references of historical facts and locations. He should, considering he was employed by a branch of UNESCO: The United Nations Educational, Scientific and Cultural Organization.

Leah knew of the great work being done by people like Emmanuel across the globe. Not only was he dedicated to the conservation of historic sites, he was also a part of saving all different types of cultures—helping to keep their beliefs and customs alive for the next generation.

But his brain was not all that was attractive about the young man, Leah noted. His tanned skin, dark hair, bedroom brown eyes, and muscular build, certainly added to his list of assets. She'd found out over dinner that Emmanuel had studied with Kathryn at the University of New Mexico, before being drafted by his dedicated employer. Leah also assumed, by the puppy dog expression that he'd aimed at Kathryn all night long, that the young man had not only pledged his help, but also his heart, to the young blonde whipper-snapper.

Leah tried to hide her amusement when Gareth slowly came to the realization that the feelings were mutual. She could barely contain her laughter as Gareth eyed the young man, like a bird of prey studies the helpless rabbit as it hops lazily across the meadow. She was quite certain, when Gareth's look of surprise turned into one of anxiety, that this was the first time he'd recognized the fact that his little sister was all grown up.

Gareth squirmed in his chair when Kathryn leaned over and kissed Emmanuel on the mouth.

"When did this happen, exactly?" Gareth's voice boomed through the bar like a clap of thunder, disturbing the patrons around them.

Emmanuel looked at Leah, clearly avoiding the angry older brother.

"Oh, please." Kathryn laughed at Gareth's expression. "I'm thirty years old, bro. Did you think I was the Virgin Mary, or something?"

Gareth winced.

"Besides, you like Emmanuel. You know you do."

Gareth mumbled, "Liked him a hell'uva lot more a couple of minutes ago."

Leah erased her smile when she saw the anger flash in Gareth's eyes. She looked down at her plate and began shoveling food into her mouth, making sure she didn't end up on Gareth's hit list.

Emmanuel took a deep breath. "Think of it this way. We have a lot in common now, you and me. I'm in the same sinking boat as you are. I used to be the smart one, too. But with your sister I can't claim anything except…well…" He blushed. "The luckiest, of course."

Kathryn's eyes shone with love.

Gareth's shoulders slumped in defeat. "Fine." He sighed. "Can we talk about something else?"

Kathryn leaned across the table and kissed her brother's cheek. "Okay, Mr. Grouchy Pants. That's probably the best I can hope for." She turned to Emmanuel and shrugged. "When Gareth changes the subject, that means he's given us his blessing."

"I didn't say that," Gareth barked.

"Whatever." Kathryn waved her hands over her plate like a gypsy over a crystal ball, closing the subject for good. Her face grew serious when she stared at Leah. "Gareth told me about Winchester House and The Ripper. I'm so sorry you had to be involved in all that."

"No regrets." Came Leah's honest reply. "It got me to where I am now, so it was worth it."

Kathryn's eyes gleamed. Her whisper was barely audible in the crowded pub. "He's been looking for you his whole life."

Leah's heart skipped at her words, and she stared across the table at Gareth. His smile was wide, as he offered her a nod.

"Well, that settles that!" Kathryn declared. "On to more important things. Demons of the past be gone!" She brought her small fist down on the table, sending her fork flying through the air into the fireplace behind her. "Whoops."

Emmanuel let out a shriek of laughter.

"This is why everyone hates us." Kathryn laughed along with him. "We Americans are so uncouth. We don't know how to behave ourselves in public."

Gareth laughed. "Not all Americans…just you."

Kathryn punched him in the shoulder and turned her attention to Leah. Her eyes were twinkling with excitement. "I know that Gareth has told you our family history."

She nodded.

The rest of the table grew quiet, as she continued, "Glastonbury, as you know, is a legendary location. And, oddly enough, a tourist trap that's home to the most remarkable artifacts in the world."

"Not surprising," remarked Leah. "The people involved in all this seem to have loved proving that humans are so wrapped up in themselves, there's no way any of them would notice the clues sitting right in front of their eyes."

Kathryn smiled. "Truer words have never been spoken." She turned to her brother. "You know? I really like her."

"Uh, oh." Gareth grimaced. "If she has your seal of approval then something must seriously be wrong with her."

"Brat." Kathryn slapped his arm, and turned her attention back to Leah. "What do you know about this area?"

Leah shrugged. "Just the regular stuff, I suppose—Arthur, Merlin, etcetera."

"Have you heard of the Chalice Well?"

"Sure," she replied. "People believe that's where Joseph hid the Holy Grail for safe-keeping. Legend says that a spring burst forth from the spot where the Cup of Christ was buried, and the water that flows from there offers eternal life to anyone who drinks it."

Kathryn tilted her head to the side. "Only if the drinkers have faith."

"There's always a price." Leah couldn't stop the sarcasm from creeping into her words. "Kathryn, many so-called believers have drunk from that well and, as far as I know, no one has yet to attain eternal life."

"Not eternal, no." Kathryn agreed. "But the spring *does* have healing properties. And the same spring—the spring that's flowed from the Chalice Well for thousands of years—still flows today."

"So?"

"There's no underground water source that feeds it," Kathryn stated.

Leah felt her eyebrows climb up her forehead. "How do you know that?"

"How *do* you know that?" Gareth asked.

Kathryn's voice remained calm. "I've been under it."

"Excuse me?" Tallent and Lowery echoed in unison.

"Turns out that Tor Hill is hollow." She smiled knowingly. "You can get into it through a tower that sits on the top; the last surviving tower of a church that was dedicated to the Archangel Michael."

"Couldn't anyone get into it?" asked Leah.

"Actually," Kathryn replied; her eyes sparkled. "They could. *If* they knew what I know."

Leah put down her fork and crossed her arms. "Okay. I'll bite. How do you get in?"

"I'm so glad you asked," Kathryn said. "Just like any door, all you do is knock."

Clearing her mind, Leah tried to prepare herself for what she was about to hear.

CHAPTER TWENTY-THREE

Kathryn looked over at Emmanuel. As if her loving stare was a cue, he began, "St. Michael is believed to have been the leader of a group of twelve angels who once walked the earth."

"One and twelve," Leah whispered.

Emmanuel nodded. "I've been a fan of Glastonbury legend for a long time. Almost everything around here—churches, monasteries, land masses—they're all named in Michael's honor. But that's not what brought me on board with the Lowery family quest." He grinned. "You see, I'm also a fan of poetry, and at one time I was fascinated with William Butler Yeats. I thought his work was extraordinary. After meeting Kathryn and forming our…bond." He glanced at Gareth warily. "Um…she introduced me to her brother and Donovan, and they told me what they were looking for. After hearing about it all, I found that their quest reminded me a great deal of the last poem Yeats ever wrote."

"*The Black Tower.*" Leah nodded.

"That's the one." Emmanuel smiled at Gareth. "Congrats on finding such an intelligent woman."

Gareth shot him a look of pride.

"Anyway," Emmanuel continued, with a chuckle, "*The Black Tower* shows remarkable similarities to the structure that stands on top of Tor Hill."

"So do a lot of other poems, I'm sure," remarked Leah. She shook her head slowly. "You needed more than that to bring you here. You needed a link between Steiner and Crowley."

Gareth spoke up. "We absolutely did. That's when we started to go back and explore their pasts. We needed a thread."

"A thread indeed." Emmanuel nodded.

Leah stared at the grinning young man. "And your link was a poet?"

"Yeats wasn't only a poet, Leah," he replied. "He was also known far and wide as a mystic. He had a life-long interest in spiritualism, the occult, and astrology. Yeats had said, that if he'd not made magic his constant study, he wouldn't have been able to write a single word. He truly believed that the mystical world was the center of all that he did, thought, or wrote.

"One night, when all of us were just sitting around talking, I mentioned the fact that Yeats was once a member of the Golden Dawn and had gone by the name of *Demon est Deus inversus*."

"Devil is the reverse of God," Leah translated.

Emmanuel pounded his fist on the table. "Right again! You *are* good at this. It would've been great if we'd had you at the beginning."

"Aleister Crowley was a member of The Golden Dawn," Leah said, staring at Gareth.

Emmanuel nodded. "There was also a great deal of in-fighting in the group between Crowley and Yeats. At one point it got so bad that Yeats snapped. He actually came to a stand-off with Crowley, who was trying to convince the other members that he was, in fact, Satan reborn."

"Yeats went out on his own then." Kathryn picked up the story with a fluidity that spoke volumes about the amount of time she and Emmanuel spent together. "Crowley made Yeats mad, causing Yeats to move further and further away from the…let's say…dark side of mysticism. He started to focus on the lighter side of life." Kathryn's eyes gleamed. "When Yeats was seventy-three, shortly before his death, he met a man by the name of Rudolf Steiner here, while he was visiting Tintagel Castle."

"Steiner?" Leah felt her blood run cold as the paths began to merge.

"Gareth thought it was spooky, too." She smiled, reaching out to pat her brother's hand. "Yeats and Steiner met each other here in Glastonbury in 1919; Steiner and Crowley would've hidden their orbs by then." Kathryn leaned forward on her elbows. "We believe that Steiner was ending his 'mission' for Carnegie at the doors of Tintagel Castle for a reason. He visited here a lot between 1919 and 1924—couldn't seem to stay away from the place." Her voice filled with wonder. "It was almost like he was an old knight guarding a secret."

Leah remained silent; her brain recorded every word.

"Anyway," she continued, with a smile. "During their meeting, Steiner told Yeats his theory about Tintagel Castle. Although, over time, his theory was lost; it became buried under the more popular legend of King Arthur."

"That one's way more fun," said Gareth.

"True," Emmanuel agreed. "When I was a kid, I would run around my bedroom half-naked with a sheet tied around my shoulders like a cape, pretending I was Lancelot."

Gareth raised his hand in the air. "Too much information."

"I would like to see that." Kathryn elbowed Emmanuel in the shoulder, and winked.

"Okay," he replied. "You can be Guinevere. I'll save you with my sword."

"Seriously." Gareth raised his voice; he sounded like a frustrated father about to kill the eager suitor who was after his daughter. "I'm gonna' throw up."

Kathryn giggled, and continued on, "I know that Gareth told you about the Akashic Records and how hard Steiner worked to prove that reincarnation existed."

"I already know all that." Leah waved her hand between them. "Tell me where Yeats fits in. I mean, he knew Crowley from the past—through the Order—but he only had one conversation with Steiner that you know of. Or, think you know of."

Emmanuel turned serious. "Years ago at auction a collection of Yeats' personal works came up for sale, and I immediately called Gareth. He was kind enough to purchase them."

Leah grinned at Gareth Lowery, entrepreneur. "Aren't you nice?"

"What can I say?" He shrugged. "I should be sainted."

"You'd have to be dead, remember?"

"We all gotta' go sometime." He winked.

A sudden chill crawled up Leah's spine at his innocent remark.

Gareth caught a whiff of her fear, and smiled. "Also, a saint probably wouldn't be allowed to run around half-naked with a sheet around his shoulders and save Guinevere with his mighty sword." He winked. "Which *we* could try sometime."

Kathryn stuck out her tongue. "Ick."

"Now you see how I feel." Gareth laughed.

"Okay," she said. "You win." Kathryn shook the creepy picture from her brain, and went back to a more pleasing conversation. She looked at Leah. "In the collection Gareth bought, there was a diary. In it, Yeats had written about his meeting with a fairly inebriated Rudolf Steiner. During their short time together, Steiner told Yeats that in every era a king had been born who helped the oppressed and fought for the people. Steiner believed King Arthur and his Knights were one group that arrived during their own era to do the job. Steiner also said there were many famous bands of brothers over time, including St. Michael and his angels."

"Sure." Leah heard the disbelief swimming in her voice.

Kathryn, like her brother, ignored her tone completely. "He even went a step further. Steiner told Yeats about the Akashic Records and how he had the ability to focus on past lives. Steiner said because of this awareness, he could actually *see* these famous groups roaming around inside Tintagel Castle. Not a surprise, really, considering how steeped in magic this area is. In addition, the castle once held a library that served as a center for learning for astrologers and astronomers—people who were behind the construction of powerful places like Stonehenge."

Leah knew the famous monument was close by. For a second, she wondered what those intelligent beings would think of their little quartet—sitting in the cozy bar and attempting to decipher the past.

Emmanuel's voice broke through her thoughts. "Steiner said that Tintagel was not only the home for scholars, but also played home to the Archangel Michael and his followers. He said that each of Michael's members—his troop of angels—represented a sign of the zodiac. St. Michael was the sun that the other zodiac signs surrounded."

"According to modern day astrologers," Kathryn interrupted. "An event on the astral plane caused the Age of Michael to be reborn in 1879. They thought that the next five hundred years would be a New Age where we would finally find peace."

"Hasn't happened," Leah snorted.

"Five hundred years is hardly up yet." Kathryn smiled. "We still have time."

"And you really believe all this?"

"Of course!" Kathryn looked at Leah as if a third head had just grown out of her neck. "There's even a place the locals call Merlin's Cave that's under Tintagel Castle. People, including myself, go into this cave and come out rejuvenated—like their souls have come back to life and are ready to take on the world again. The people who stand inside this cave reincarnate their faith, not their bodies. It's truly amazing. The power is here, Leah. You can feel it."

Leah muffled her sigh, and stared down at the table. No matter what she'd seen in the Upper Room, she still needed facts…not faith. "So you came here because Yeats wrote a story of a drunken encounter with Rudolf Steiner. And that basically Steiner had revealed—without actually revealing—the existence and location of Heaven."

Kathryn gazed at her; devout faith burned in her eyes. "Yeats wrote in his diary that Steiner showed him the way. He wrote about going to the tower with Steiner and watching him knock twelve times on the door. One knock equaled one request, asking permission from each member of Michael's group to enter."

Leah trembled slightly in her chair. Everything in Kathryn's story seemed far too easy.

"Yeats also wrote about going to the wall."

"What wall?" asked the completely confused librarian.

"A place where all religious beliefs were turned into fact," Kathryn declared. "You'll see it too." Her eyes glittered with excitement. "The locals agree with Emmanuel. They think Yeats' last poem, *The Black Tower*, was really about the lone tower on top of Tor Hill; the tower that protects and guards the secret of a lifetime. I think that Yeats' love of mysticism, King Arthur, and astronomy was so great, that he wanted to write himself into the story. His poetry and his diary acted like a map that led Emmanuel and I to what we know is Heaven's door."

Gareth reached across the table for Leah's hand. "You look worried. I know that all this information is confusing." He grinned. "Even for a brilliant mind like yours. But this isn't as crazy as you may think, Leah. There's an old Celtic legend that says Tor Hill, and the tower at the top, is the entrance to the Underworld. Yet another red herring, most likely invented by people who knew what was really in there. They believed that if they pronounced the place evil, then no one in their right mind would ever go down there to find the Kingdom of Heaven. This puzzle has been hidden and re-hidden for centuries."

He took a deep breath. "A lot of people believe that no good can come from opening it up. Unlike the Holy Grail, and the Spear of Destiny, the wall is a little known artifact that could be used by bad people to further their own horrible pursuits."

"Yes!" Leah's voice came out loud and strong. "And if you get *your* way, it *will* be opened, and all the bad people will come out of the woodwork to do just that."

"We don't want to use the site for evil purposes," Kathryn spoke quickly, seeing Leah's disgust.

"I'm sorry." Leah stood from her chair. "I'm completely worn out. I think my brain has finally reached its limit. You'll have to excuse me."

Turning quickly, she worked her way through the small, packed tavern. Taking a deep breath, she entered the cooler air of the lobby, and headed up the red-carpeted staircase to her small room. A hand touched her lightly on the shoulder and she turned around, meeting Emmanuel's boyishly handsome face.

"Sorry about that in there." He smiled warmly. "We have a tendency to forget everything else when this subject comes up."

"You're *really* sure that you're making the right choice?"

He leaned against the wall. "What do you mean?"

"I've listened to your theories, and I have to say, all of you have made more than a few leaps of faith here. Are you sure there's nothing you missed along the way?"

Emmanuel tilted his head. "I thought after your trip to Mt. Zion that you believe now?"

"In Jesus, yes…maybe" Leah sighed. "But, excuse me for saying so, every single one of you at one time or another have pointed out the fact that this secret—these orbs—have been hidden for centuries for a damn good reason. Yet all of you want to go into a mountain tomorrow and expose this secret. Why?" She threw her hands in the air. "If this wall, or gate, or whatever, was built to hide the Kingdom of Heaven, who are you to open it? That's not your job. And it wasn't Gareth's parents' job before him. If these gates are real, they're for Jesus to return when *He* feels it's time—not when you do."

Emmanuel looked confused. "Leah, let me ask you a question. If you knew that the answer to peace was right around the corner, would you keep walking in a straight line?"

Leah bowed her head, as the seeds of doubt blossomed inside her soul. "Heaven's not an archaeological find, Emmanuel; it's not King Tut's tomb. It's hope. That's what Gareth taught me. It's a belief that there's something better out there. You want to dig it up like buried treasure. I think you're all missing the point." She sighed. "Isn't Heaven a treasure because we *can't* see it? It's not tangible—it's faith—and people need that to survive."

"We don't want to *dig* up Heaven, Leah." Frustration laced Emmanuel's defiant words. "We don't want to sell tickets for admission. We're trying to help. By showing this to the world we'll finally have peace."

"Peace?" Fear clogged Leah's throat. "Trust me, Emmanuel. When you take something that's pure and perfect and place it in a world of chaos and pain, it becomes flawed. There's no way to stop it—that's human nature. If you expose perfection day in and day out to evil, you'll destroy it."

Confusion filled his dark brown eyes.

Leah tried to offer him a comforting smile. "I'm not saying your intentions are bad. But have any of you ever thought that by opening this gate you just might let Hell inside? There have been two sides to this story at every turn. Yet here we are at the end, and you're all doing just what Crowley thought you'd do. You're once again underestimating the power of evil."

Emmanuel offered her a troubled stare. "Are you leaving us?"

Leah shook her head. "I made a promise to Gareth Lowery, and I keep my promises. I actually hope that I'm wrong about the whole thing. I just want you to weigh every option you have. Keep in mind that scientists have been bashed throughout history for being so eager to make a discovery, that they didn't think through the consequences.

"People have discovered plutonium, lead, uranium. These things have healing properties and have helped humanity. But with the discovery of these wonders also came the power to build bombs and blow up countries. You get the bad with the good; there's no way to get around that. Right now you're dealing with the most powerful good in the universe." She tried her best to swallow the lump of fear in her throat. "You can bet your ass that the most powerful evil in the universe will be coming to the party, too."

Leah walked up the staircase, leaving the young man in a state of shock. "Goodnight Emmanuel," she whispered.

She could feel the cold draft on her back as more visitors arrived at the small tavern. She didn't know what chilled her blood more—the cold hand of winter, or her own frightening words.

CHAPTER TWENTY-FOUR

People knocking on doors were far worse than the buzzing of an alarm clock. With the clock, you could press the snooze button or hurl it across the room. Unfortunately, you couldn't get rid of people that easily.

Leah raised her exhausted head off the pillow, and proceeded to smash it into the low ceiling. With profanity spraying from her mouth like a geyser, Leah threw open the door, ready to take out her aggressions on the rude person who quite obviously wasn't going away.

Gareth's bright and beaming smile met her gaze. "My goodness, the mouth you have. Didn't sleep, my princess?"

"Go away."

"Now, now. That's no way to treat someone who has struggled up three flights of really tiny stairs—with a hangover, mind you—to bring you this lovely offering of food." He produced a silver tray from behind his back, and waltzed into the room.

Leah slammed the door. "What time is it?"

"It's almost six o'clock."

"In the *morning*? I just went to bed!"

Gareth laughed. "Now, that's not true. You've had a whole five hours to yourself. Besides," he continued, reaching out and twirling her curls between his fingers. "You're the last woman in the world who needs her beauty sleep."

Leah tried to step away, but he pulled her against him and claimed her mouth with his own. The breath left her body when Gareth, the eternal scientist, began to explore. She clung to his shoulders as his warm body pressed against the length of her, erasing any intelligent thought from her brain. Leah was angry at herself when the mutiny began. Her soul screamed out for him, and every part of her body sprang to life beneath the flimsy gown.

Suddenly, Gareth released her. He stepped back and proceeded to slam his head into the small, slanted ceiling. Closing his eyes, he let out a painful groan.

"Serves you right." Leah took deep breaths, attempting to smother the animalistic passion that threatened to tear her apart every time he was near.

Gareth rubbed the back of his skull. "Well," he said, moving his gaze over her body appreciatively. "This *is* a good morning."

Leah snatched the heavy robe off the foot of the bed, and wrapped the tie around her waist. "You're a real pain in the ass, you know that?"

Gareth grunted, "Eat, and come downstairs."

"Yes, sir."

Closing his eyes, he took a deep breath. "I'm sorry. I feel like a caveman around you sometimes. I can't really help it, you know. I am a man, after all. We have no self-control."

"I love the testosterone card," she grumbled.

"Oh." Gareth reached out and took her hand. "I wanted to give you something."

"I'll bet," she sneered.

"Well…that, too, of course. But I actually came up here to give you something else. I've been waiting for the right moment. But something tells me, with my sister downstairs—who I swear is the reincarnation of Hitler—we're never going to have a moment's peace from here on out. So...I wanted you to have this."

Leah took the small, silver package from Gareth's hand, and sat down on the bed. She tore through the ribbons and wrapping like a kid on Christmas morning. Opening the beautiful black velvet box, her hand fluttered to her chest. She stared down at the gorgeous green jewel in its perfect case. "My God, Gareth. Where did you get this?" She held the necklace up to the light. The early sun's rays burst through the large green teardrop. Emerald beams lit the room; the points of light danced across the wall like a herd of happy leprechauns.

"I bought it during our lovely stay with Trish, the shopkeeper extraordinaire of Whitechapel fame. She picked the clothes out, but I thought this would be a nice touch. Green is definitely your color."

Leah stared up at the most handsome face she'd ever seen, and smiled. "It's beautiful."

"You're not going to say that you can't possibly accept it, are you?"

She clutched the necklace to her chest. "Just try and get it back. You'll have to wrench it from my cold, dead hand."

His face filled with an emotion that Leah didn't quite know how to handle...yet. She stared into the brilliant green stone that stood for luck and life, trying to speak the words that she knew he wanted to hear. Giving up, she cleared her throat. "Thank you."

Gareth bent down, kissed her forehead, and walked to the door. "Don't take too long. My sister can make that hand of yours cold and dead before its time, if you have the nerve to keep her waiting."

Leah grinned, as the door closed behind him. Her prayers, which came often these days, lifted through the ceiling and out into the dawn.

She hoped beyond hope that she'd be able to hang on to Gareth Lowery after this strange, dangerous quest came to an end.

*

Leah couldn't help but laugh when Gareth's description of his dearly beloved sister came true. Like a little general, Kathryn led the way through Glastonbury, pointing out all the historical and legendary sights to better educate her group.

Her small voice boomed loud and strong as they walked down the path through Arthurian legend. "Glastonbury is one of the most powerful places on the planet. Prophecies were made here. And Merlin, the ultimate magician, still seems to hover over this place like a UFO."

She kept marching forward, oblivious to her amused students. "This land is one point of a triangle of power that's dedicated to the Archangel. St. Michael's line is the invisible line that links Glastonbury to the circles of Stonehenge and Avebury. Astronomers believe that the energy of God sits on top of the triangle like a beacon on top of a lighthouse, calling the lost souls back home."

Leah stared into Kathryn's excited eyes. "So where's the top of this triangle of power?"

Kathryn pointed up at the earth covered mound. "You're standing on it."

Without waiting for a response, Kathryn turned away and continued her educational talk. "We're on Dod Lane right now. It means Dead Lane in English, and it goes right past the Chalice Well. It's been said that this is the path for the departed. From here, they journey to Avalon—the isle of mystery where the chosen come to rest."

Leah looked down. She wondered if she would see the imprints of the dead who'd made their way to Paradise on this small, unremarkable trail. As they turned the corner, the Chalice Well came into view.

The monument was lovely. There was a small, peaceful garden surrounding it, where someone could take a seat and talk to their Creator. The serenity was magical; soft music floated in the breeze, and the heady scent of roses filled the air. As they entered the garden, Leah noticed the lovely circle of stone in the grass.

Kathryn pointed at it. "That's the sign of Pisces. Gareth thinks that the 'powers that be' picked the best and most holy sign for the garden." She rolled her eyes. "Like he needs another thing to increase the size of his ego."

Gareth punched his sister playfully in the arm. "Be nice. I have the orbs. I can run away at any second."

"I'll shoot you where you stand." Kathryn giggled.

Gareth stuck his tongue out and brushed past her. Taking Leah by the elbow, he led her away from the tiny tyrant to the holy Chalice Well. "People see this place as a gateway to the spirit world. It's believed that here, in the presence of the famous water, the barrier between life and death falls, and people can actually communicate with Heaven."

"It's very beautiful," said Leah. "I suppose this is the place that Yeats spoke about in his poem?"

Gareth smiled. "Well…we think so."

Leah stared down at the wrought iron well cover, as Gareth continued, "See the Pisces design? Those interlocking rings represent the overlapping of worlds—spirit and human." He winked. "The sign is actually referred to as the Vesica Pisces."

"You're just all over the place." Leah laughed. "Surrounding me on all sides."

Gareth's lips broke into a wide grin. "It's like God is trying to tell you something, Leah. After all, I believe it was He who saved the best sign for last."

After the traditional rolling of her eyes, Leah peered down at the water racing from the fountain head carved in the shape of a lion. Leah looked over her shoulder at Gareth. "Leo?"

He nodded. "Look at the bowls."

Leah leaned over further. Upon closer inspection, she saw that the water leaving the mouth of the lion spilled into a series of stepped bowls. She could barely make out the signs of the zodiac that were carved into each stone, but they were most definitely there. Her voice came out as a whisper, paying respect to what might have gone on in this sacred spot so long ago, "The water's red."

"Geologists have done studies on the water that flows here," replied Gareth. "It's highly magnetic—that's what they say causes the orange-red hue. Of course, most people don't accept the scientific analysis. They prefer to believe that when the Holy Grail was buried beneath the Well by Joseph of Arimathea, the water pouring from this spout ran with the blood, life, and power of Jesus."

"Much nicer explanation." She smiled. "All that scientific garbage gets a little boring."

Gareth's eyebrows reached high up his forehead, like downhill skiers readying themselves to attempt the treacherous slalom. "What happened to the cynical skeptic I've grown to know and love?"

"Still not saying I buy it all." She clarified. "I just think it's a more pleasant explanation."

Kathryn's voice broke through their peaceful moment. "For goodness' sake, Gareth, come on! We can't get in that way."

Leah stifled her giggle when she stared at Kathryn's agitated face.

"See?" Gareth shook his head. "I'm telling you. We're being led into the most religious place on the planet by a Nazi."

"I heard that!" Kathryn's voice disturbed the peace of the exquisite garden once again.

Emmanuel let out a roar of laughter. The young man hung back, joining Gareth and Leah as they all marched behind their petite leader. "You know, Leah, the most intriguing thing about Tor Hill is that many locals have reported seeing balls of colored lights—orbs, if you will—spiraling around the hill at night. People believe that knights or angels are responsible for their appearance." His voice floated in the air like a dove of peace. "This place holds more power than we can possibly imagine."

Emmanuel patted Leah's shoulder and rushed off to Kathryn's side, looking a bit worried that his true love might get angrier if they didn't speed up.

"You know which stories I'm most fond of?" Gareth's eyes twinkled.

Leah waited, as his arm slipped around her waist and they began their ascent up the hillside.

"The romantic ones," he said. "Arthur saving Guinevere from the clutches of the horrible King Melwas who reigned over Glastonbury. The love of poor Tristan and Isolde, who met on these very shores and found their soul mate in each other's eyes. That's good stuff."

"Yak, yak, yak." Kathryn doubled back and ripped Leah from Gareth's grip. "Woo the lady on your own time, sparky. We've got tracks to make."

Leah let out a laugh, as Gareth and Emmanuel walked behind the women, relegated to the back of the line.

Gareth let out a deep sigh. "This is exactly why I've never married, you know. My darling sister scared me off women years ago."

Kathryn marched Leah up the unique terraces that wound around the sides of Tor Hill. Now eroded, Leah could still see that at one time the terraces must've formed a path—an ancient avenue for the procession that journeyed to St. Michael's church.

The lone tower loomed over the brilliant, green landscape. Kathryn reached out and lovingly pressed her hand against the stone of the reverent structure. "The last tower of the church built for the Archangel Michael. He's regarded as the Angel of Light, you know? He was the revealer of mysteries and the guide who would bring people safely home. Seems fitting that the entrance is here."

"And, see over there?" Kathryn turned and pointed toward a strange landmark that took up at least ten miles of the beautiful landscape. "Those are the twelve zodiac rings. Each sign appears in the same order as they do in the sky. The rings are formed by hills and outlined by rivers and roads to separate one from the next. There are some who believe the rings represent Arthur and the Knights seated at the Round Table, but I know better." She smiled wide, like a child with a secret. "It's the zodiac—the map to the most powerful place in the world."

Leah shuddered at her absolute faith.

The excited woman continued, "Do you see what's beside the rings there? That hill is over five miles long and is believed to be the great watchdog that oversees the rings, guarding them from any evil that tries to get inside."

"What's that clump in the center of the circles?" Leah stared at the small, dark forest inside the rings.

"That's the center of the zodiac that represents the Pole Star; the point that remains still as the heavenly wheels spin around it. It's like a sanctuary; people can sit in the center and feel the power of the zodiac circling them, but be safe inside its core."

Leah felt the chill race down her spine as she stared at the dark forest. It seemed completely out of place inside the clean lines of the symmetrical rings, like a hiding place for something evil. She moved her gaze to the strangely-shaped hill and her imagination sprang to life. Leah watched as the so-called, protector of the gathering, transformed into a snarling dog before her eyes. Turning its head, it aimed its ugly fangs in her direction, and growled—warning her to stay away from his protected charges.

Kathryn's knuckles rapped on the tower door, and twelve hollow echoes reverberated in Leah's ears. The sound reminded her of drumbeats, keeping time with her footsteps as she walked toward the gallows. Swallowing her fear, Leah followed Kathryn through the door, and began her descent into the depths of Tor Hill.

CHAPTER TWENTY-FIVE

Further and further they went, traveling slowly into the hollow belly of dirt and rock.

Leah was amazed that the air wasn't filled with the scent of mildew after being closed up for centuries. Instead, fresh oxygen permeated the space, making it seem as if there were wide open windows buried deep underground that were continuously filtering in the fresh air. It was… peaceful, until the familiar voice rang out in her ears.

"Welcome, Madame Librarian."

Leah turned quickly and came face to face with Donovan Barker's midnight eyes. He seemed absolutely exhilarated to see her again. In fact, the strange light of the cave seemed to make every inch of his face and body pulsate with joy.

"Did you miss me?" He winked.

Leah turned on the sarcasm switch inside her. "Almost as much as I miss the gallbladder attack I had when I was a kid."

He laughed; a long drawn out sound that fell somewhere between a snarl and a scream. "I do love your wit. You certainly are one of a kind, Leah." He bowed. "May I call you Leah?"

"That depends," she answered in a threatening voice. "What should I call you?"

Donovan offered a slightly evil smile. "Yes…" His voice seemed to hiss through his lips. "You're one of a kind."

"I wish I could say the same." She stared into the blue light beaming from the depths of his eyes. "But you remind me of someone."

Donovan took a step closer to her, and lowered his voice. "Believe me, Leah. I am like no one whose ever come before."

"I wouldn't bet on that if I were you," she shot back. Choosing to ignore him, Leah stared over his shoulder at the torches burning on the wall. "Did you light these?" she asked, counting the thirteen flames.

Donovan shook his head.

"No," Kathryn spoke. "When Emmanuel and I discovered this place they were already lit. We stayed here at night waiting for someone to show up. We wondered if there was someone in charge of taking care of this place."

"And…no one?" Confusion filled Leah's brain.

"Not a soul." Donovan smiled.

Leah kept her gaze firmly set on Kathryn. "Doesn't it seem strange to you that a secret of this magnitude would lay here virtually unprotected?"

Gareth walked up beside her. "People want the legend to be true, Leah. They don't want to see it because, if it failed to open, their hope would be lost forever. Sometimes, to save a person's faith, the smart thing to do is walk away."

"You should heed your own advice," she snapped.

Donovan cut in. "Not necessary." He smiled. "Gareth already knows it'll open."

Leah felt an overwhelming fear at the determination staring back at her from the eager black eyes.

Donovan held out his hand toward the opening, ushering Gareth and Leah through a large open door. "After you," he said in a sticky-sweet voice.

Gareth practically ran, as Leah followed slowly behind him, trying to delay the monumental event for as long as possible. She gasped as she entered the round room. Separate panels of rock had been fitted like picture frames, side by side, into the large chamber walls. The signs of the zodiac each sat in their own frame, carved into the rock by a master's hand.

Leah stopped before the regal lion. His mighty paw was raised in the air as if he were swearing an eternal oath to the Almighty—to protect and preserve the secret. Leah felt respect flow through her veins as she thought of Patience and Fortitude, protecting the steps of her own beloved sanctuary in the City far away.

When she glanced at the carved effigies of the bull and the ram encased in stone, she waited for the bad feelings to surface. But nothing did. It was as if, with her belief, had come the ability to understand and not be afraid.

Her own sign had its deadly tail held high, as if waving welcome to the new visitors, and the twins of Gemini stood stock still; their cherubic rock faces offered sanctuary. Walking past the twelve signs, Leah circled the outer wall of the chamber, admiring the amazing craftsmanship as if she were touring the Louvre.

Waves of excitement rippled in Kathryn's voice. "Well…this is it. Before us stand the gates of Heaven."

Leah felt the cold breath on her neck. She jumped when Donovan whispered in her ear, "Just think. Without you, none of this would even have been possible."

Standing still as a statue, Leah watched in silence as Emmanuel and

Gareth retrieved the blinking orbs from the knapsack. Gareth walked up to the mighty Taurus and placed the blinking orb into the hole that someone had carved out between his massive horns. When the orb snapped into place, a burst of green fire illuminated the panel. Right before their eyes, the bull came to life in the rock face. Lifting his head, he sent a snort toward the heavens.

Emmanuel plugged in the second orb between the joined hands of the Gemini twins. Their heads flew into the air, and a yellow beam as bright as the sun warmed the cave. The sign of youth and vitality began to dance. Arms intertwined, the twins giggled with the spirit and hope of the children they represented.

Leah moved her gaze from the boisterous girls when a bright silver flame suddenly emptied into the chamber. The crab of Cancer glowed like moonstone, and a nurturing feeling descended over the group.

Leo's mane erupted into golden flames, as he sat back on his haunches and issued a deafening roar, banishing evil from his sight. The charismatic sign began to prance inside his panel. His head was held high in the air, like the King's chosen Knight that he most assuredly was.

Kathryn retrieved the glowing pink orb and placed it on Libra's scales. The panel turned to opal, and the refined picture of justice came to life, showering the souls in the chamber with her elegance.

The men crossed over to Scorpio and placed the topaz orb on top of his dangerous tail. The venomous creature sprang to life and walked slowly inside his panel of rock. The hypnotic hum emanating from the orb of Scorpius shouted out to the people who held mystery in their hearts, demanding them to rise up and march behind him into the world of magic.

Leah felt her heart quicken, feeling the passion for life that Scorpios possessed in spades.

Gareth walked over to her and gave her the bright, blue orb that perfectly matched her eyes. Leah held it steady in the palm of her hand, and felt the controlled order that came with the purity of knowledge. Crossing the room to the tall figure of Virgo, Leah placed the orb in the cradle of rock; an amazing azure flame flew from the virgin's robe.

The electricity was so powerful that the human inhabitants of the chamber gasped for air. They watched Sagittarius, the archer, draw back his bow and send a flaming purple arrow into the room. Beside him erupted the garnet flame that represented the tireless workers of Capricorn. Aquarius sprang to life and produced a beautiful amethyst rainbow into the sky, calling out to the creative people that the sign defined. The ram awakened and sent his shower of red sparks into the cave. And, last but not least, Aries awoke to summon the leaders of the world.

A blast of cold air suddenly rushed into the chamber, and twelve of the thirteen torches dimmed. The signs came to an abrupt standstill. Everything—human and supernatural, alike—ceased their movements when Pisces, the final sign, crested the waves inside his panel and called out to the romantics of the world.

The orbs continued to hum, but the signs stopped their celebrations and turned to stare at the final wall. It was as if they were waiting with bated breath for the big finale. Leah joined with them to gaze at the masterful representations of the zodiac signs that'd been carved around a large star. She gazed at the round globe that jutted out from the center of the work of art, and wondered if there was still time to run.

She felt the frigid draft on her back. She could feel Donovan standing directly behind her; his excited breaths sounded like the hiss of a serpent in her ear. A scream caught in her throat when Gareth walked slowly toward the wall and stared at the handprints carved in the rock beneath the star. Taking a deep breath, he pressed his palms into the strangely shaped prints, throwing his weight against the immovable stone.

Leah felt the air in her lungs release when warmth returned to the room. The brilliant colors of the orbs began to fade with Gareth's attempt, and twelve of the thirteen torches were suddenly extinguished. The topaz pinchers of the scorpion, the golden eyes of the triumphant lion, and the deep blue robes of the Virgin, all began to dull. Leah watched as a light film of red dust covered them, transforming them back into the inanimate stone pictures. The orbs turned to rock as well, and the lights blinked no more.

Turning around, Leah stared at Donovan. The bright blue flames pulsed brighter in his angry black eyes.

He reached out quickly and grabbed her wrist, squeezing it like a vise. "What did you do?" he snarled. "*You* did this. I know you did."

Leah felt the grin on her face. "I guess it just wasn't meant to be."

"Bitch," he hissed. "You know something."

"A hell of a lot more than you do," she replied smugly.

Letting go of her wrist, Donovan grabbed her by the shoulders and began to shake her. Her leather coat fell open, and her assailant jumped back as if he'd been struck by a bolt of lightning. She followed his gaze and stared at the sparkling emerald around her neck.

Donovan looked like he'd seen a ghost. "Where…? How…?" He returned his gaze to her face, and Leah's heart stopped. She'd never seen such a look of pure hatred in all her life.

"He was right." Donovan took a step back. "I did underestimate you. But this isn't over."

"Who's *he*?"

Without a word, Donovan turned and raced from the cave.

Gareth's angry voice brought Leah to her senses and she quickly turned back to the other members of the group.

"Where's Donovan going? What the hell is going on?" Gareth dismissed his strange friend and stared up at the immovable wall. "Nothing happened!"

Kathryn raced to this side and placed her hands in the carved prints, pushing against the door with all her strength. "I don't understand," she whispered.

All Leah wanted to do was run, but she was overpowered by the love flowing through her veins. She struggled between her heart and her mind; the latter was screaming at her to keep her mouth shut.

Focusing on the round object protruding from the mural of rock, Leah stepped forward. Reaching up with a trembling hand, she opened the ball and peered into the dark hole. "It's empty."

"What is *that*?" Gareth looked up. "What could possibly go into that one?"

Leah stared at the carved handprints that rested on either side of the star. She placed her hand over one, feeling a slight beat coming from deep inside the stone. One hand print was large, and looked like a man's. The other was dainty in size, expressly made for a woman with small, delicate fingers…like Kathryn's. Two for everything on this journey, Leah thought to herself.

She turned and faced Gareth. Her heart broke at the sight of the discouraged soul. All he'd fought for, all he'd believed since childhood, seemed to be going up in smoke. The eyes she truly loved were filled with despair, and the faith visibly began leaking from his soul. This man had strived to find the Kingdom of Heaven to offer it to a world that, Leah knew, simply wouldn't care. Now he was left only with a supernatural image of jumping rams and roaring lions. A beautiful light show, certainly, but without the grand finale that he and his parents had paid so dearly to see.

Leah buried the fear and doubt inside her soul. Her choice was simple—she loved him. The man had brought her to life, and her job was to stand beside him and do everything within her power to make his dreams a reality. This was Leah's vow before *her* Creator, and she took the leap of faith.

Gazing over at the thirteenth torch, she watched the eerie blue flame bounce up and down, like laughter rattling in the Devil's throat. She checked to make sure that Donovan was truly gone before she opened her mouth. "There's another one," she whispered.

Gareth's head shot up. "What did you say?"

Kathryn rushed from Emmanuel's side. "What was that?"

"One and twelve."

"Come again?" Kathryn pushed.

Leah let out a deep sigh and sat down. Gareth knelt beside her, and Kathryn joined them on the floor. A feeling of dread fell over Leah like a shroud.

Emmanuel leaned against the wall and gave her a solemn stare. Leah's stomach churned as she read his strange gaze. He looked like he knew she was about to relinquish everything she believed in for two obsessed people. Breaking their gaze, Emmanuel closed his eyes and moved his lips in silent prayer.

Leah hoped with everything she had that his prayer would be strong enough to save her soul. "One and twelve is thirteen. That's what you keep forgetting," she said. "Crowley used the number thirteen in all his clues. Jesus and his apostles made thirteen, not one and twelve. Arthur and his knights total thirteen, not one and twelve. There were thirteen angels—not St. Michael and twelve others. They aren't separate entities… they're groups. The *team* was always thirteen."

"But there are only twelve zodiac signs," said Gareth.

Leah shook her head; her voice caught in her throat. "No. There are thirteen."

Kathryn glanced over at her brother's confused face, and turned back to Leah. "You mean the sun?"

"No." She swallowed. "There are thirteen signs. The thirteenth comes between Scorpio and Sagittarius in the constellations. It was called Ophiuchus by the ancients—the bearer of the serpent."

"That's impossible," Gareth said, clenching his fists at his sides. "My father was an astronomer. He never mentioned this…thirteenth sign."

Leah stopped his tirade before it could begin. "Your buddy Ptolemy discovered Ophiuchus. He found it in the Milky Way between the scorpion and the archer, but it was erased from his writings for acceptance by the Vatican. By then the number thirteen represented evil, like I told you back at the hotel, so the constellation was eliminated."

She felt the tears run down her cheeks. "Gareth, the zodiac your father worked with was the tropical zodiac—the one we use today. The thirteenth sign only appeared in the sidereal zodiac, which Hindu and Western astrologers used based on Ptolemy's works. Probably another reason why Christianity wiped out any reference to it. At that time, Hinduism was seen as a pagan religion."

Leah's voice was robotic. She felt as if she was supplying her avid listeners with the information necessary to commit suicide. "It's one of the brightest stars in the galaxy. Different religions believe that Ophiuchus was the actual Star of Bethlehem. It was so bright that it guided three wise men to a stable to meet their King."

"My God," Gareth stammered. "It's…the true star of Heaven…like in the carving?"

Leah shook her head, as the tears cascaded down her cheeks. "There are two sides to every story, remember? Ophiuchus is a serpent-bearing god who was, and still remains today, the most highly recognized image of the Devil."

Her tears turned into a waterfall of pain. "The missing orb will be that powerful, Gareth. It most likely represents Heaven *and* Hell—the best and the worst of the whole damn thing." Leah took deep breaths, trying to steady herself as the pain and fear ate away at her heart.

"But where would it be?" Kathryn thought out loud.

"If you needed to hide the master key that would open the Kingdom of Heaven—who would you give it to?" Leah sighed. "Where would you possibly hide the most sought after treasure in the Christian world…in *all* the world?"

Gareth whispered in the dry, stale air, "To get to Heaven—"

"You've got to go through Hell." Leah finished.

Kathryn continued to stare back and forth between them; her face was a mask of confusion. "What are you two talking about?"

Leah shivered. The blue torch pulsated on the wall and produced goose bumps on her now sweat-soaked flesh. "Crowley was in charge of hiding the final orb because he was, for the purposes of his era, the Devil. He would've put the orb of ultimate power in the only safe place he could think of."

"The folds of his robe?" Kathryn's voice was weak with exhaustion.

"Close," Leah whispered. "Crowley's been leading us all through his twisted little game and screaming the answer the whole time. The only place you wouldn't find Heaven is *in* Hell." She sucked in a breath of stale air. "I think that Crowley hid the orb in his own home; the place where he practiced rituals and summoned demons from their graves. His place of worship…on the shores of Loch Ness."

The light of hope sprang back into Kathryn's eyes. "Boleskine House.

I've read about it. You're right!" She vaulted her small body into Leah's arms.

Gareth grabbed for his sister. "Kathryn, stop. Give her some air."

Leah stood up and ran from the chamber. As she passed by the zodiac carvings, she noticed their accusatory glares. It was as if they were telling her she'd made the wrong choice. She'd sold them out.

Guilt clogged her throat, as she tore up the staircase and out the tower door that'd once belonged to an Archangel. Her long legs took her further and further away from Gareth's frantic pursuit. Leah could almost make out the figures of King Arthur and his mystical knights glaring at her. And she found herself praying for the all-powerful Merlin to appear and shoot a bolt of lightning through her heart—take her out before the real suffering could begin.

CHAPTER TWENTY-SIX

As the warm, salty tears fell from her eyes, Leah thought about the Chalice Well. It was a pretty story. But after what she'd just witnessed, Leah was more than willing to believe that the endless stream of water came from the tears shed by the ones who'd lost their loves, lives, and innocence at the hands of the Devil.

There are two sides—always two. Perhaps that room hidden far below an Archangel's tower could be thought of as a passage back to peace. But, to Leah, as she'd watched the signs of the zodiac come to life inside their cages of rock, she'd felt only grief. She knew that once the gates opened, the only person who'd ever really mattered to her would be lost. The gate was simply an exit from a life that she wasn't ready to leave—a life that was just beginning to get interesting.

The door to her small bedroom flew open, like the Angel of Death had just pulled her name from his hat and was in a hurry to get the job done.

A blast of cold air blew Gareth's wavy blond hair across his forehead, forming a golden shroud that framed his worried face and blocked out his beautiful eyes. He raced into the room like the proverbial knight, and knelt on the floor beside her. "Are you okay?"

"Am I *okay*?" Leah's voice crackled with anger. "Was I the only one in that room back there?"

"What?" He looked confused. "It was amazing."

"I should know by now to trust my instincts." Leah cursed loudly, and pushed against his broad chest. Marching to the small window, she turned back to him. "You *are* crazy. I knew it the first time I met you."

Gareth's eyes grew wide. "What are you *talking* about? We found it. We actually found it. Everything's true. You should be…ecstatic!"

"Ecstatic?" Leah glared at him. "The power in that room was suffocating."

He reached out for the hand she refused to give. "Of course, it was. The power of God was in that room."

Leah shook her head furiously. "You *still* don't get it!" Anger fused with her pain, forming a huge ball of hopelessness that weighed heavily on her chest. She felt like her heart was mounted on the bow of the Titanic, waiting for the iceberg to slice it in half. "The Devil is *here*!"

"For crissake sake, Leah. Crowley's dead."

"Screw Aleister Crowley," she shouted. "I'm talking about the real deal. Wake up!"

Gareth put his head in his hands, and let out an exasperated sigh. "I don't understand you."

She stomped her feet on the floor like an angry child. "Gareth, I *told* you what Lucifer said to me in the Upper Room."

"You were just caught up in the moment, Leah. It was a powerful thing you went through. Your whole belief system was upended. Remember, you were the one who said that the mind sees what it wants to see."

"Do not dismiss me, Gareth!" she screamed. "Not when I finally understand what you've been telling me this whole time. *You* were right. I didn't imagine it. The Devil said he'd see me again. And he did! He was in that cave with us."

Gareth shook his head. "Leah, we were standing at the gates of Heaven. That's the last place the Devil would be."

A frustrated scream exploded from her throat. "Are you *nuts*? Think, Gareth! The gates that lead to Heaven and the gates that lead to Hell are the same gates! *It just depends which side you're standing on when you walk through them!*"

Gareth's head snapped up.

She stared into the desperate eyes, knowing her statement had hit its mark. "You said it yourself. The worst case scenario *is* the right one. God's people let Him down. Lucifer was right, and he's used the time to prove that humanity would be on *his* side when those gates re-opened. He was trying to re-write the Second Coming." She pleaded with him to understand. "He wanted a different ending, Gareth. And if you open that thing, he'll get it!"

"Jesus, Leah," he groaned.

She clenched her fists, determined to beat the truth into him if she had to. "Only one percent of the entire population could even *tell* you what the Ten Commandments are, let alone live by them. People are shedding their neighbor's blood; they're fighting over dirt. You think you'll usher peace into the world by giving them this discovery? You won't. Not a chance." She shook her head violently. "In less than twenty-four hours after opening that gate every faction of every religious group will be here—bearing arms—claiming that *they* are the chosen ones. Your discovery will only lead to more killing—*more* bloodshed. And, trust me, Lucifer will be right there. He'll cross over the threshold into Heaven, laughing his ass off all the way."

Gareth's voice was loud and strong, as if he was attempting to bury her words underneath the flame of faith that burned inside him. "You're being cynical, Leah. You've been a non-believer most of your life. You just didn't grasp the power of it all and it scares you. Which is *normal*. There are millions of good, decent people out there."

"They're outnumbered!" Leah slapped her open palm against her forehead. "There are reasons why man has free will and why God chose to *hide* the keys to Heaven. *You* don't possess the answers to these mysteries. Do you know why? Because *you're* not God!"

"I don't want to be," Gareth fired back. He threw himself down on the foot of the bed. "If you felt this way then…*why*? Why did you say anything back there about the thirteenth orb? Why tell me at all? We would've eventually just given up and walked away."

Leah's shoulders slumped. Closing her eyes, she slammed shut the card catalogue in her mind. There were no answers there. This was uncharted territory, and no heavenly map or ancient text could guide her. Leaning against the window, she stared into the stunning eyes. "I watched you in that room, Gareth. The look of defeat when it didn't open was so immense that I thought it would kill you. I actually could see the faith drain from your soul—like somehow God had let you down. I had to tell you."

"Clearing your conscious?" His voice broke with sadness.

Leah took a deep breath, feeling like the fat lady right before she blew out that last fateful note. "I would go head to head with anyone." An image of Donovan Barker flashed in her mind. "Even the Devil…if it meant I could save you."

He raised his head; a look of pure love shone in his eyes. Love and… pain.

Leah hesitated. She'd dipped her toe into the freezing waters of the unknown and now it was time to take the final plunge. "I've used sarcasm all my life to keep people away. I've hid in the shadows of my stacks of books for years. The day you unearthed that metal book from the cornerstone of my library, you dug me up with it. I can't thank you enough for that." Her voice was soft and genuine. "I need you to know that whatever you decide to do—for the first time in my life—I am completely and unimaginably impressed."

*

Gareth felt like he'd been transported to Vegas, as the room began to spin with the power of her words. He'd gone so far and given up so much to continue his journey. He knew there was a part of him that just couldn't stop and walk away.

Guilt and shame for using Leah to fulfill his destiny weighed heavily on his shoulders, as almost everything he'd ever wanted stood before him in the fading twilight. Was she his olive branch? If he took her hand would he be saved? He would certainly know heaven in her arms, but would it be enough?

The pressure was too great. Gareth stood up and walked slowly to the door. Turning the knob, he stepped into the hall, and looked back at the woman of his dreams. "I can't live with regrets, Leah. I have to know."

Closing the door behind him, he disappeared into the dimly-lit passage, unable to let go of his quest.

*

Gareth could barely feel the stairs beneath his feet, as he struggled to take the next step away from her. Spotting the familiar face, he crossed the floor and sat down beside his silent sister, who was all alone at the small table by the roaring fireplace. "Have you seen Donovan?"

Kathryn shook her head. "His room was cleaned out."

Gareth sighed. "I really wish I knew what the hell was going on. My whole world is upside down. Donovan's disappeared. Leah's…" He hung his head.

"Is she okay?" Guilt swam in Kathryn's eyes.

Gareth shook his head. "But better than me, I think. She knows exactly what the right road is. No doubts. No regrets."

"Will she go to Crowley's house?"

"Yes." He choked on his tears. "For me."

Kathryn's voice was filled with pain. "Emmanuel's angry too. He wants us to stop. I think he agrees with Leah. He says we've gone far enough and we've proven what we needed to prove. He said that we don't see the shadows. He thinks we have our eyes closed, Gareth—that we're only seeing what we want to see—and it's time to move on."

"Is that what you want?" he asked.

"No," Kathryn replied. "I want to solve it. I want that last piece of the puzzle."

"And, then?"

She shrugged. "I haven't thought that far ahead. Funny, isn't it? I guess in the back of my mind I never thought we'd get far enough to have to make this decision."

Gareth studied the old water rings imbedded in the antique wood. The round table was a relic that probably had played host to many conversations over the decades. Perhaps even Steiner and Yeats had sat and discussed the Divine Truth right here in this spot, sharing the mysteries of the zodiac map.

"Do you love her?"

Without hesitation, Gareth nodded.

"Then you owe her the truth," Kathryn stated. "After all, you've spent your entire life searching, and if anyone can offer Heaven to you on a silver platter, it's her."

"Tomorrow we're going to the Devil's house," he said.

"So tonight stay as far away from him as you can get." She patted his hand. "Choose your own path tonight."

"I have to finish this," said Gareth sadly. "But…I'm using her."

"Than let her choose her path, too. You never know, it just may turn out to be the same one as yours."

*

The click of the lock echoed in the small room.

Leah hadn't moved; she still stood by the window staring out into the night. The moonlight lit her beautiful face.

Gareth closed the creaking door and leaned against it. He stared at her stoic figure standing in the sliver of light from the winter moon. "When I left the library in France," he spoke softly. "I checked into a small bed and breakfast like this one. I sat in my room alone with the lights off and watched the orbs blink on and off. I was so excited and so scared all at the same time. I knew that I had come halfway, but I had no idea where to go next." He kept his gaze locked on her stunning face. "The humming from the orbs got louder, and I realized that I recognized the tune. *Rock of Ages*. Do you know it?"

Leah turned to face him, but remained silent.

"Anyway," he continued, "I got out my laptop. After a little help from those lovely search engines you're so fond of, I found out that the writer of that song was a man by the name of Hastings. He was the grandfather of Thomas Hastings, of Hastings and Carrère—the architects that Andrew Carnegie hired to build your library."

Leah remained a quiet shadow in the corner.

"I was so excited." he smiled. "Another library—*the* library. I knew I was right but, where to look? I went to sleep and, I swear to you, that night I walked through the gates of Heaven. I saw one amazing room after the other." His voice was reverent. "But it wasn't the Archangel Michael guiding me that night. My escort had hair the color of a summer sunset, and eyes as blue as the ocean. I could've stayed locked in those eyes forever, drifting on those glorious waves for eternity."

He took a deep breath. "That's the first time I saw you. You held my hand, and it was the most overwhelming feeling of love that I've ever had in my entire life." Strength. Truth…beamed from his eyes. "No matter what happens, I needed you to know that."

Gareth's breath caught in his throat when Leah finally moved. Like a vision, she walked across the floor. Wrapping her arms around his waist, she rested her head against his chest. He was afraid to move—scared that the silent phantom would disappear and take her warmth and protection away forever.

Leaning down slowly, he captured the velvet lips with his own. A jolt of electricity shot through his body. It was as if her touch awakened his soul, letting him know that he'd finally found the other half he'd been searching for all his life. "What about tomorrow?" he whispered.

"Tomorrow we go to Hell," she replied.

Gareth buried his fear. Taking her in his arms, he carried her to the bed, choosing to explore Heaven first.

CHAPTER TWENTY-SEVEN

Donovan paced back and forth inside the cave, screaming at the inanimate signs. Shaking his fists at the silent panels, he slammed his body against the frozen scorpion.

He stared at the horrible sign that stood for the one who had brutalized his plans. Her! It was all her fault! Leah Tallent had come into his world and ruined everything. Destroyed everything he'd fought so hard to achieve.

Donovan could feel the ultimate power leaking from his soul. He couldn't breathe. Tears of frustration filled his eyes and choked the oxygen from his lungs. He'd been the chosen one. Him! Donovan Barker! The one and only choice of the Beast who needed a human to open the gates and let him return home. Now…just like that…the dream was over. Killed by a librarian. A non-believer, no less. It was a hypocrisy!

Exhausted, Donovan slid down the wall and landed on the stone cold floor. The door to Paradise stood solid in front of him, as if mocking his failure.

"I hate you," he said, hoping beyond hope that the beloved beings on the other side could hear his words.

Donovan tried to ignore the annoying beep coming from the Blackberry. What was there to say? His brother had been right; Donovan had completely underestimated the team of Tallent and Lowery, and he would now pay the ultimate price. He wondered what method of death his evil brother would choose for him. It wouldn't really matter, of course. Whatever his evil sibling devised, Donovan just hoped the end would come fast…and soon.

Sighing, he removed the Blackberry from his pocket, ready to face the music. Before he could punch in the sentence that would get him killed, text appeared on the screen.

There's another orb. It's not over.

A small ray of hope began to beat inside Donovan's soul.

What?

Leah Tallent is going to find it tomorrow.

The evil darkness began to seep once again into his soul, filling him with a power that could only be described as perfection. Donovan punched in his next line.

Where is it?

It doesn't matter. You stay there! Don't follow them.

You'll just screw it up again.

Donovan's rage grew, but now was not the time to voice it. If Leah Tallent solved the puzzle, his brother would be the one cast into the pit of Hell—while Donovan reigned over Heaven. He sent his reply.

I'll be here when they get back.

You better be.

Feeling the slight dread in his soul, Donovan suddenly thought of something.

How do you know what Leah Tallent is doing?

The smiley face returned to the screen.

I know everything about Leah Tallent. I'm her future.

She has no future. She'll die in this cave!

Maybe... Do you have the necklace?

Donovan hesitated.

I need that emerald!

Slowly, Donovan pushed down on the power button, disconnecting from his all-knowing brother. Leaning back against the cold stone, Donovan felt the fire warm his soul. He gazed at the lone torch shining its blue light into the room, and illuminating the entrance to Heaven.

He'd been right, Donovan thought. This wasn't over. Not by a long shot.

CHAPTER TWENTY-EIGHT

"When I look back on my life, I will regard my decision this morning as the worst I've ever made." Gareth wrapped his arms around her. "We never should've gotten out of bed."

"Amen to that." Leah clung to his warm body as the horrendous winds whistled over the murky waters of Loch Ness.

Gareth shuddered when he stared out at the large jagged rocks jutting from the frightening lake. "Do you think that thing is really in there?"

Leah giggled. "One monster at a time, please."

Unable to force the SUV any further up the ice-covered mountain, they'd gotten out and walked up the stone driveway. The bitter wind pummeled their backs, forcing them forward, pushing their bodies through the tall, brittle grass that felt like sharp needles.

Leah winced. Like a rusty razorblade scraping across her skin, she could feel the warm drops of blood appear on her legs when the frozen spikes sliced through her pant leg. It was a true blessing to reach the front door of the unassuming white house with beige shutters.

Gareth turned the knob, and they entered the abandoned homestead.

He slammed the door behind them, banishing the high winds of Scotland that were just about ready to release a barrage of snow and ice.

Leah tried to stop trembling. Rubbing her hands together, she forced the circulation to return.

They walked through the rooms, hand in hand, checking every open door that led to yet another empty space.

Leah tried to be serious, but the smile felt like it'd been pasted on her face with Krazy glue. She knew she should fear the evil house, but all she could think of was the amazing night she'd spent in Gareth's arms. The symphony that they'd created was breathtaking. Leah's body still felt like a tuning fork, remembering the breathless crescendo as their bodies came together in the ultimate climax.

Staring up at him, she focused on Gareth's glazed stare. Perhaps he, too, was lost in the same wonderful memory. Watching the incredibly handsome man, Leah tried to hush the woman who screamed inside her, begging for more. Clearing her head, Leah tried to focus on the danger that should be lurking all around her, but the home of the wickedest man who ever lived was completely silent.

"There's nothing here." Her voice echoed in the vast empty space. It wasn't only the lack of furnishings—the house, itself, was missing the feeling of evil that should've been buried inside it for the last hundred years.

Down into the cavernous cellar, she walked by his side, but they were met only with the rodents who'd braved the Devil's home to get out of the harsh winter winds.

When they went back up to the first floor, they walked through the musty kitchen and stared out the large bay window overlooking the famous Loch three hundred feet below.

Gareth's strong hands encircled her waist. "I don't get it," he muttered in her ear.

Leah shrugged. "This place is over forty-seven acres. Could be anywhere, I suppose."

A chill crawled up her spine, as Leah stared out at the wooden fence circling the property. Just beyond it, another barrier of barbed wire was visible, ready to slice anyone to ribbons who tried to trespass on Satan's property. The dark gray clouds obliterated the sun, and the waters of Loch Ness turned black as pitch.

"I really hope he didn't hide it in there," Gareth remarked. "There's no way I'm swimming in that."

Leah turned around in his arms to face him. "What now?"

"Well—." Gareth raised an eyebrow; a look of pure lust beamed from his emerald eyes.

She grinned. "Not the most romantic place."

"Could be." He winked.

Scanning the area, Leah shivered, wondering if the tiny rosebuds on the faded wallpaper acted as eyes for the damned. "I'll pass."

Gareth laughed, and tapped her on the forehead. "Okay, Miss Smarty-Pants. What do you know?"

"There's really not much to know." She sighed. "Crowley bought this house in 1899, and stayed here on and off until 1913. He told his followers that he was working on a ceremony that would bring forth an army to do his bidding."

"And?"

Leah shrugged. "Never happened. Crowley admitted that the ceremony was never completed, but that demonic entities were released during his attempt and had become trapped inside the house."

"Sounds like a silly ghost story," Gareth snorted.

"Could've been." She agreed. "When Crowley left this consecrated ground, he took up the Ouija board. He started telling his followers about the conversations he was having with the Holy Guardian Angel. Knowing what we know now, I think the job was simply getting to him." She smiled. "He loved publicity, and I think keeping all this a secret was starting to get boring. I'm sure he didn't want to live day in and day out with the orb; it would be a constant reminder of what he knew he could never reveal."

"You still think the orb's in here?" asked Gareth.

"Nowhere else makes sense."

Walking around the small kitchen, Leah stared into the adjoining, empty rooms. At the far north end of the house, she spotted a small door with a tiny window that looked out across the rocky terrain of the backyard. Moving closer, she felt the eerie pressure begin deep inside her body. Her hands tingled as she reached out and twisted the knob.

The wind barreled in, knocking her back into Gareth's sturdy frame. Lowering her head, she stepped out on to the stone terrace.

Gareth's boots scratched against the strange substance that covered the ground. He screamed, trying to be heard above the howling winds, "There must be a caretaker. Looks like someone's put salt down to break up the ice."

Leah bent down and grabbed a handful of the strange gravel. Her stomach clenched. The fine, powdery sand flowed through her fingers like the soft grains in an hourglass. She shook her head; the strong wind blew her curls around her face. "This was Crowley's starting point. From here, he would lead his followers to the ceremony.

"I read about this." She raised her voice above the thundering winds. "The gravel is actually sand. Crowley's procession was supposed to be symbolic, like Mary and Joseph crossing the desert to the Holy Land to bring about the birth of the King."

She raised her head and stared through the sudden blinding snow.

"See that?"

Gareth squinted. "Garage?"

"Cottage...Crowley's temple. That's where he tried to bring about the birth of *his* king."

Leah forced her legs to move. She stared at the hard, white snowflakes that looked like miniature ghosts raining down on her from above. Unlike the billowy snow of the perfect English evening, the flakes on this mountain were like shards of ice. They sliced at her cheeks like finely-honed knives as she made her way to the small, white cottage.

Gareth reached out for the knob and stepped over the threshold of the small house.

A black sign hung from the side of the decrepit building. Leah pointed up at it. "He called it, *The Gate*." Sending up a prayer to her newfound friend, Leah hoped that whatever was born here a hundred years ago had already left home.

*

Calm. Quiet. Still. Every adjective for peace perfectly described the room they were standing in, yet the bare walls felt like they were alive with evil.

Leah held her breath as she surveyed the small area. Not a stitch of fabric, not a leg of furniture, and the cabinets were bare. But the space felt almost like it was holding its breath, waiting for the right moment to reveal the horrors that were lurking inside.

The room was freezing, like they'd stepped into a basement morgue. *But the bodies are invisible here*, Leah thought. *And...very much alive.* She felt like the undead were waiting in breathless anticipation to announce their presence.

Leah tried to close her ears and pretend that the music she suddenly heard was simply the wind playing tricks on her, but the tune wouldn't go away. She stared into Gareth's wide eyes; he heard it, too. Stepping carefully over the creaking floorboards, sending white clouds of dust into the air, Gareth grabbed her hand and reached out to open the black cellar door.

A light came from the bottom of the dark stairwell. Gareth turned and kissed Leah's frigid lips. "For luck."

She responded with a whimper when the strange voices floated up to the landing where they stood. It sounded like musicians were waiting down below to welcome them to a party.

Together they took a deep breath and descended the staircase. Gareth turned the corner and immediately jumped backward. Leah screamed. She reached out and ran her hands frantically over his body, searching for a wound.

He grabbed her. "I'm okay. Just surprised, is all."

Leah peeked over his shoulder, as they hit the final step and entered the basement side by side.

It was as if they'd walked onto a movie set. The cellar walls were lined with empty book shelves; cracked, bent, and twisted, the wooden shelves looked like a row of old coffins that'd been set against the peeling paint, ready to accept the next body into their rotted arms. The floor was cement, but a thin layer of the fine river sand had been scattered across it; the tiny grains were trapped in the cracks of the hard floor.

Gareth and Leah walked past the dozen or so people that appeared before them. All were dressed in colorful robes with opulent masks covering their faces. The revelers didn't seem to notice the new arrivals; they continued to dance, talk, and raise their glasses in the air, offering a toast to their happy futures.

The ghosts moved of their own accord, stepping aside and creating a path for Gareth and Leah to follow. As the crowd parted, Leah gazed at the strange quartet in front of her. Sitting in rickety chairs were four men clothed in robes, staring at the center of the table.

Leah crept closer. The ghostly figures were staring at a Ouija board. And in the middle of the child's toy, sat a large orb. A rainbow of colors came from inside the glass and lit the room like a disco ball.

Her stomach turned over.

"Don't you get sick of being right all the time?" Gareth mumbled.

The card catalogue opened inside Leah's head and the answers began pouring out, filling her terrified mind. Ironically, her favorite author delivered the final blow. Leah choked on her fear. "I know what this is."

Gareth turned to her and waited.

Leah repeated over and over again inside her head that this was simply a picture she was staring at, and there was absolutely nothing to fear. The four demonic figures were just images created by a psychotic man who'd left the earth years ago. Her lips trembled. "This is the *Masque of the Red Death*."

"Movie?" Gareth asked.

"P-P-Poe's famous story." Her teeth chattered; she felt like she'd been stuck in a walk-in freezer for days. "The Red Death was a plague. People in town were dying, so the upper class ran to the local abbey for protection. They threw a masquerade ball and celebrated how smart they were to have evaded death."

She swallowed hard. "But someone came to the party dressed in robes of gray, and a hideous red mask covered its face. When the person was revealed, it wasn't a person at all. It was the bearer of the Red Death, and the people at the party began to die…violently."

"These people are already dead." Gareth practically yelled, as if trying to remind them both that this was only a picture. "Isn't that our friend from Whitechapel?"

Leah looked closer at the seated phantom. His robe was black, and his elegant gloves rested on the table. When Gareth spoke, Jack the Ripper raised his head and bowed to Leah—a woman whose life had begun too late to be one of his victims. The monster smiled. The blue flame pulsed in his black eyes as he opened his robe to reveal the empty, ragged hole. Although he'd spent his life ripping the hearts from many, he'd apparently never found one that fit.

Turning her gaze away from the truly heartless killer, Leah stared into Gareth's comforting, green eyes.

He shook his head. "They're dead." He announced once again.

Leah wanted with all her heart to believe Gareth's declaration, but the sweat had broken out on his upper lip and the blood had drained from his cheeks.

Forcing herself to stay alert, Leah moved her gaze to the guest at the table dressed in the brown robes of a monk. His eyes stared into hers. The familiar blue flame in his frenzied pupils seemed to swirl in his eye sockets, and he looked like he wanted nothing more than to bury her where she stood. A frothy glob of red foam stuck to the corners of his mouth. Leftovers, Leah knew, from the poison that'd been administered by his killers. As she watched, the crazy man turned his attention back to the orb with a gleeful grin on his face.

"Rasputin," whispered Leah. Her mind delved deeply into the card catalogue and conjured up a picture of the murdered fanatic. He'd tried to bring Russia to its knees by controlling the mind of the Tsarina Alexandra—a mother who'd been desperate to save her dying son. Rasputin. Yet another self-proclaimed prophet who'd used his black magic to control the world.

The next man at the table was so small that his robes seemed to consume him. The crude symbol of the swastika gave him away immediately. And even though Adolf Hitler made no attempt to welcome the living visitors to his table, Leah knew in her heart that if he were to look up, she'd see the eternal blue flame of evil burning in his eyes.

Gareth spoke, "I assume the other chap is our pal Crowley?"

Leah stared at the figure directly in front of her. The robes were gray, and the mask of the Red Death concealed the monster's face. The being stood from his chair and placed the orb in the palm of its hand. The myriad of colors that blinked inside the glass globe immediately froze, and transformed into a single bright beam of black light. The robed creature walked toward them and stretched out his arm.

Without a word, Gareth stole the orb from its hand. When the beam changed to violet before Leah's eyes, her stomach lurched. She grabbed the orb from Gareth and a white beam burst from the glass, filling the room with an angelic light.

The figure bowed. As he stood back up, the grotesque mask morphed into a familiar face that burned her soul.

Gareth yelled, "Jesus…it's Donovan!"

A clock began to tick loudly on the wall behind them, and torches burst into flame around the room.

Grabbing Gareth's hand, Leah pulled him up the stairs. The clock continued to tick off seconds like a bomb ready to explode. When they reached the landing, Leah slammed the door behind them, shutting out the sudden bone-chilling screams that came from the revelers down below.

CHAPTER TWENTY-NINE

The harsh winds meant nothing now. The sharp needles of grass still punctured their skin, but they couldn't feel the pain.

Racing back to the warmth of their vehicle, Gareth turned the key and the engine sprang to life. Reaching for the knob, he blasted the heat into the leather-scented space.

He laid his head on the steering wheel, and struggled to catch his breath. "I never liked Poe. That bird…the Raven? Always creeped me out."

Bolts of fear shot through Leah's body like lightning.

"Is Donovan…dead?" Gareth's voice shook. "Is that why he was in there?"

"That wasn't Donovan," she whispered.

"What?" He stared at her confused. "Of course it was. You saw him."

She shook her head. "No. Donovan's just the chosen one this time out." She swallowed hard. "You just came face to face with the real thing."

Gareth's skin turned as green as his eyes. "Are you telling me that we just crossed paths with the actual…Devil? The real one?"

Leah nodded, trying desperately to erase the ticking noise from her brain.

"Jesus," Gareth breathed.

"Not even close." Leah turned in her seat, and grabbed his cold hand. "I thought Donovan was my…friend. All this time?"

"He knew your father was right," Leah spoke softly. "He had to push you…egg you on so that you'd continue down the path. Gareth," she choked. "I think the reason that Donovan felt nothing when he touched the orbs was because he'd already been chosen. He was already…demonic. He was never with you when you found the good ones. He couldn't be. If he'd touched those, he probably would've been…burnt to a crisp, or something. And the bad ones. There was no way for him to find those. You're never attracted to what you already are. Evil."

He shuddered at her words.

She took a deep breath. "Gareth, the Red Death—"

"I don't want to know," he said quickly.

"I don't care." She pressed on, forcing him to hear the truth. "Poe used seven colors in his story, which represented the seven stages of human life. Blue was the beginning, white was the middle and, of course, black was the end…death." She swallowed hard. "When I touched the orb it turned white."

"Leah…it was just a story."

"Damn it, listen to me!" she screamed "Your whole journey has been about stories and signs. I'd say this was a pretty big one."

Gareth raised his hand in the air. "The orb didn't stay black when I held it."

"No," Leah cried. "It turned violet. Violet comes right before black in the story. It's violet right before the Devil drops his mask and devastates the world; right before the crowd comes down with the Red Death and chokes on their own blood."

"Jesus, Leah…please."

"At the end of the story the clock stops ticking and the candles are snuffed out. Life just ends."

He turned to her. "So what's your point? The orb is the power of the Devil that will kill us all?"

"No." Leah sighed. "The orb holds *all* the colors—*all* the stages of life. The orb represents humanity, which is the most powerful of all. It's more powerful than God or the Devil because it represents free will. It stands for the millions of souls—the largest and most dangerous army in the world, by the way—who have the ability to choose which side they want to fight for."

"I understand." He nodded. "But, please…no more."

"You're going to die and you don't even care!" She slammed her fists against the dashboard.

"No one is going to die!" Gareth threw the SUV into first gear and crept down the mountain; the icy path threatened to deliver them into the depths of the freezing loch.

Leah buried herself in her coat. "A book is only images…words on a page. What we just saw was the same thing—pictures left behind by a maniac. But the moral of the story is still true, Gareth." Her voice was filled with anger. "The people hid in an abbey—a *haven*—that was all about protection. Death. Came. In!"

Gareth stared out the window, as the blinding snow suddenly came to a halt.

"There's no such thing as an invulnerable man," said Leah. "Poe knew there was no one and nothing in the world that could stop death. Not even a miracle can make death go away. A miracle can delay it for a while, but never stop it completely. It's just like Poe said: *a thief in the night*, that's what Death is and it'll get us all…eventually. The only thing we might be able to do is choose when."

Leah stared out at the gloomy landscape. She wasn't looking forward to boarding the creaking puddle-jumper that would fly them back to the Kingdom of Heaven. "Clock's ticking, Gareth. And, I'm telling you, the Devil is more than ready. He's already picked his evil soul in this era to bring him in." Donovan's hiss returned to her mind. "I saw the serpent in the garden. I just never thought it would literally be true."

As the vehicle bounced along the pitted road, the large black stones seemed to shift on top of the flat surface of the mysterious loch. Leah turned on the radio, trying to break the eerie silence.

Lost in fear, she closed her eyes—completely missing the mythical beast. It reared its mighty head into the sky and sent black waves thundering against the icy shore.

The legendary monster let out a shrill cry that joined forces with the powerful winds, announcing the Devil's return.

CHAPTER THIRTY

The venomous stinger of the scorpion moved back and forth like an evil pendulum.

Out of the corner of her eye, Leah saw the lion gnash his teeth together; his fangs glistened. She knew that the mighty animal was getting ready to leap from his panel and tear her apart.

In fact, every sign stood at attention, glaring at her. Even the wholesome, fun-loving twins of Gemini had pure, unadulterated hatred beaming in their youthful eyes. The blue flame of the lone torch still flickered in the dim cave. The pressure was suffocating. Leah could feel the anger all around her, waiting to explode. The zodiac signs could sense the presence of evil, and they were ready to defend their home at all costs. Leah begged them to forgive her for falling in love and giving up their secret to the man with the green eyes, and more than worthy heart.

She hadn't said a word on the flight back. As they'd walked past the Chalice Well, down into the depths of the dimly-lit cavern, she'd kept her mouth shut. Besides, after everything she'd already said, Gareth and Kathryn had still chosen to continue—march to the final panel—and insert the multi-colored orb into the stone.

Emmanuel stood by Leah's side in the center of the room. They waited—terrified—as the carved star came to life. The energy of the ancient orb burst through the shell of rock, and the swirling colors that represented humanity lit the room. As the star began to rise up the panel, the zodiac signs waited to defend the Kingdom from the evil they knew was close by.

With every inch the orb moved into the red-rock sky, the demanding clock ticked louder inside Leah's head. The blue flame of the torch burned and dimmed; the Devil was breathing behind her. But there was no point in telling them. After all, she deserved to burn. In this room, it was her sin that was the greatest, and Leah knew that no amount of bright light or forgiveness would change the fact that she was on her way to Hell.

Emmanuel stood silent beside her. She could feel his desperation and fear. Upon their return from Loch Ness, he'd told Leah that he'd begged and pleaded with the woman he loved to walk away, but it hadn't worked. Kathryn stood beside her brother, staring up into the light of the Star of Bethlehem. Yet again, it was calling out to the human race to come bear witness to their King as He re-entered the world. But this time, Leah knew, there would be no saving. This time, because of her bad decision, the heavenly entity would be walking into a trap.

The room filled with the sounds of a choir. A million angels screamed into the cave, using their powerful voices to scare the evil from their doorstep. The handprints carved in the wall shimmered with white light, waiting for the two souls to place their hands in the final keys, and open the gates.

"Don't!" The scream tore from Leah's throat when Gareth reached out to touch the wall.

He turned to her; sadness filled his gaze. "We've been over this… again and again. I've heard everything you've said, but I have to *know*.

My whole life has been about this moment. You can't ask me to give it up," he pleaded. "I can't…not even for you."

Leah cringed. The hot breath came from the panel, and she heard the deep growl of the lion. He was coming for her. He'd sworn to protect his King, and he was ready to do just that.

Leah stared straight ahead, trying to find the words of reason that would stop this from happening. The ticks of the clock grew louder inside her brain, keeping time with the Scorpion's deadly pincers as he, too, prepared to uphold his oath to the Son.

"Gareth." Leah tried again. "There's so much more you have to do before you get to this moment. Heaven is the end. Remember? The only bad part about it, is that you have to be dead to get in." She moved her gaze to Kathryn. "None of us are done yet."

Kathryn stared at Emmanuel.

His voice came out as a whisper, pleading with the love of his life, "Kathryn, what you're doing is wrong."

"No!" Gareth shouted. "This is right! We can help the world. Our parents knew that. You just don't understand."

"But *you* do!" Leah yelled back. "You have the information in your head, Gareth. You're just coming to the wrong conclusion. You see only what you want to see. …Just like you did with Donovan."

Gareth shook his head. "Leah…please. Donovan is just…"

"The Devil's choice!" she screamed. "A soulless entity that the Devil tried to fill. Just like the other horrible monsters at that table, Gareth."

"If he's the Devil than where the hell is he?" Gareth shouted back. "Answer me that!"

Her skin turned to ice. Her teeth began to chatter, as the blue light of the torch swept over her. "Oh…he's here. You've just never been able to see him."

Gareth and Kathryn stood in the light that beamed down on them from the Orb of Humanity—the final key. But they couldn't see it for what it really was. It wasn't the key to the Kingdom; it wasn't the final piece to unlock the mysteries of Heaven. "It's the key to the end of the world," whispered Leah.

Emmanuel's breathing turned ragged when the evil blue light crept over his terrified form. Leah twisted her neck and watched the life literally fade from his eyes. She could feel the hope—the faith—leaving his body as the Devil came closer.

Her throat burned. She couldn't give up. All her life, she didn't believe. And now, after living in the darkness for so long, she was the only one who could see the truth. Fighting through the oppressive weight that was suffocating her, she shook off the icy fingers of the Devil. "Gareth." Her voice sounded dead in her own ears. "You were the one who told me about that night…the night the Devil met Jesus. God forgave him, but left him down here. That night, God gave humanity the one thing He wanted us to have—free will. It was up to humanity to decide who to follow. He forgave the fallen angel, but he would *never* be allowed back into Heaven! That was his punishment."

The blue light pulsated around her; Donovan's hissing laughter met her ears. Closing her eyes, Leah summoned the image of Jesus placing his hand in hers. Heaven and Hell battled inside her, as she forced the words from her mouth. "*You* said the Devil would never open this gate because he needed time to get humanity to follow him. But there's something you forgot, Gareth. God only gave him six orbs for a *reason*. God knew the Devil would never keep his end of the bargain. He knew that if the Devil had possessed all the orbs he would finish building his army and come after the Father and Son. He'd make Them pay for what They'd done to him."

"Leah...They win," Gareth said; exhaustion filled his voice. "The Second Coming...They win. The Bible says so."

Leah struggled to breathe. "They win because *He* decides when it's time to come back. The Son will return—the King of Kings—when *He* decides! The Devil will destroy Heaven, Gareth. And you're helping him do it."

She heard the whimper beside her. Emmanuel's face had turned blue; his fingers were almost black, like he'd been buried in a block of ice for years. He looked at Leah with understanding in his eyes. "When you take something that's pure and perfect and place it in a world of chaos and pain, it becomes flawed."

"If you expose perfection day in and day out to evil, you'll destroy it." Leah nodded.

Kathryn's face filled with despair at their words, and she fell to her knees.

Leah swallowed hard, trying to fill her lungs with the oxygen she needed. She could hear the choir behind the wall. They were shouting—mobilizing—preparing to rush into Hell and meet the Devil head on.

"He's been biding his time, Gareth," she cried out. "He's been collecting souls one by one through war, greed, murder—anything he could do to make sure that he had the numbers. You're going to bring about the Second Coming...right here...right now. The orb was placed in your hand by Satan...not Jesus." Her voice turned cold and hard. "If you do this you'll switch sides. Make no mistake, Gareth Lowery. When those gates open...you're working for the Devil."

Kathryn sucked in her breath at the horrifying words, as Gareth fell to his knees beside her. He whispered, "Dear God...please—"

"No!" Emmanuel screamed. "Open your eyes! You and Kathryn need to see. You've waited your whole life to prove the Divine Truth, but you can't! Not unless you open your eyes. The truth is that God exists and Satan exists, *too*. You can't have one without the other. You know that by now!"

The life drained from Emmanuel's face, and he fell to the floor. His words continued in short spurts, as his lungs struggled to find air. "You have free will. Please make the right decision."

Gareth stared up at the wall. "Tell me what I'm supposed to do."

Leah's heart broke. "It's over," she whispered. Nothing had gotten through. Gareth simply couldn't see the bad. He was asking the One who'd given him free will in the first place to make the decision for him.

Her knees buckled when the mighty paw of the lion struck her in the back, pinning her to the floor. Leah almost reveled in the sudden warmth of his hot breath when he lowered his open jaws to her neck. It was time. Like Poe had written so long ago, they'd run into the safety of an abbey… and death had gotten in.

"Funny." Leah stared up at the gates of Heaven. "You're the one who wanted it for so long. But after all your hard work…I get to go first."

CHAPTER THIRTY-ONE

The strange words stopped the prayers running through Gareth's head. The wind in the chamber turned cold, and pummeled his flesh. Leah was leaving. Gareth spun around and faced the center of the room.

Blink. Fear caught in his throat.

"No!" he screamed.

Rays of color shot from the orb on the wall. A golden beam hit the lion's fearsome eyes, as he stood on top of the broken body. The mighty animal lifted his head; his jaws dripped with Leah's blood.

A purple beam hit the panel of Sagittarius and the archer leapt from his stone. He pointed his bow at Emmanuel and shot an arrow through his head.

Taurus broke free and raced toward Kathryn's weeping figure, holding the man she loved in her arms. A bright green light burst from her eye sockets when the bull's sharp horns pierced her heart.

Gareth's eyes were burning. He couldn't think. He couldn't move. He watched in silence, as the eyes of the Gemini twins turned a bright, hot pink, making them look like demonically possessed children.

The gentle fish of Pisces grew inside his stone panel, transforming into a Great White before Gareth's eyes. The mighty jaws opened wide, ready to tear him limb from limb.

In response, the scales of Libra tilted and her face, once beautiful, turned into a grotesque mask of pain and death.

The ram's eyes glowed like red hot coals, as the enraged animal scuffed his hooves against the ground, ready to tear out of his panel and toss Gareth's lifeless body into the pit of Hell.

As the Orb of Humanity lit each panel with beams of color, the signs of the zodiac transformed into minions of death.

Gareth's body turned into a block of ice. The blood of the people he loved pooled at his feet. Life was truly over. The thirteenth sign appeared in the cave…the killer had arrived.

The blue light coming from the torch on the wall turned black when Donovan Barker made his way across the floor. The face of his friend was twisted into a macabre mask; his forked tongue flew from his mouth as he slithered over the stone floor like a snake. He smiled at Gareth as he moved closer, eager to enter the gates of his old home. And, suddenly, Gareth understood. He flicked his gaze to Leah's blood-soaked body. "You were right. You saw the serpent in the garden." He wanted so much for her to wake up and tell him what a jerk he'd been.

Gareth could hear the clock ticking and felt the strength drain from his body. "I guess you do have to go through Hell to get to Heaven," he whispered.

His mind suddenly exploded. That was it! Leah! Up until now he'd been saved from seeing the dark side of the world by Leah. She was the one who'd held the orbs of the Devil in her hand and witnessed the horrible images from the past. There were always two—Yin and Yang. That was it. Leah had seen the evils of the past, but he was being shown the future—his very own Hell.

This *was* his decision. All They wanted was for Gareth to see what would happen if he made the wrong one. His prayer had been answered. His eyes had been opened. And, more importantly, his faith burned brighter than it ever had before.

Gareth could feel the hot, rancid breath of the serpent as it closed in on him. With all his might, he turned his back on the Devil and ran to the great wall. Jumping up, he ripped the Orb of Humanity from its place inside the star. Grabbing the archer's bow that now lay on the ground beside Emmanuel's corpse, Gareth sent an arrow of fire into the serpent's body.

Blink. The Devil was gone. In its place lay the body of Donovan Barker, pierced through the heart.

The Orb of Humanity burned his skin, as the bright white beam burst from the glass, banishing the Devil back to Hell. The signs of the zodiac innocently stared down at him from their homes inside the rock. The ticking of death's clock disappeared, and was replaced with the sound of Leah's beating heart.

Kathryn lifted her head off the floor, and fell into Emmanuel's outstretched arms.

Gareth ran to Leah. Watching the color return to her cheeks, her skin transformed from the purple hue of death into the golden flesh of life. Her sapphire eyes filled with what he could only describe as the light of Heaven.

He smiled. "I want to stay here…with you. If you'll have me."

Leah covered her face with her hands, as the sobs wracked her body.

A jolt of fear raced up his spine. "Please say that's a yes."

She threw her body into his arms. "God," she said, smiling through her tears. "You are *such* a pain in the ass."

"Is multiplying still out?"

"Absolutely." She smiled. "Do you really think I want kids as slow as you?"

Gareth reached out and took her face in his hands, pulling her into a kiss that was filled with the promise of an incredible future.

Kathryn's eyes filled with tears. "Leah…thank you."

"Thank your brother. He knew."

"I love you." Kathryn smiled up at him.

Gareth's heart was filled with joy, as he held his little sister in his arms and thanked God for her life.

Standing up, he lifted the Orb of Humanity off the floor. The mighty lion stretched out his paw, and bowed to the man who'd made the right decision. The Gemini twins clapped their hands, and Libra's scales leveled out; the world was once again balanced. The ram and the bull—the archer and the scorpion—all followed suit, bowing their heads in gratitude.

The twelve torches came to life, as a sudden breeze snuffed out the thirteenth flame. With the disappearance of the strange blue light, went the bloody body of Donovan Barker.

The carved faces said their goodbyes and turned back to stone. The orbs fell from the panels to the floor and Gareth gathered them up one by one, placing them back into the knapsack. The colorful flames dimmed and the humming stopped. The keys once again became dormant, waiting for the next to arrive who wished to solve the greatest mystery mankind had ever known.

Gareth offered up a prayer. He hoped that the next time the orbs rested in this place, they'd be put here by the One who'd created them. He stared over his shoulder at the gates of Heaven where the power of that One remained protected, waiting for the day He would open the doors and welcome His people home.

Leah stared down at the strange black box lying on the floor of the cave, where Donovan's body had been. The tiny light beamed up at her and she stared at the picture on the screen...completely confused. The smiley face gazed back at her and, as she watched, a small line of bold, black type appeared on the screen below it:

I will <u>never</u> underestimate you. DB

Stepping down on the small device, Leah smashed it underneath her boot.

*

Walking through the twists and turns of the cave, the group gasped in awe as they passed by St. Michael and his angels, who'd magically appeared from a dark corner of the cave. The illustrious group bowed, as their leader stepped forward and placed his hand on Gareth's back.

From another corner, King Arthur rose with Excalibur in hand, and touched Gareth's shoulder. The other Knights fell to their knees, honoring the newest protector of the people.

Gareth led his own group by the small, dark corners that'd once been empty cracks in the stone walls. Yet now they were the home to treasures. The Spear of Destiny leaned against the wall; the Holy Grail gleamed in the light of the torches; and, the Crown of Thorns rested in an alcove—worn by man's very first protector.

Tears of joy flooded Leah's eyes when they turned the next corner and saw the Son. He smiled at her. "There's more."

"I'll be there," she replied.

He offered a look of pure love. "So will I," he promised.

The emerald grew warm against her skin, as they exited St. Michael's tower. She felt rejuvenated, like the power of life was flowing through her veins.

An old man with white hair and silver eyes walked toward them. He bowed, and pointed to the beach that lay just outside the opening of

Tintagel Castle. The sight of a brilliant new day met their eyes.

Leah knew the images that'd come to life inside the cave had done so for Gareth. They'd come to bless him. But there were other things, Leah knew, other mysteries that were waiting to be solved. Donovan Barker's words sprang up inside her mind. *It's not over.*

Burying the memory in the card catalogue of her brain, Leah turned her thoughts to the other words that'd been spoken to her: *There's more.* The Son's statement overwhelmed her. Leah knew that the incredible beings inside that cave had chosen Gareth to be the next protector of humanity, and she would do her absolute best to help him find the peace that the world was waiting for.

CHAPTER THIRTY-TWO

The blanket of new snow was already muddy and the streets were crammed with holiday traffic. The sidewalks were bustling with last minute shoppers on Christmas Eve, struggling through the crowds to get home to their loved ones. Tonight they would celebrate the birth of Christ, not to mention the magical man in the bright red suit who was already making his way across the globe, delivering his presents to all the good little boys and girls.

Leah rushed out the front door; her face was a mask of annoyance. Turning back, she looked up at the crooked sign hanging from the building's façade. "Every time! These people *seriously* need to invest in glasses."

"Hello there, gorgeous."

Leah turned on her heel and caught a patch of ice with her stiletto boots. Falling into his outstretched arms, her kisses came out like rapid gunfire.

"Goodness." Gareth pulled back. "I've only been gone for five days. What do I get if I stay away ten?"

"A kick in the teeth." Leah punched him playfully in the chest. "So I wouldn't advise trying it."

Gareth's face was flushed, as the cold New York City afternoon quickly drew to a close. "I missed you, too."

"Is everything…finished?" asked Leah. She wanted to make sure that the orbs were back in place and the secret was once again hidden from prying eyes.

Gareth nodded. "All back where they belong. What about Kathryn?"

Leah laughed. "Kathryn and Emmanuel flew in this morning. All the bad orbs are home. Your sister really got a kick out of the Winchester House. She loved Mt. Zion, too."

"What about Trish?" He grinned from ear to ear. "Did my sister kill her? Was there another murder in Whitechapel?"

"Trish wasn't there." Leah smiled. "Kathryn and Emmanuel did a little breaking and entering. But I would bet that Trish would rather meet The Ripper, himself, before dealing with your sister."

Gareth let out a roar of laughter. "I can just imagine my sister scratching Trish's eyes out of her head. She wasn't so bad, though." He winked. "If I recall, she had extremely good taste in lingerie."

A strange, eerie feeling erupted in Leah's soul.

"What is it?" he asked.

"I don't know," she whispered. "You know that creepy feeling you get sometimes…?"

"Like someone's walking over your grave." He nodded.

Shaking off the weird moment, Leah turned and caught sight of her regal friend. The frown spread across her face like a plague across the land. She snorted at the ugly wreaths that'd been thrown around the necks of her favorite statues. It looked like they were sitting in a horseshoe pit at a backyard barbecue, instead of guarding the most majestic library in the world. "Why must they do this?"

Gareth grinned. "New exhibit?" He pointed up at the horribly crooked sign waving precariously in the breeze.

Leah glared at him. "Myths and Legends: Fact versus Fiction."

"That should draw in the crowds." He laughed.

"I think I'll skip this one." She stared into the green eyes that held her future. "I've got better things to do with my time."

"You bet you have." He smiled. "So…what did you end up doing with the last one?"

Leah offered a wicked grin. "I'm not supposed to tell you, remember? You said that if you knew, there would always be that small part of you that would want to try again."

"I know what I said." Gareth sighed. "But, really…tell me. You can trust me. I won't go near it, I swear."

"No worries, Mr. Lowery. The metal book is back where it belongs. And…as for humanity's orb, I hid it in the most evil place in all the world. Even Crowley would be proud of me."

Leah knew that he'd entrusted her with the orb for a very good reason. The powerful key could never be put back into the cellar at Boleskine. After being there, it was quite clear during Crowley's ceremony long ago that he'd succeeded in opening a portal inside the dreaded lodge; a door that would allow the Devil to enter with ease, and use the infinite power of the orb to gather more followers to his side.

Not to mention, Leah still thought about the words etched into the small black box by the hand of DB. It couldn't have been Donovan, he'd already been killed before the strange message had been typed right before her very eyes. She wondered briefly if he'd had a partner. And if he did, Leah knew someday, somehow, somewhere that mysterious partner would appear and try to torture the secret out of Gareth Lowery.

Leaning back, Gareth stared at her. "What could be more evil than

Crowley's place?"

A bright yellow bus pulled up to the steps; a plume of black smoke burst from its tailpipe. The multitude of screaming voices sounded like cats walking across hot coals.

Leah's stomach lurched. "Disneyland."

"*Disneyland?*" Gareth laughed.

"You heard me."

"My apologies, Madame Librarian, but isn't that commonly referred to as the *happiest* place on Earth?"

"Don't let them fool you." Leah shook her finger in his face. "There are hordes of those little demons running all over that place day and night. I was lucky to get out alive."

Gareth offered a teasing grin. "You know, this kid issue you seem to have—"

"Yes?" Leah shuddered, as the screaming mob ran by.

Bending down, he grabbed her bottom lip between his teeth. "Let's just say that there may be a compromise coming in your future."

Leah fondled the necklace that lay beneath her leather coat. "We'll see." The card catalogue sprang open, filling her brain with the facts she'd need in order to prove that motherhood was definitely not in her future. "So…where to?"

"Well," Gareth began, taking her elbow and leading her down the steps. "Lately I've been thinking a lot about *The Library Hotel*."

"Oh, yeah?" Leah grinned, as her heart beat wildly in her chest. "And?"

"I've been contemplating what exactly they offer in that *Erotic Room* of theirs." He winked. "Care to hazard a look?"

"That could prove interesting."

Gareth pulled her to his side. "Do you think we'll live happily ever after like Disney always claims?"

"Not a chance," Leah replied, planting a huge kiss on his inviting lips. She pointed at the lions behind her. "Patience and fortitude, sweetheart. We're gonna' need loads and loads of patience and fortitude."

Gareth swung her into his arms and walked swiftly down the sidewalk, leading her to a room that, Leah knew, would soon become Heaven on Earth.

EPILOGUE

The setting sun lit the lion's eyes with a brilliant red glow. As the herd of children raced up the stairs in between the regal statues, their heavy footfalls completely obliterated the eerie humming sound that came from deep inside the pedestal.

Shadows danced across his elegantly carved features and, for a split second, Patience looked as if he held the answer to mankind's greatest mystery…behind his marble eyes.

LOOK FOR

"THE SAPPHIRE STORM"
COMING 2013

Coming down from their incredible adventure, Leah and Gareth find themselves heading for the 'next step' in their romance…going home to meet Leah's parents. As Leah spends time rolling her eyes at her own ridiculous DNA, Gareth receives a frantic phone call from his sister that leads the team of *Tallent & Lowery* down yet another astounding path. A well-known artifact has been found under an archaeological site in the famed desert world of Petra, and from a very famous staff to odd clues found in the diary of the "real" William Shakespeare, Leah and Gareth must find a way to 'link' age-old mysteries together to solve a truly haunting puzzle. But as Leah's nemesis draws near, she must put her faith in the hands of everything from a saint named Gregory to an ivy-league school in Britain that houses one of the best-kept secrets in the world, in order for she and Gareth to stay alive.